THE
PLAN

A Novel

Kevin P. Chavous

Also by Kevin P. Chavous

Serving Our Children: Charter Schools and the Reform of American Public Education (2004)

Voices of Determination: Children that Defy the Odds (2011)

Building A Learning Culture in America (2016)

ISBN - 13: 978-1548992088
ISBN - 10: 1548992089

www.kevinpchavous.com

For Amber

PROLOGUE

Deep in the hills of southern Pennsylvania, just south of Harrisburg, a small group of scientists huddle in a windowless building, shielded from the outside world. The top secret nature of the scientists' work require that the building has security, but there is little concern that information about their research will be leaked. The leaders behind the project have gone to great lengths to protect their plan. They possess an impenetrable commitment to each other and to the cause that has brought them together. Over the years, they have gone step by painstaking step to ensure their success. Patience has served the leaders well. It has allowed them to consider every possible scenario, every potential twist. Before long, it will be time for implementation of the plan.

The scientists are poring over the most recent data on the toxic nature of a newly refined poisonous chemical agent. They are pleased with the data. Their progress has been stunning. Soon, the scientists will be able to control the poison's dosage based on the body weight and food intake habits of the targets. The plan leaders will be pleased. Once the science is correct, the only variable left is the politics. Unlike science, politics is inexact. It is also malleable, subject to the twin challenges of ego and emotion. The leaders constantly remind themselves of that fact. For the plan to work, all involved must remain disciplined and focused. Any deviation from the ultimate goal will result in failure.

In the meantime, the scientists continue to check and recheck their research to prepare for their upcoming presentation and report. The leaders will welcome and embrace the scientists' conclusions. The plan will be ready to move to the next phase.

MONDAY

ONE

Jackson Lowery was being gently shaken. Once. Twice. Then, a third time. He wanted to open his eyes to get his bearings, but his head was killing him. Instead, he kept them shut and remained motionless, only to be shaken again. Jackson tried to lift his head and felt a cold uneven surface under his face. His senses were coming back. He could feel the wind. He heard the swishing of water. He smelled the pungent smell of fish. He began to open his eyes. It was night. The first thing he saw was a large green eye looking back at him, three inches away. The green eye did not blink. Jackson closed then reopened his eyes and finally began to pull himself up, noticing as he did that the green eye belonged to a frog. He noticed that he was laying on gray concrete. The left side of his face was cold, wet and numb. He looked around and realized that he was on the last of several wide steps leading to the Potomac River. Slowly, it was coming back to him. He had been hit on the head. But who was shaking him?

"Jeremy likes you," said a hoarse, husky voice. The voice then laughed so hard, it began to cough an old smoker's hack.

"They just left here and boy, they didn't mean you no good," the voice said. "Me and Jeremy saw 'em bring you down here. We thought they were gonna toss you in the river, but then they just started pouring liquor or somethin' down your throat. Guess they wanted it to look like you had passed out. I made a noise, which I think kinda spooked them because then they took off. But they dropped you hard on that bottom step. You ok, fella?"

Looking up, Jackson saw an old heavy-set white man with a large gray beard. He wore a big blue coat and worn brown boots. He was sitting on one of the steps right above Jackson, four feet away. Jackson knew instantly who he was. This man was one of the homeless people living in and around the Georgetown Waterfront Park underneath the Whitehurst Freeway, which cuts through Georgetown in Washington, D.C. Jackson knew this man's face because he saw him several times a week. Jackson lived in an apartment right down the street on Cecil Place.

"Yes, I think so, thank you" Jackson said. "My head is killing me. How long have they been gone?" Jackson began holding the side of his head, which was hurting even more now that he was regaining consciousness and coming to his senses. He also started licking his lips, tasting the alcohol and knowing that he had not willingly had anything to drink.

"They left about five minutes ago. Jumped in a black van and hightailed it outta here. You know it was the government, don't you? They gonna snatch each of us up one by one and place us on another planet. Me and Jeremy saved you."

Jackson looked at the frog, who was still looking at Jackson sitting on the concrete steps. "Well, I owe you and Jeremy my life," Jackson said. "Thank you."

"No problem. They were in your house too," the man said, looking at Jackson with a twinkle in his eyes. "Didn't stay long, but they went in there. You may want to check it out. Let's go, Jeremy."

With that, the man held out his hand and the frog jumped into it. The man then put the frog in the breast pocket of his coat and turned to amble down the path parallel to the river.

"Thank you! I won't forget this!" Jackson yelled after him.

The man didn't turn around but lifted his hand and said, "Watch the government, son. Watch them, cuz they are watching all of us."

Jackson gathered himself, and unfolding his lean, six foot four inch frame, painfully climbed up the concrete steps and jogged as best he could to his house. He crossed over K Street, went past Wisconsin Avenue and turned right on Cecil Place. For the first time since he came to, he checked his pockets. No wallet, no keys. Cecil Place was a hilly one-way street going south a couple of blocks from M Street to the north. The clustered three story townhouses facing the small, secluded street gave Cecil Place an old European flavor. Most people in D.C. weren't even aware of the street's existence. For Jackson Lowery, the quiet, historic anonymity fit his tastes.

As Jackson got closer to his apartment, he noticed that his front door was partially open. *Damn*, he thought. What if someone was still in there? Jackson walked as quietly as he could and pushed open the front door. His place looked to be in reasonably good shape. He looked around and couldn't see anything missing. Still, his mind was racing. *That would make sense,* he thought to himself. *They would want it to look like I did something to Amy--not that I was a victim.*

Amy Duncan.

Just thinking of her made him sick. He ran to his bathroom and threw up. It was all coming back to him. Being hit on the head and seeing the look of shock and fear on her face. That was his last image before being knocked unconscious. *Lord, I pray that she is alright*, Jackson thought. But the old prosecutor in him sensed that the only reason why he was still alive was to be the fall guy for something. It was the only thing that made sense.

Jackson went into critical thinking mode. He wiped the vomit off of his mouth, brushed his teeth and began to think. The truth was, he guessed that he had a little time on his side since they were probably expecting him to be laid out on that concrete for an hour or two longer than he was. Jackson thought about calling one of his former prosecutor friends to talk through what had just happened. Or maybe one of his former law firm partners. But none of that felt right. If there was any truth to what Amy had been telling him, this thing was bigger than anything he had ever seen. Should he run? Where would he go? He could not stay in his house.

"Think, Jackson, think!" he urged himself, feeling stalled and wanting to just lie down in his bed, hoping that when he woke up it would all have been a dream. Snapping to, he quickly changed clothes and grabbed a few credit cards from the underwear drawer in his bedroom. As he was walking to the door, it struck him that credit cards could be traced, and they wouldn't allow him to fully disappear. Plus, with the folks he was dealing with, those cards could be blocked soon. Jackson put the credit cards back in his drawer and pulled down the ceiling fan in his kitchen. Buried near the tiny space between the fan blades and the motor was Jackson's emergency cash, $5,000. Jackson had kept the money there for years and never thought he would actually need to use it. He needed it tonight.

Having walked briskly out of his apartment, Jackson had to keep his head clear. Just as he was walking north up Cecil Place, he looked over his shoulder and saw two D.C. Metropolitan police squad cars pulling up in front of his apartment. They had driven the wrong way on his one-way street. Their lights were on, but not the sirens. *Not good*, he thought. Jackson scooted up to Grace Street, made a quick right, crossed Wisconsin Avenue, and navigated his way to the footpath bordering the Georgetown C & O Canal. He prided himself on working well in a crisis. At least that was what all his colleagues used to tell him. But it sure felt different when the person in crisis was you. As much as he did not want to run, just based on what Amy told him he was dealing with something bigger than anything he had ever seen. He was being set up and turning himself in to the authorities would not help things at all. The people who knocked him out and grabbed Amy were the real deal. While he sure hoped that Amy was alright, he did not hold out much hope. Just thinking about her made his heart sink. But he had to be smart. They were all looking for him. Some probably ready to kill him on sight.

Being in personal crisis mode made him think about the only person on earth who he knew well enough and trusted completely, who also had the skill set needed to help him in such a dark moment. He remembered hours of conversation with this person, who had often talked with Jackson about how to drop off the grid if you needed to. Jackson was formulating a plan in his head. But the first thing he needed to do was hide in plain sight. He needed to get out of Georgetown fast and head to far southeast, D.C., east of the Anacostia River. His days as a prosecutor at the D.C. U.S. Attorney's office taught him one thing: for a crime like this, the last place the authorities would look was in far southeast. It would be assumed that Jackson would seek safe haven somewhere in northwest D.C. or Virginia.

Soon, every police officer in town would see his picture pop onto the laptop in their patrol cars. D.C. had more police monitored cameras on the street than any city except for London and New York City. With that information in mind, he had to pick the right way to head across town without being seen. Cabs and Ubers were out of the question. Same with the metro system. But, a city bus could work. Jackson recalled that there were a couple of bus lines that went from far southeast to Georgetown and back. He needed to check the bus schedule.

But wait, he thought. He needed to call his son. He could not have Eddie find out about all of this through CNN, while he was unreachable and on the lam. Jackson had planned on getting a few throwaway phones from some random store in southeast, but now he needed to get at least one phone here in Georgetown before catching his bus. He knew he would be caught on film by the store's cameras, but so be it. Jackson kept walking east along the canal, turning left on 30th Street before crossing M Street. He headed for the CVS store near 28th and M. He kept his head down the whole time he was walking. He had grabbed an old Redskins cap from his apartment and made sure not to make eye contact with any other pedestrians. As usual, Georgetown was full of people, which helped him walk along unnoticed.

Once inside the CVS, Jackson grabbed one of the throwaway phones along with some Tylenol and paid at the self-service kiosk. With help from one of the store clerks, he loaded minutes on the phone and then hustled out of the store. While he worked to get the phone going, he walked quickly up 29th Street, headed to Wisconsin Avenue and P Street NW. Having lived in Georgetown for so long, he had seen folks waiting for a bus at that bus stop late at night for years. He arrived just before 10 pm. There were five other people waiting for the bus. He started to ask someone what time the bus would arrive, but then thought the better of it. He just casually hung toward the back of the stop, waiting like everyone else.

By now, Jackson had the phone working. Stepping away from the group, he called his son, Eddie. When his son answered the phone, Jackson jumped right in.

"Hey, son, you alone?"

"Uh, yeah, dad. You sound out of breath and weird. You okay?"

"I am okay. But I cannot talk long and you need to listen to me very carefully. You hear me?"

"Okay, dad. Now, you are kind scaring me."

"Well, the worst is yet to come, son. Look, there is no easy way to say this, but by morning, my name and picture will be on every news channel in the country. While I don't know for sure, I believe they are going to say that I hurt, maybe even killed someone. No matter what you hear, I did not do the things that you will hear. Do you understand, Eddie?"

Silence.

"Eddie?"

"Dad... if what you say is true, why not turn yourself in? I mean, you are a former prosecutor. You know the judges. If it is like you say, wouldn't that make a difference?"

"Eddie, you are right. It should make a difference. But, in this case, it won't. I am dealing with something bigger than all the people you mentioned. I don't know all of the connections yet, but the only way I can clear my name is to be out of jail. I gotta go, but just hold on to the man you know your father is, no matter what you hear. I will find out what all this means and clear my name. Can you do that?"

"Of course, dad! Do you need help? Can I go with you?"

"Son, I would love to have you with me, but it is far too dangerous. As you will soon see, whoever is causing all of this will stop at nothing. I cannot have you in the line of fire, I love you too much."

"Okay, dad. You can count on me. Hey, if you cannot call me, you know..."

Jackson interrupted. "The reality is, Eddie, I will not be calling you until this is done. No way. Gotta go. Love you and give my best to your mom. Try to keep her positive during all of this. Bye, son."

With that, Jackson hung up. He didn't give Eddie a chance to respond. What he could not say was that his son's phone may already be tapped. Jackson was so glad he cut his son off from saying what he was going to say. Eddie was going to suggest that they could meet at their favorite place, Dumbarton Oaks, where Jackson used to take Eddie for lunch on his son's early dismissal days. They would buy sandwiches and hang out at the park for a couple of hours. Eddie loved these times and said it was his and his dad's secret place. Jackson certainly did not want whoever may be listening in to be stalking Eddie, hoping that he and Jackson would be meeting. Jackson was glad that the call had gone well, but continued to harbor extreme guilt over his relationship with his son and ex-wife, Pam. Sure, he and Eddie get along great. But Jackson knows that the family break-up was his fault. He had betrayed his wife, his son, and his career. That betrayal followed him like a loyal dog follows its master.

When the bus arrived, Jackson quietly boarded and paid his fare, walking to the back where he settled in for the ride. He was going to ride the bus to the end of the route, wherever that may be. He would then buy a couple more throwaway phones and make contact with the one person who could help him. As his bus neared the White House, he took the phone he had just used to talk with his son and discreetly tossed it out the window.

While on the bus, Jackson must have fallen asleep. He was awakened for the second time that night by a friendly shake. He looked up and saw a matronly woman with a kind face. She had the look of a domestic worker. "Time to get off the bus, sir," she said with a smile.

"Oh, I'm sorry. Thank you, ma'am."

Jackson got off the bus, pulling his baseball cap down over his face as far as he could. He then got on another bus that would take him to the Minnesota Avenue Metro Station in northeast D.C. The bus was over half full and everyone on it looked beaten down. Bus riders heading into the far eastern part of D.C. at this time of night have more challenges than most. But they are, without question, some of the most resilient people in the city. Jackson needed some of that resiliency. *Maybe it will rub off*, he thought.

As he traveled across the Anacostia River, however, his thoughts quickly settled on Amy. His head was still pounding from the blow to his head. He was trying to remember all the details of what had happened but was having a hard time. The more he tried to concentrate on his memory, the more his head hurt. He closed his eyes and leaned his forehead on the bus window.

"Amy Duncan," he whispered out loud to himself, as he slumped down in his window seat near the back of the bus, deep in thought. Jackson vividly remembered that first day when she walked into the U.S. History class he was teaching. He was instantly attracted to her. But he had also strictly followed his rules regarding improper conduct with his students. He had disguised his attraction for Amy even as he accommodated her various requests for help; first by agreeing to meet with her study group, then by way of advising her on her semester abroad, and finally, through several one-on-one career counseling sessions in his office. Soon, it became obvious to Jackson that Amy was attracted to him, as well. During one of those supposed career counseling sessions she let it be known.

"Professor," she had said, "I really like you and I think that you like me. Why don't we go out on a real date?" She had even batted her eyes while she asked the question.

Jackson was caught completely off guard and thoroughly taken with her forwardness and her beauty. That day, she was wearing his favorite outfit of hers: a cream colored turtleneck and jeans. The jeans fit snugly on her hourglass figure. He did not know how to respond.

"Come on, Jackson," she continued, purposely calling him by name for the first time. "I am twenty-three years old, and graduating this year. Don't you like me?"

Jackson recovered, leaned forward on the desk separating them and said, "Amy, yes, I am attracted to you. But I will not have a relationship with a student. I just can't. I will help you..."

Amy cut him off and matched Jackson's body language by placing her chin in her hands and propping her elbows on the desk. She was face to face with Jackson, less than two feet away.

"Okay, I know what you are going to say, but that is not what you want to say. Can we at least see each other somewhere off campus? We can be friends without a relationship and figure it out from there." Her green eyes sparkled as she suggested the arrangement. She was smiling.

Jackson leaned back and sat upright in his chair. Then, he started to laugh.

"Let me say this. I think you are the one who should be offering me career advice. I am convinced that there is nothing I can teach you." He regretted the statement as soon as it came out.

Amy did not miss a beat. She crossed her arms across her chest, tilted her head forward suggestively and purred, "Oh, I am sure there are some things that you can teach me, professor."

He laughed good-heartedly in response – her forward nature was disarming, but relaxed him as she laughed along with him.

For the next several weeks, Jackson and Amy became close friends. He talked to her several times a week and saw her off campus frequently. But, the relationship remained platonic. Whenever she pushed the issue, he consistently demurred, reminding her that they could not go to the next level while she remained a student. Jackson also limited their off campus meetings to coffee shops, visiting museums, and casual food joints. He kept his distance, but was slowly allowing her into his life and was enjoying every minute he spent with her.

Frankly, Jackson's pent up guilt about the break up of his marriage a few years earlier had catapulted him to the world of a recluse. Amy Duncan was opening up something in him that had been closed for a long time.

A few days before the tragic night, they were sitting at a Starbucks on Wisconsin Avenue when Amy proclaimed, "Jackson, you know that I am graduating in December, just a couple of months from now. Plus, Friday is my birthday. How about that real date?"

Jackson studiously considered what she had said, thinking of a way to challenge her statement. In reality, he had been fooling himself. Over the previous few weeks, they had been on many 'dates'. They had an initial attraction for each other, which had only grown as they spent more time together. The only thing missing in their relationship was physical intimacy.

Both knew that by agreeing to have an official date, they were crossing the line and going to the next level. As had been the case throughout their acquaintance, Amy continued to call Jackson's bluff. She was raising the stakes, and controlling the game. Jackson looked at Amy and relented, realizing that he was all in, hook, line and sinker.

"Alright," he responded. "I have the perfect place. Let's meet Friday night."

Amy smiled broadly as she got up from her seat to squeeze in next to Jackson and give him a bear hug. That Friday night dinner was just three days ago, but to Jackson it felt like an eternity.

Jackson's thoughts were disrupted when the bus driver jammed hard on the brakes and swerved a little to the left apparently to avoid an accident. The bus passengers remained stoic and unmoved, each immersed in their own worlds. Jackson went back to his musings, listening intently to that voice from deep inside his head. *I hope that you are okay, Amy. Please be alive. Please be alive.* He whispered the words repeatedly to himself, not letting go of his hope that Amy Duncan was still alive.

TWO

Earlier that day

Idaho Senator Rex Duncan enjoyed the rare moments of quiet time in his senate office. The longtime Chairman of the powerful Committee on Agriculture, Nutrition & Forestry, Rex cherished sitting in his high back chair, putting his boots on his desk, and leaning back and thinking, without any distractions. His staff knew that their lives were better when they were able to give the senator that kind of space. Of course, it has been increasingly difficult for the senator to have any uninterrupted time with himself these days, not since the implosion of President Barry Coleman.

Now with the family insider trading scandal virtually making the sitting president unelectable, Republican leaders had been aggressively looking for the right candidate. More and more, the focus was zeroing in on the senior senator from Idaho. Rex was getting closer and closer to making his decision on whether to run. For weeks, everyone had been consumed with whether he would pick up the mantle and rescue his party from a badly battered and damaged Coleman Administration. Updates on the status of his decision were on all of the news channels every day, even when there was nothing to report.

Interestingly though, while he was as ambitious as any politician, Rex had never really coveted the job of president. His ambivalence towards the position along with his easy-going Westerner demeanor, had made him even more appealing as a candidate. As an added asset, he was on good terms with and respected by many Democrats, a far cry different than the current situation with President Coleman. As the upcoming presidential election neared closer, Senator Rex Duncan's ambivalence was waning. Being politically fawned over can be overwhelmingly intoxicating. Rex Duncan was slowly beginning to warm to the idea of running for president of the United States.

One strong positive from Rex's standpoints was his family life. His wife Reba was completely on board with a presidential run and his daughter Amy was even more open to the idea. He would often shake his head when thinking about Amy. She had a wild streak and there was a period of time a few years back when he thought he had lost her for good. Drinking, doing drugs, hanging out with the wrong crowd. Rex and his wife were at their wits' end. The relationship between the family members was even more complicated because of the ongoing fragile health of their oldest child, Kyle, who was born with cerebral palsy. Amy had always felt left out as a child and she had rebelled in response. Seeing her turn her life around had been the biggest blessing in Rex's life.

Amy was going to join them in their Kalorama home for dinner that evening and Rex couldn't wait to see her. Even though she was in her senior year at American University less than a couple miles away, he didn't see his daughter much. She lived in an apartment near the campus and, well, was living her own life. He was always happy to see her.

Suddenly, the senator's quiet time was interrupted by his executive assistant's ringtone. "Yes?" Rex barked.

"Sorry to interrupt you, senator, but I just wanted to remind you that Steve Mills and Bill Merchant are scheduled to have dinner with you tonight. Do you know where you want to meet them?"

Rex wanted to scream, but caught himself. He had forgotten about the dinner with two major Republican donors. Mills was a hedge fund billionaire and Merchant was the CFO of, a leading U.S. technology company. They had raised untold millions for Coleman and their willingness to sign on with Rex early would send a powerful message.

"No problem, Rita. Tell you what, Amy is coming to the house for dinner tonight. Please tell Steve and Bill that dinner will be with me, Reba, and our daughter at our home. Be sure to let my wife know that she should prepare for a couple more settings at dinner. Afterwards, Reba and I can spend some quality time with Amy."

"Yes, sir. Will do," said Rita, in a voice that sounded relieved over avoiding a potential scheduling issue.

Rita then called Steve Mills' assistant to confirm the dinner plans.

Steve Mills was pleased and could hardly contain himself. He was having a great day. His assistant had just informed him that dinner with Senator Duncan was confirmed. But he was also especially excited to hear about the progress of the scientists hard at work in the Pennsylvania mountains. For months, the scientists were struggling with how to apply their poisonous agent for its maximum targeted effect. But now they were close. Mills could hardly sit still. *This really will happen*, he thought to himself. He leaned back in his high-back chair in his D.C. Connecticut Avenue office, and looking to the ceiling, he exhaled loudly.

In addition to being arguably the most successful and respected hedge fund manager in America, several years ago Mills, along with Bill Merchant, had organized the exclusive, clandestine group that developed the plan. Recruiting allies and refining strategy had been a tedious, painstaking process. Other members of their group had hired the scientists, who had been struggling with their mission. But now, even they were making headway. Getting an unknowing Rex Duncan in the White House would seal everything.

"Soon, there will be a new day in America," he mused, smiling to himself. "Very soon." He picked up his phone to call Bill Merchant.

For Mills, the rest of the day continued to go well. That afternoon, he treated himself as Sarah, his able and reliable assistant mixed his favorite afternoon cocktail. The vintage scotch and water drink was prepared to perfection.

———

Amy Duncan was in good spirits as she drove her beat up Cabriolet to her parents for dinner. Happy as she was to be seeing her parents, all she could think about was Jackson Lowery. She kept thinking about their dinner and how sweet it was. Amy remembered their long passionate kiss, smiling throughout. *I should have gone home with him right then,* she thought. Yes, Amy was going to have Professor Lowery, age difference be damned.

She had wanted Jackson since she first walked into his U.S. History class and patiently waited until he was comfortable with the relationship. Amy could see herself settling down with Jackson. During their time together, even the coffee shop meetings, she felt a level of comfort that she had never felt with anyone else. In spite of her looks, Amy had always been a loner with very few friends. Having a well-known politician for a father did not help.

To Amy, it seemed as though what little free time that her parents did have was invested in her brother Kyle, who needed constant care because of his Cerebral Palsy. Amy had always felt guilty about being jealous of her brother's time with her parents and in high school, she started dating a drug dealer and quickly became an outcast at school. A caring teacher stepped in and helped Amy see the value in herself. While Amy was not sure what she wanted to do after graduation, she had plans to graduate with a major in American History and a minor in African American History. Amy was considering grad school, but she just wasn't sure. Things were going to get a lot more complicated if her dad chose to run for president. But that would be okay. She and her parents had made their peace. She loved them dearly and adored Kyle. Right now, however, her attention was on Jackson Lowery.

In the meantime, Amy was looking forward to seeing her parents for dinner. It had been a while since they had been together. Too bad Kyle wouldn't be there. Amy sure hoped that he was doing better with some of his treatment in Boise. Kyle spent most of his time in Idaho and stayed there with Reba's mother, Lucy. The doctors all agreed that Kyle needed a stable and secure environment, something not possible in many D.C. political households.

Pulling into the driveway of her parents' Kalorama estate overlooking Rock Creek Park, Amy noticed two other cars in the driveway. Knowing her dad, he could be finishing another meeting. Amy rarely went into the house through the front door and seeing that other guests were there, she certainly was not going to do so on this evening. Amy walked around back and entered by way of the side door leading to the kitchen. As soon as she walked in, she heard whispering voices. Not wanting to interrupt, Amy began to tip-toe across the kitchen, hoping to make it to the door on the other side of the room that led to a back stairway to the upstairs. If her dad was going to be tied up for a bit with his other guests, she could possibly have a little time with her mom.

She was going to tell her mom about Jackson, she thought to herself. She had talked to both parents a lot about how great a teacher he was, but Amy had no idea how they would react to her romantic interest in a man twice her age. The way she felt now, she did not care. She was going to be with him and her parents would understand.

As she got halfway across the room, one of the whispering voices got louder.

"I'm telling you, he doesn't need to know about everything or be onboard, we just need him to be there to keep things on track. Chances are he won't sign off on our plan, but it is going to happen anyway. We are so close to finally being able to exterminate a generation of dark and brown babies and no one will see it coming. Not even Rex. We just need to stay the course and keep connected to him."

On hearing those words, Amy gasped loudly. Before she could get out of the kitchen, two men came into the room, saw her, looked at each other and walked toward her.

"Well, hello, Amy. I am Steven Mills and this is Bill Merchant. We are joining you, your dad, and your mom for dinner."

Both men extended their hands, but Amy refused to shake them. In fact, she was still in a state of shock. Her first instinct was to run upstairs and tell her father to stay away from these men no matter how much money and power they had. Then, she thought about begging off like she was sick and find a way to talk with her mom. But while standing there watching these ghastly men look at her expectantly, she felt herself start to get sick. She wanted to throw up and she could not be in the same house with them for another minute - even her parents' home. She ran past the men and went out the kitchen door.

Crying uncontrollably while backing out of her parents' driveway, she called the one person she knew she could trust. He would know what to do, she kept telling herself as she called Jackson Lowery.

———————

Steve Mills did not become successful by panicking whenever something went wrong. Indeed, he had built one of the most lucrative hedge funds in the world by deliberately assessing any problem that arose and specifically removing it. Still, he had to admit, since he had been the one leading the conversation, it was a little intemperate of him to speak so frankly while in the senator's home. After all, anyone could be listening - like the senator's daughter. His friend and fellow co-conspirator, Bill Merchant had to state the obvious. "You got a little too carried away, Steve. Now what do we say to the senator and his wife when they come back downstairs?"

"First, I just put the word out on our network. They will find her and deal with her. Unless you disagree, we cannot have any loose ends."

"How do we explain her leaving so quickly," Merchant pressed on.

"Let's think about this, Bill. She was upset, right? Let's say we introduced ourselves and then she got a phone call. Though we could not hear the conversation, we could tell it was getting heated. Then she hung up, told us to tell her parents she was sorry, but had to take care of something and would call them later."

"I don't know Steve. What does that buy us?" Merchant said, uncertain of the approach.

"This is what it is buys us, my dear friend. There is no question when she got into that car, she called someone she felt she could trust. More than likely, it was a boyfriend or close friend. Whoever it was, we will find out and will have her phone log any minute now. If we can make it look like she was fighting with her friend while she was walking out the door, we have the perfect fall guy."

Finally, Bill Merchant saw the insight in Mills' thinking. "Let's hope we get that name soon. We can even mention hearing her call the name out as she was heading out the door."

"Exactly, my friend," Mills nodded knowingly. "Exactly!"

Merchant then thought about their colleagues. "Shouldn't we let Roger know?" Merchant was referring to Roger Tyler, one of the plan collaborators.

Mills recoiled a bit, but quickly recovered, saying, "Of course, but in due time. We are both here, in the here and now. As a result, we are in the best situation to assess and fix this problem. Plus, we really do not have time to let this spin out of control, do we?"

"I get it," Merchant acknowledged. "We are getting so close, though, I want to make sure everyone is in the loop."

"They will be, Bill. I guarantee it."

All at once, Reba and Rex Duncan bounced into the dining room. Reba, a slender attractive woman with green eyes and an hourglass figure looked radiant. Bill Merchant could not help but think that she would present well as a First Lady. Reba also matched well with her husband, Rex. He was a wide-berthed man, well over six feet and more likely to play a center or offense tackle than a skilled position in football. Both had broad, infectious smiles.

Reba immediately apologized. "We are so sorry we were detained. We were talking with my mother in Boise about our son Kyle. He has had a few more challenges lately and we needed to fully understand where things stood. Again, we apologize."

Steve Mills responded. "No need to apologize at all. We are honored that you actually invited us to your home. That is very generous of you. Bill and I are humbled by the request."

Rex then asked, "Did either for you see Amy come in? We thought we heard her old car and were expecting her to join us upstairs."

Again, Mills took the lead. "Oh, yes. What a lovely girl! She did come in and was actually heading upstairs when she received a phone call. She stepped away a bit and was in the middle of a rather heated conversation. She then hung up the phone, headed for the door and told us to tell you both that she had something to take care of and would call you later."

Mills was so taken with his own performance, that he did not see the joint text message that had, at that very moment, been sent to both him and Merchant.

Like any good partner, however, Merchant saw the message immediately and stepped right in.

"Yes," Merchant replied. "Steve is right. I thought I heard her refer to a car jack, like maybe someone had a flat tire. But, she could have been saying, Jackson."

Rex and Reba turned and looked at each other with puzzled faces.

"Oh, well," Reba said. "It will all work out. Gentlemen, shall we eat?"

As he was sitting down, Mills looked at his phone and saw the text message that had been sent to both he and Merchant. The message had two simple words: Jackson Lowery. Mills nodded and smiled slightly. He knew that young Amy Duncan would call a friend as soon as she left the house. Now, because of their access to resources, they knew exactly who he was. He sent a text response to the message and sat down to eat dinner with the next president of the United States.

It was just past 7:30 pm on Monday night when Jackson's cell phone chirped. Ironically, he had been thinking about his lovely dinner with Amy on Friday night. Was he in high school or what? It was obvious that she was a focused lady and was clear about what she wanted. For some strange reason, she wanted Jackson. Jackson liked the idea, but was that the responsible thing to do? He had decided early in the weekend to tell Amy he was fine with them going out, but the romance would have to wait until she left his class. By Sunday night, he was ready to invite her to spend the night. *Take charge, Jackson*, he thought to himself.

Looking at his ringing phone, he knew that it was Amy's number. They had texted each other a few times over the weekend. Sitting on his living room sofa in his Georgetown apartment, a smiling Jackson Lowery answered the phone.

"Hi, Amy! How are you?"

"Jackson, I need your help! It is all so wrong, Jackson. These are evil men and my father doesn't even know it. Please, Jackson, please help me!" Amy was hysterical. Jackson could tell she was driving so his first thought was to get her to settle down somewhat so that she could drive safely.

"Amy, I am here. It is alright. Try to stay calm. I am here to help you," Jackson said.

"I need to see you right away. These bad men are going to do something horrendous. I need your help."

Jackson tried to think quickly about where they could meet. He did not want her driving far in her current state of mind. "Remember where we had dinner, Amy? Across the street? Where we kissed? Can you meet me there in ten minutes?"

Hearing Jackson refer to their date did serve to calm Amy a bit.

"Of course, I know where you mean. How could I not," she said, laughing nervously. "I am on my way."

Jackson hung up the phone, slipped on his shoes, checked to make sure he had his wallet and keys and bolted out the door. He would be at the Exorcist steps in less than ten minutes.

Jackson had been leaning against the wall just a few feet from the top of the Exorcist steps on Prospect and 36th Streets, NW. He heard Amy before he saw her. She was running hard and burst into tears when she saw him. She jumped into his arms and they embraced like lovers who had been separated for weeks.

"Oh, Jackson, it was so horrible. I don't know what to do," Amy stammered.

"I am here, Amy. Just tell me what happened and then we can take it from there." While he spoke, he wrapped his arm around her and walked back toward the 1789 Restaurant, where they ate just a few nights ago.

"Let's not cross the street, Jackson. I am terrified. There is no telling what these people will do," Amy shrieked. They leaned against the brick wall that encompasses the Car Barn office buildings. Then, she told him about the men she had met at her parent's home. She then told Jackson what they had said. All of it. Jackson took it well, but he too was stung by what Amy had heard. Hadn't we gotten rid of that garbage during the civil war? Or the 60's? Jackson had always figured that the Alt-right, white nationalist group thing was a fringe element. Could Jackson have been wrong?

Jackson calmly asked one question. "Amy, are you sure you heard the words 'close to finally being able to exterminate a generation of dark and brown babies and no one will see it comin'?"

"Yes, Jackson, I am positive. That is how I got caught. I could not believe those words. I sort of yelped and startled both men when I did."

"And, their names were Steve and Bill?"

"Yes, I am sure about the first names, not about the last names. Maybe Steve's last name was Miller or something like that." She shuddered. "The look he gave me was so scary."

At this point, both were arm in arm pacing back and forth between the top of the Exorcist steps and Prospect Street. Understandably, neither could stand still.

"Amy, we will figure this out. There are some folks I can call. You need to stay with me tonight. Where is your car?"

"I parked it a couple blocks away from here. My lucky day. I found a parking space in Georgetown." Both smiled.

"Okay. Leave it there. We can worry about that later. The more I think about it, if these folks are saying the kind of things you mentioned, they are dangerous. We should take a deep breath. We can go to my place and figure out what to do. We also need to decide how to approach your dad."

For the first time since seeing her that night, Amy actually smiled a real smile. "Thank you, Jackson. I knew I could count on you. You know, I think I am in love with you."

Jackson smiled back. "One step at a time, young lady. First, we need to figure out what all of what you just told me really means. Again, are you sure you heard things exactly as you just told me?"

They had just turned from Prospect and were heading toward the steps down the path Jackson usually took to get to his apartment whenever he ate at the Tombs or 1789. Amy was about to respond to Jackson's question when suddenly, a black van screeched to stop on Prospect and two men jumped out of the car. While trying to shield Amy from the men, Jackson was pushing her toward the steps. He then saw two other men running up the steps headed toward them.

They were trapped!

Amy looked at him with a face filled with terror. Jackson clenched his fists and turned to face the men charging from the van, when suddenly he felt a jolt to the side of his head. Then, everything went black.

Rex and Reba were having a generally uninspired dinner at their home with Steve Mills and Bill Merchant when they got the call. The four of them were in the midst of talking about Taiwanese cuisine when Rex finally got up to answer his cellphone, which would not stop ringing. The look on his face said it all. The man looked as if he had been punched straight in the gut. All the color left his cheeks. Reba, after over thirty years of marriage knew that Rex had not just taken an ordinary call. She also had the benefit of women's intuition. She dropped her fork on her plate, pushed back her chair and ran toward her husband.

"It's Amy, isn't it, Rex? It's our precious daughter. Please tell me she is alright!! Please, Rex!"

The senior senator from Idaho just shook his head and slumped back in his chair. "Reba, my love, they found her in Georgetown. She is dead." He got up from his chair, grabbed his wife and held her close. Reba began screaming and weeping uncontrollably.

Mills and Merchant acted surprised, shocked and distraught.

"Dear God in heaven!" Bill Merchant said. "My dear God in heaven." He then covered his eyes with his hands and began shaking his head.

Steve Mills' response was more muted, but still respectful. "I am so very sorry for your loss." He stood up at the same time that two of the senator's aides entered the room to escort the two men out.

"Your family is in our prayers," Mills said, as he and Merchant were leaving.

Rex nodded slowly and continued to hug his wife.

Walking to their cars, Merchant turned to Mills, looked around, making sure that they were alone and said, "God, are we doing the right thing, here, Steve? Really? Did it have to go this far?"

Mills, while fishing out his car keys, looked at his friend and simply said, "We may not have gone far enough, Bill. We are in a war and nothing is more important than the cause, than the plan. There will be collateral damage. This is all just beginning, my friend."

With that, he looked at his friend, gave a slight nod, got in his car and left.

THREE

Having arrived at the Minnesota Avenue subway station in northeast D.C., Jackson went to a nearby phone store and now had three more throwaway phones. Standing in the shadow of a convenience store on the northeast corner of Minnesota and Benning Roads, Jackson began dialing the number he had memorized years earlier. He was told at the time that one day the number could mean the difference between life and death. The phone rang one time before it was picked up.

"Talk," said the voice who answered the phone.

"Do you know who this is?" Jackson replied.

"Yes, I do," said the voice.

"Do you know what is going on? How bad is it?"

"It's everywhere. Bad. Just hit within the hour."

"Part of me feels like I should turn myself in, try to explain things," Jackson said, hoping to get the advice he had called to get.

"Negative. It's past that. Come to me," the voice said.

"Come to you?"

"Right now," the voice said, giving him quick, cryptic instructions. The phone then clicked dead.

Jackson had to think. Where he needed to go was at least a five to six hour drive. He couldn't fly and using his car was out of the question. Jackson had to think fast, because some of the neighborhood boys were eyeing him, sizing him up. Looking in the parking lot, Jackson noticed three parked cabs. *Great*, he thought, noticing that it was a hang out for cabbies. Jackson went into the store, grabbed some coffee and raised his voice, saying, "Does anyone want a $100 cab fare?"

Two older men hanging by the cash register jumped in his direction. The first one who made it to him said, "At your service, sir. Just tell me where you want to go."

Jackson told the cab driver to take him to the New Carrollton subway station. From there, he could get to Baltimore and catch a Greyhound westward. While in the cab, Jackson remembered again about subway cameras. He also thought about all the cameras at bus stations. He kept brainstorming in his head, realizing that his best option was to drive. He looked at his watch. Nearly midnight. Where could he get a car this time of night? Would it make sense to camp out somewhere and try something new in the morning? Then, it hit him. He knew exactly where he could get a car. With no questions asked.

Rahim Singleterry was the best car thief in the D.C. Metropolitan area by far. While countless stories exist around his legendary thievery, the best one centered around then fourteen year old Rahim stealing a Ford Taurus from a train full of new cars being shipped across country. Somehow, Rahim got in one of the cars up front on the second row, hot wired it, and drove it off the train while it was slowing down and maneuvering through southeast D.C. The car was not missed until the train was half way across the country.

In the meantime, Rahim was driving his fellow block boys all around southeast for several days. He got caught when police saw him speeding down Nannie Helen Burroughs Avenue. He pulled over and asked the officer, "What took y'all so long?" It wasn't until the car's serial number was matched with the serial number from the missing car on the train that the authorities were able to put two and two together.

Jackson met Rahim when Jackson was prosecuting a high profile murder case. The evidence against the defendant was decent, but not overly strong. At the time, Rahim was awaiting trial for another car theft. He was facing ten to fifteen years if convicted. Rahim's lawyer reached out to Jackson to tell him that Rahim witnessed the murder and could recall things that only an eyewitness could recount.

After talking with Rahim, it was evident that his lawyer was right. Rahim did witness the murder and his testimony would help immensely. Rahim's lawyer was asking that his sentence be cut in half in exchange for Rahim's testimony. Rahim, on the other hand, being a seasoned criminal, wanted his case dismissed. Jackson's superiors left it up to him, but were not inclined to see Rahim walk away scott-free. Jackson pushed for and got the deal Rahim wanted. Rahim gave sworn deposition testimony, which Jackson shared with the alleged murderer's counsel. The defendant pled to a murder two charge and was locked away for a long time.

When Jackson told Rahim of the outcome, Rahim devilishly said, "Guess it pays to be at the right place at the right time, ain't that right, Mr. DA? I owe you, sir!"

That exchange occurred nearly fifteen years ago, but knowing Rahim the way he did then, Jackson was betting on the fact that the master car thief was not in prison and could be found.

Jackson gave the cab driver another destination change, to a corner in Fairmount Heights, Maryland, just off of Sheriff Road. The cabbie kind of grunted in response to another changed destination as if to say, "I thought this would be an easy $100."

After being dropped off, Jackson walked down the still familiar street and saw the bungalow house where Rahim grew up. Back then, Rahim had other haunts, but always considered his momma's Fairmount Heights home as his place of residence. With the time approaching 1 am, Jackson hesitated before knocking on the door. He continued, however, when he heard voices inside.

The door was answered right away. Rahim looked older, heavier and with less hair, but that infectious smile was still there.

"My, my, my! If it ain't my favorite D.A. You in some shit, ain't you boy?"

An elderly woman's voice yelled from inside, "Who is it Rahim? Who's knocking on the door at this hour?"

"Chill, momma, it's just Jo Jo. I'm just gonna be a minute," Rahim yelled back.

She had an edge in her voice now, "You're not going anywhere are you, boy?"

"Naw, momma. Just gimme a minute."

To Jackson, he said, "Let's walk to the street, so we can talk. Momma hates Jo Jo. That's why she didn't even say hello. Also, why she didn't come to the door. Anything to avoid contact with him."

Jackson, who hadn't been able to get a word in edgewise up to that point, tried to jump right in.

"Rahim, sorry to come to you this way, but I need your help..."

Rahim cut him off. "Ya think, Mr. D.A.? Your shit is all ova the news, CNN, MSNBC, everywhere. And man, that student of yours was finer than shit. She looked kinda like that girl in Will Smith's movie, Hancock---"

Now, Jackson cut Rahim off. "You said *was* fine. What do you mean *was* fine?"

Rahim looked at Jackson with quiet, compassionate eyes. "You really didn't know she was dead, did you? They found her propped up on the Exorcist steps in Georgetown, like she was sitting down for a minute or something. She had been hit on the head and was strangled. Everyone thinks it was you."

Jackson felt lightheaded and lost his footing a bit. He did not even notice that Rahim was holding him up with both arms. "Sorry, Mr. D.A. They gunning for you now. When I first saw it, I didn't think you would do some sick shit like that, especially with a fine motha like that. But since OJ, if a successful brother walks out of line, his ass is grass. You remember I told you that, right? Way before Black Lives Matter."

"Yeah, I remember, Rahim. You used to say, 'but for the grace of God'... but that is why I am here. I need your help. I need a car."

Rahim smiled broadly. "Glad you remembered me and my skills. Of course, you came to the right spot."

At that point, Jackson looked in the driveway and noticed there was not one car parked in it or on the street in front of the house.

"I see you looking, Mr. D.A. My rep is so strong, I can't keep any vehicles on my premises." Leaning forward, Rahim started to whisper conspiratorially to Jackson.

"Look, go to the end of the block and make a right turn. Then walk two and half blocks and turn into the alley on the left. Wait for me there."

Jackson looked at Rahim and nodded. Inside, his emotions were taking over. He wanted to cry - for himself, his son, for Amy. A few hours ago, his life was steady and comfortable. Now, he is a wanted man, believed to have killed the pretty daughter of the next President of the United States. Again, his legs were feeling wobbly.

Once again, Rahim, snapped him out of it. "Fuck it, Mr. D.A. Meet me at my spot so I can get you this car and you can go clear your name. See you in fifteen." With that, Rahim walked back to his momma's house and went inside. Jackson did as ordered and walked down the street to get the car.

Rahim met Jackson in the alley, walked halfway down and then opened the gate to a fence leading to the backyard of a house, right next to a garage. He opened the gate, then unlocked the door on the side of the garage. Jackson followed him inside. Once inside, Rahim turned on a small light by the door. Jackson noticed that Rahim had a trash bag in his hand.

"I don't need to know details, but are you headed south, toward the Midwest, or north?" Rahim asked.

"Toward the Midwest."

"Cool, these will work."

Rahim then opened the trash bag and pulled out a gray cardigan sweater, a blue down vest, a blue, gray, and white scarf, and some nerdy looking glasses. He also tossed Jackson a Kangol hat similar to the kind worn by the old golfer Calvin Peete.

"These things will match your car and make it less likely for you to get stopped by some redneck trooper on the road. Wear the cardigan at all times, along with the glasses. The lenses are clear, with no prescription, but they help a lot when you want to look non-threatening. Now, let me give you your car."

With that, Rahim lifted the cover off of the only car parked in the garage. The Volvo was about ten years old, with a dark green color and beige leather interior. It was in good shape, but there was a dent or two on the passenger side. The car had Pennsylvania tags.

"Registration is in the glove compartment, but, honestly, if you get stopped, you are probably done. Oh, one other thing, don't buy gas on the interstate. Always stop in one of the Podunk towns off the beaten path."

Jackson was floored. For the first time all night, he felt hopeful. If he made it to his destination, he could figure out a way to fight back. "I don't know what to say, Rahim."

"Shit, I owe your monkey-ass! My lawyer wasn't shit. If it weren't for you, I would have been in the joint for five to ten years. You saved my black ass. Oh, one more thing. How did you get to my house?"

"I caught a cab near Minnesota and Benning."

"Ummm," Rahim said, fingering his chin. "Where did the cabbie drop you off?"

"At the corner, on Sheriff Road. Why?"

"No sweat. But the folks after you got cameras, satellites, all kinda shit. They want a brotha bad enough, they will keep lookin'. I'm glad I asked. Gonna send momma to see her sister in North Carolina for a few weeks. If those motha-fuckers do come a-calling, me and my crew will be a-waiting."

Jackson nodded, but didn't say anything.

Ever upbeat, Rahim just laughed heartily. "I 'spect we even now, Mr. D.A, ain't we?"

"I would say so, Rahim," Jackson said, forcing a small smile.

"It's close," Rahim said, still smiling. "Five to ten years is a long damn time! Go avenge that fine student of yours, Mr. D.A. I'll holler!"

With that, Rahim gave a wink, turned around and opened the big garage door.

Jackson put on the cardigan, glasses and Kangol, jumped in the car and started it up. The Volvo purred as if brand new. Jackson inched out of the garage, gave Rahim a thumbs up and headed to Ohio, where he could begin to avenge Amy's death.

FOUR

Former Texas Ranger and Green Beret Brent Livermore was the lead military strategist for the plan. His responsibilities were simple. He was in charge of executing the appropriate response of force needed to keep the mission on track. At Livermore's disposal were fifteen former special ops, navy seals types who worked with him around the clock. With the resources and connections available to his superiors, Livermore was able to access almost any piece of information or resource accessible to any law enforcement agency or military branch in the country. In real time. This included the use of satellite technology.

Before tonight, there had been little need to utilize those contacts. As far as Livermore could tell, things were moving expeditiously and without any stumbles. That all changed when Steve Mills called him earlier this evening about the senator's daughter. Livermore had to get six of his best men together ASAP and had the rest of his team on full alert. He was proud of the way they responded. They obviously had been listening when he had repeatedly said to them over the past few months that this was the quiet before the storm.

"When things get hot and heavy," he had told them, "it will come quick, with virtually no warning." To his team's credit, they got the Duncan girl's phone records in minutes, before she even met her black professor.

Livermore was on the scene when they found the couple. Indeed, he was the one who knocked the professor out with the butt of his gun. His second in command put the girl to sleep - permanently. That all went well. But now, several hours later, the black professor was still free. How could that have happened? The media team had done their part well - Jackson Lowery was now public enemy number one in the D.C. region. But how was he still free?

Livermore had called together all fifteen of his team members, along with a few tech guys. Their location was a secure spot in Fairfax, Virginia with a giant satellite screen in front of them. The screen had access to every satellite and camera image maintained by D.C., Maryland, and Virginia authorities. Livermore knew it was time to crack some heads.

"Let me have your attention! Everyone! All eyes on me. First, great job by the tech folks and media folks early tonight. We found the target quickly and the ground team took care of business."

A few folks in the room started to clap, which led to an incensed response by Livermore.

"Don't you dare clap for doing what you are supposed to do! Never. Especially, when the main job is not done! Tell me how a college professor with no money, no wallet, no car, no phone, no identification and no help can elude capture for seven hours? How? Can someone hazard a guess?"

One tech raised his hand. "He obviously is getting help from someone."

"Okay," Livermore responded. "Let's say that is true. Who is it? And how did he connect with that person or persons? Didn't you run all of his contacts?"

"Yes, we did, boss."

"How far did you go back?"

"Three years. We checked each and every call he has made from his cell, office and house phone. He has not called any of those numbers since the ground team dropped him off at the Georgetown waterfront."

"Alright. Go back ten years. And, check the phones of his son and ex-wife. We should have done that earlier." Not doing so was a mistake. I am going to let you all get back to it, but this is what I want. When we reconvene at zero three hundred hours we are going to follow his movements, both known and possible, step by step, with timelines. In order to prepare, drill down on satellite images and cameras accessible to local authorities. Let's go to work, people!"

FIVE

Jackson drove all night. As bad as his night had been, he was actually traveling a near perfect route, leaving the D.C. area and hiding at the same time. After getting on the Beltway, he took I-270 to Frederick, Maryland and planned to maneuver his way west until he reached his destination of Marietta, Ohio. By now, Jackson had Rahim's Volvo on cruise control. He gripped the steering wheel with both hands as he struggled to remember Amy's every word before they were attacked.

She had said something about a killing, but he just could not remember all that she had said. Something was telling him that the government was involved. He kept trying to focus but the pain in his head was coming back. Push yourself, he reminded himself. Dig in on the details. Jackson then got a sharp, stabbing pain in his head. The Volvo jerked to the right as he grabbed the back of his head with his right hand. Fortunately, there were no other cars in sight.

Jackson had to regroup. He forced himself to stop trying to think about last night. He intuitively understood that he was still experiencing the after effects of the trauma. He decided to think about his relationship with Amy and how it has evolved over time.

Although he was on the run, with an unknown future, Jackson smiled at that memory as his headache started going away.

Nearly a third of the way through his trip, Jackson slowly started reflecting on his Friday night dinner with Amy. It was pretty special and Jackson remembered every detail. The 1789 Restaurant was located in the same building as another restaurant, the Tombs. Both are two of Jackson's favorite haunts. The Tombs had more of a burger and fries menu, while 1789 is upscale. Friday night was upscale in every way. Jackson had been coming there for so long that they always prepared something to suit his tastes. When he set his reservation for his dinner with Amy, he told Pablo, the longtime 1789 chef, that she was vegan, so he had promised to whip up a nice meal for her.

Jackson had waited for Amy outside and when he saw her walking up the street, she looked radiant. A natural blonde with shoulder length hair, Amy had her hair in an elegant looking bun. Her green eyes were glistening. Strikingly beautiful, she was wearing a tasteful black figure-hugging dress, with a classy, silky shawl hanging over her shoulders. As she walked, it seemed as though the flowing shawl and her well toned legs were in sync. *Simply beautiful,* Jackson thought as Amy smiled broadly at him. For his part, Jackson wore blue slacks, a cream colored shirt and a blue, gray tweed jacket. They warmly embraced when she got to the restaurant door.

Pablo greeted them as soon as they walked in and joked about Jackson getting younger every day. Jackson wasn't sure if the joke was good or not, but both he and Amy laughed heartily. Yep, it was going to be that kind of night. When they were seated in a private spot, Jackson could tell that Amy was waiting for a menu.

"Uh," he began. "I took the liberty of having Pablo put together a meal for you. I hope you will like it. Vegan, right?"

Amy looked flabbergasted. "I am impressed," she said. "I guess you know a lot about me."

Jackson shrugged.

"Well," she said. "I still bet that I know more about you than you do about me."

"Hey, that's not fair," Jackson feigned anger. "I am kind of in a disadvantaged situation here. Clearly, I have lived longer and have a much more public footprint. Knowing that, I feel honored that you still wanted to have a real date with me," he smiled.

"Life is about the journey, not the destination, my dear professor," she slyly said.

For the next two hours, they traded many stories about their lives. He heard about her challenges with drugs, her parents, and her guilt about her brother. For his part, Jackson was more forthcoming about his life than he had ever been. He told her about his son, ex-wife, and his life as a prosecutor. But, he also dug deeper.

He told Amy something he had never told anyone else about why his marriage ended. He confessed to her about the affair that he had with a fellow prosecutor. He related how his betrayal cost him his wife, his son, his family. Pam, his wife, had a nervous breakdown. She had even attempted suicide. Eddie was young then, but the scars still ran deep. For the first time, Jackson also admitted that his ego led to both his affair and challenges in the office.

"I was so determined to be the best in the office that I became selfish and singularly driven. I lost my way," he said.

The transgression also nearly cost him his career. Jackson ended up leaving the U.S. Attorney's office after having been there six years, but only a handful of people knew the truth and he resurrected his career with a stellar private practice. With each success, however, he remained haunted by his own guilt and by the types of clients he began to attract.

Amy seemed unfazed by Jackson's candor. She had been listening intently. The freshness and honesty of her youth made her impervious to judgment. Though Jackson did not know it, Amy found herself falling more deeply for him because he chose to be honest with her about his past. She then asked Jackson about why he would give up a successful and growing practice to teach history at the college level.

That very question had gnawed at Jackson, his ex, his former colleagues, and friends for the last ten years. Sitting at dinner with Amy that night, Jackson felt that he could, for the first time, articulate why he had changed careers.

"Early on, as a prosecutor," he said, "it was pretty straightforward. Nearly everyone was guilty so I cut deals and honed up on my trial skills against mainly guilty defendants who had nothing to lose by going to trial. I developed a nice reputation and my confidence grew. When I left the U.S. Attorney's office, I had a certain buzz about me, so I was getting some really good retained clients.

"And, I really enjoyed representing the roguish client who was not trying to hurt anyone, but was just a criminal because that was all they knew. One client like that was Luther. Luther was an out and out crook. He stole from banks, broke into rich folks' homes in northwest, wherever he thought there was something he could steal. But Luther was a lovable rogue. He was good looking and the women loved him. He had his main girlfriend who would visit him the most while he was in jail and then he had at least two other women visiting him as well.

"As his lawyer, I began to feel like I was running interference for him. But none of the ladies ever crossed paths. Well, Luther was up for a felony for stealing a bunch of jewelry from a jewelry store on upper Wisconsin Avenue. He went to trial and because some big Hollywood actress, who happened to be in D.C. at the time witnessed the crime, all the major news outlets covered the case. Both Luther and the starlet testified at the trial. Luther absolutely loved the attention.

"Well sure enough, the jury believed the Hollywood starlet more than Luther and he was convicted on all counts. As I was walking with him leading him out of the courtroom, with about twenty cameras following us, a reporter yelled out, 'Luther, any final words?' Luther stopped suddenly, looked straight into the camera and said, 'I just want to say one thing and this is something I told my lawyer. I want to send all the love in the world to my woman and I am going to fight to get back into your arms. Love you, baby!' He then blew a kiss into the cameras."

Amy, who was clearly enjoying Jackson share so much of himself burst out with a girly laugh. "What happened after that?" she asked.

"I swear to God," Jackson said, "my office got calls from about ten to fifteen women wanting to hear directly from me what Luther had told me about them. That guy was something else," Jackson said shaking his head and sipping a cup of after-dinner coffee.

"So," Amy pressed, "what made you give it all up?"

Getting serious again, Jackson answered directly. "Yes, Amy, the lovable rogues were fun clients. But in that field of criminal law, the more success a defense lawyer has, it seemed to me like the more despicable your clients get. I had always thought that all people had a good side. But, I ran into a couple of clients that were just plain evil. It got to the point where I would throw up before going into a room with them. Pure bad seeds. I started to have health issues, and I lost weight - my doctors said that all it was stress. So, I quit. I gave it all up after just three years.

"To this day, my ex never understood and said it was another example of me being selfish and selectively self-righteous. She may have been right to some degree. But to be honest, I was trying to save my sanity. After the hurt that I had caused, I could no longer be an advocate for those who also hurt others so maliciously."

Jackson looked up at Amy, whose eyes were tearing up. "You are a good man, Jackson Lowery."

After dinner, Amy was going to call an Uber to take her back to her apartment, and Jackson was going to take his regular jaunt down the Exorcist steps to his apartment near the Whitehurst Freeway.

"Sorry for the generational question," Jackson said. "But you do know about the Exorcist and the steps here in Georgetown, right?"

"Of course, I do! That is one of my favorite old school movies. I'll admit that I have always been leery of the steps, so I have never actually visited them. Are they close by?"

"Right across the street," he said, smiling.

By now, it was dark. Jackson grabbed Amy's hand and pulled her catty-corner from the restaurant and walked her to the front of the steps.

Amy acted frightened and grabbed him. "Please protect me, Jackson!"

They both started laughing.

Jackson then cupped her face, bent down and kissed his student. It was a long, tender and sweet kiss. Over the past few weeks, they had spent countless hours together. But, all of those hours had well defined limits. The boundaries were clear. They had been like two dancers mirroring each other's movements without any touching. That one kiss exploded the boundaries and all of the previous limitations. The two dancers were ready to touch, to slow dance in each other's arms.

When they finished that first kiss, they stared into each other's eyes. Both were wondering if tonight would be the night. They were about to kiss again when they were interrupted by the Uber driver blowing his horn. Even he was smiling when they looked in his direction.

Jackson put his arms around Amy as he walked her toward the car.

"Happy Birthday," he said, while looking in her eyes.

Amy was beaming. "Thank you, Jackson Lowery. And, thank you for a lovely dinner."

"My pleasure, Amy Duncan. We must do it again."

"I am sure we will, sir!"

With that, Amy climbed into her Uber and left.

Jackson's thoughts were broken by the horns of a couple of eighteen-wheeler trucks. At first, he thought that they were honking at him. Looking in his mirror, however, he could see that they were actually honking at each other. One truck had drifted into the lane of another. Jackson plowed on toward Ohio.

SIX

"Okay, people, let's walk through it," Livermore yelled out while standing in front of his team. "Time to see how much progress we have made tracking that black bastard down."

Pointing to the satellite and digital imaging screen in front of him, he said, "Here we go, step by step. We drop him off at Washington Harbour a little after 8, say 8:15, right?" He points to the Harbour image on the screen map while most in the room are nodding their heads. He gets up, has no wallet, money, keys or phone and stumbles into his apartment."

He points to Jackson's residence on Cecil Place. "Joanie," he says, pointing to a heavy-set woman sitting on the third row. "Keep track of the mistakes as I call them out." Joanie nods.

"Mistake number one: we assumed that he would be unconscious on those steps for at least an hour, maybe two. That mistake gave him the head start he needed to get away."

Several people were taking notes.

"Let's walk through it," Livermore continued. "The professor goes to his house, which has been searched thoroughly by us, correct?" Heads nod.

"And we take care to make sure it does not look like a break-in, since we want him to look OJ-like, in panic mode. That is why we left the door open. Since we had made that decision, we also searched wanting to make sure that he had no money, nothing at all that could aid him in flight. Ladies and Gentlemen, by now, isn't it fair to say that we missed something?" Livermore's voice is rising now. "Is it reasonable to

59

assume that he had cash hidden in his house that we missed, enough cash to help him escape?"

No one moved.

"I need an answer!"

Several people yelled out, "Yes, that's fair."

"Joanie, write that down as mistake number two."

"Back to the professor's movements. He changes clothes, leaves his house, uses the money we missed to buy a throwaway phone at the CVS on Pennsylvania Avenue and 28th Street, right?" Everyone nods.

"The time of purchase is twenty-one twenty-two. Joanie, put the CVS camera on the screen." Once it is in view, Livermore proceeds. "There he is. Now, he calls his son at nine twenty-eight and the phone is found near the White House some time later. Question for the room. Where did he go and how did he get there?"

Several people were shifting in their seats, but no one said anything. Deep down, Livermore hoped that his team had some ideas, because he was stymied. He looked directly at his second in command, R.J., who had served with him on several assignments in the Middle East. R.J. had a much softer touch than Livermore, at least on the surface, and the team adored him. Truth was, R.J. had a sadistic side to him. He liked to kill. It was at his hand that Amy Duncan lost her life.

Fortunately for Livermore, R.J. was completely loyal to him. Speaking in R.J.'s direction, Livermore said, "Come on people. What did he do? Where did he go? He made no other calls from that phone."

Looking at the nerdy techies, R. J. said, "Sir, let's give our tech team a chance to share their thoughts."

Livermore looked at the group. Slowly, a hand was raised near the back. It was one of the techies.

"Yes, Mason, right?" Livermore said.

"That's right, sir. I was checking the bus schedule and the last 30 south bus leaving for east of the Anacostia River - where most of the black people live - leaves Wisconsin and P at four past ten. At that time of night, the bus contains mostly black riders. The bus passes near the White House, ends up at the Potomac Avenue station on Capitol Hill, where some of the riders catch the subway or use a bus transfer to cross the river. Sir, I am thinking that he took a transfer which would send him to the Anacostia section of southeast D.C. or the Deanwood area of northeast D.C."

By now, Mason was pointing to the map, recreating Jackson's possible routes.

"In sum, sir, I think that this professor is a lot smarter than we think."

On hearing that, everyone in the room jerked their heads in Livermore's direction to see if he would explode. To the contrary, Livermore had his hand on his chin and looked like he was deep in thought following with his eyes the route Mason laid out for them.

"Good job, Mason. You are right. That son of a bitch went to the one place in the city where he would most blend in. He isn't so dumb after all. The bastard is in the wind!"

Gathering himself, he thought of next steps, and finally continued, "Folks, let's check the cameras at the Potomac Avenue subway as well the various drop off points in Anacostia and Deanwood. By the way, did we get anywhere with the calls from the past ten years?"

"Negative, chief," came a voice to the right.

"Time to stop playing around, people. Let's uncover this and get it done. Now!"

Four star General Michael Brock called Roger Tyler after midnight.

"What the hell is going on? What happened tonight? I know this family."

General Brock and Rex Duncan were college roommates at Harvard. They had remained close friends since.

Tyler was calm. As the board chairman of Hampton-Powell, the largest microchip computer processing firm in the world, he had learned to lower his voice when others raised theirs. "Yes, I know you do. A little intemperateness from our friend Steve Mills led to some rash decisions."

"I'll say. And, judging by the news, it is still unresolved, wouldn't you agree?" asked the general.

"Yes. He says he has it under control, but, frankly, I am not sure. I am not sure that Livermore is competent enough. Suggestions?"

The general hesitated. This was not how things were supposed to go. For the past couple years, there had been smooth sailing as they waited for the political timing to work in their favor. Now, it was getting messy. Messy was never good.

"You know what to do and who we need. Make the hire. We can bring it all together later, but immediate containment is key. Excuse me, but I need to call my best friend. He lost a daughter tonight."

"Of course, General. I will take care of it." Both men signed off.

TUESDAY

ONE

In a driver's daze, Jackson tried once again to shift his thoughts to all that had happened earlier that evening. Relishing the memory of Friday night had helped. His head was still hurting, but not as much.

Looking at his clock, Jackson realized that it was nearly 4:30 am. He was nearing Wheeling, West Virginia. He still had about an hour and a half to go. There was something about driving a car late at night that was stabilizing and settling. Jackson had given his situation a lot of thought. As sad and traumatized as he was, he had forced himself to get back into the "lawyer mode" mindset he relied on while practicing law and working a case.

For the first hour or so of the drive, he was consumed with grief, anger, and guilt about Amy, her family, his son, his ex, his students who all will be freaking out about this crazy news, and all the people who had supported him over the years. They say Karma is a bitch. Jackson was hoping that whatever he had done to deserve this Karma was now paid in full. Thinking of his relationship with Amy helped to fuel his energy. It not only removed the blocks from his memory, it fortified him to face whatever he must to stop the madmen who had murdered her.

Jackson went back to thinking about his conversation with Amy in front of the Exorcist steps. Now that he was in a calmer state, he realized that she heard the men talk about more than just killing, they had used the words extermination. As close as he could remember, Amy told him that one of the men had said that they were close to finally being able to exterminate a generation of black and brown babies and that no one would see it coming. Jackson had pressed Amy as to whether or not she was certain of the words. But she was too horrified, too frightened to have heard differently.

Jackson found himself getting excited and anxious as his memory of Amy's words came back to him, especially when the men's names popped into his head. Steve and Bill, he remembered her saying. She thought that Steve's last name was Miller. Jackson also recalled the man saying that Rex Duncan did not need to know about things, but they still needed him. They had acknowledged that he was not a part of their plan.

Extermination. Black and brown babies. Rex Duncan was needed, but not part of the plan. What on earth were these men up to? Jackson had to direct his thinking. For that to happen, he had to keep his emotions in check.

Since he now remembered his conversation last night with Amy, Jackson began to dissect the who, what, when, where, why, and how of his situation. Who was behind all of this? Based on what Amy overheard, this white nationalism stuff extended far beyond anything he had imagined. Jackson was one of those who thought that the true believers were primarily working class, disaffected white men.

Could it be that active participants also included an established group of higher thinking, well-heeled business types? Jackson made a mental note to find out more about who Bill and Steve were. It seemed plausible that it was at their behest that Amy was killed - all while they were having dinner with her parents! Whatever he was dealing with, it was large, and if they were indeed responsible for her death, just plain evil.

The what? Exterminate a generation of black and brown people? Jackson smacked the steering wheel and shook his head over that one. It seemed far too outlandish and sinister for him to wrap his head around. How could someone undertake something so expansive and racially targeted without getting caught? Whoever was behind this was powerful, and he presumed at this level, the government must also somehow be involved.

The when? Now this was a very important question. Was all of this imminent? Or did certain things need to take place beforehand? Based on Amy's recollections, Steve and Bill need Rex Duncan to be president, even though he had no knowledge of their intentions. Did that mean that several of the 'right' people were already positioned and that they would be gone if Rex were not president? Did any of this have anything to do with his senate committee chairmanship? Again, Jackson made a mental note to table his thinking for further discussion.

The where? Certain cities. Most cities. States. Obviously inner cities. Jackson's head was beginning to hurt.

The why? Probably the easiest question to answer. These perpetrators must have had a deep-rooted belief in white superiority and nationalism. But what about the many people working together to make this happen? For such an undertaking, there must be dozens of people working on the plan. Were others unknowingly supporting the leaders towards the goal? Or were there really that many people out there who were so racist that they would go as far as murder to assert their dominance?

The how? Relates closely to nearly all the other questions. Jackson rubbed his eyes. He had been ruminating on these questions for over an hour. He was still on adrenaline and not really tired. More than anything, he was looking forward to having someone who could talk through all of this with him. Jackson passed a sign informing him that Marietta was ten miles away.

Ronnie Thomas knew Jackson Lowery was nearby. He could feel it. Sitting in his Ford truck five miles outside of Marietta, Ronnie was on alert. Twenty minutes later, a dark green Volvo passed by Ronnie. The driver wore glasses along with a funny hat. Jackson Lowery. *Nicely done, counselor*, Ronnie thought.

Ronnie pulled out from his hiding space, easily caught up with Jackson, and sped up to pass him on Jackson's left. Even with all he had been through, to his credit, Jackson did not panic. He kept looking forward, stoking a sense of pride in Ronnie. When Ronnie pulled beside Jackson, he paused, waiting for Jackson to look in his direction. Once he finally looked and saw who it was, Jackson dropped his head in relief. The two men smiled broadly at each other and Ronnie made a circle with his forefinger and slowed to make a U-Turn. Jackson waited and did the same. No other cars were on the road during the friends' rendezvous. Upon seeing Ronnie, Jackson felt that he had passed the first step to freedom. He followed his friend down the road, noticing that Ronnie had a fishing boat in the back of his truck.

Just a few miles later, Ronnie ended up crossing a bridge that led to West Virginia. After a few more miles, Ronnie turned his truck right onto a dirt road, partially blocked by foliage. It was nearly dawn, but they had not seen a house for miles. A quarter mile down the dirt road, Ronnie stopped his truck and got out. Jackson did the same. The two men embraced, backed away, looked at each other, and embraced again.

"How fucking long has it been, Jack?" Immediately, Jackson remembered why he liked Ronnie so much. He never liked being called Jack, and would correct those who used it, except for Ronnie – who had been calling him Jack as long as they'd known each other.

"Well, it has been about twelve, thirteen years. Man! Time flies. How's my favorite soldier of fortune? Which war you fighting for the good ole red, white and blue these days, my brother?"

Both men laughed. "Look at this gut, man," Ronnie said, patting his belly. "I probably could not even pass a physical today."

Both knew Ronnie was exaggerating. He had a little bit of a stomach, but he looked almost the same as he always had to Jackson. Ronnie, a slender build by nature, stood at an even six feet, with close cropped hair and guns that always popped through any shirt he wore. He was black, but very light skinned. In fact, most people who met him took him to be white. That was another by-product of living in the southern Ohio, Kentucky and West Virginia areas. Most of the people looked alike and were probably somehow related down the line, black and white. Once you picked your side of the fence, you placed the generations that followed you on that same side forever.

Ronnie threw it back at Jackson. "Don't talk about me. Look at you, boy. No gut, slim, and you still got hair. You look good, Jackson. You really do."

"Thanks, man. First, I don't know where to begin to thank you..."

Ronnie cut him off. "Jack, we are going to get to all of that. Let's take things one step at a time. First, I am going to give you a lay of the land. General rules of the road, if you will. All relating to how we need to operate here. As you know by now, this stuff is on a whole different level. By the way, I must commend you on getting here, period. You made it inside of eight hours of our call. I don't know many trained men who could have done a better job."

Jackson smiled and nodded.

Ronnie kept talking. "We cannot do all of our talking here. Listen to me very carefully. I am going to drive fifty yards down the road, get out of the car and remove some things that I have in place that blocks one of my hideaways. I am telling you this because you won't be able to see me from here. The spot is around the bend. No one is around, but I need you to be on lookout. I usually enter this hideout by boat from the Ohio River, just another fisherman on the water."

Jackson nodded, fascinated, but not at all surprised by what Ronnie was saying. Ronnie was a marine for nearly twenty years when NSA and the black ops folks snatched him up. He then spent three years undercover trying to bring down a growing white nationalist group in Montana. Yep, that's right. Ronnie Thomas, African American, posed as a white man for three years to snuff out our biggest local terrorist threat. Ronnie's heroism led to forty-five arrests. He also had half a swastika carved in his chest. Fortunately, the FBI raid took place before it could be completed.

"Alright, Jack. I know if has been rough, but don't zone out on me. Wait ten minutes. If for some crazy reason, you see or hear someone before that, blow your horn. When the time is up, drive to the bend, take the slight turn right. You will see me holding open what looks like a garage door. Don't stop, just keep driving straight into the space. I will have the lights on inside for you to see. The drive will feel pretty long, so don't panic. After almost seventy-five yards, you will see the road end. Pull all the way to the front, get out of your car and go straight to your right. Hanging down near the passenger's side of your car will be a cord. Pull down hard on it. A door straight ahead will open up. Go inside. Close and bolt the door. Then, my brother, you can relax. No one can find you here." Jackson was shaking his head.

"Dude, you need to run the CIA."

"Who says I don't?" said a smiling Ronnie. "I am going to take my car back to my spot, unload my fishing boat and will join you within the hour. Feel free to snack and have a cup of coffee, but don't eat too much - I am making us breakfast. When I get back, we can catch each other up about family, then talk through getting your life back."

"Okay. But first I gotta ask, how are Rose and Ronnie, Jr.?"

Ronnie was nodding his head. "Both are fine. Glad you couldn't wait to ask." Ronnie then went to his truck on the passenger side, opened the door and pulled out what looked like a copy of a news article. He walked back to Jackson and handed it to him.

"Read this. When shit hit the fan with you, I had Rose and Ronnie go stash up in one of my bunkers. One of the first things we need to do is make sure that Eddie and Pam are secure. They are somewhat safe now. It is unlikely that the nut jobs would want them hurt, it would substantiate belief that the senator's daughter was killed for some political reason."

Jackson had his head down. "Hey, man, about the stuff with Pam and our marriage, I am sorry..."

Ronnie gently squeezed Jackson's shoulder. "Hey, Jack. Stop beating yourself up. I understand. Life is life, man. Everyone has their journey. I know you are a good man, Jack and right now, we don't have time be dealing with anything in the past. You gotta be focused on survival."

Jackson nodded but did not say anything. He then looked at the article Ronnie had just given him. It was a copy of a New Yorker magazine article about the bunkers being built by the super rich.

"Just read it. We can talk later. Lastly, for now, take this," Ronnie said, tossing Jackson a phone. "It's clean. Always look at the color of the light at the top when you turn it on. If the light is green, you are good. If it is red, the phone has been compromised. Toss it immediately. When calling me, always use the same number I gave you all those years ago. Good thing you remembered." His grin was wide when Ronnie smiled this time.

"No argument from me," Jackson said, feeling more and more like he could relax.

Ronnie walked back to his truck, turned as he was entering and said, "Remember, ten minutes and don't stop when you drive through the door."

Jackson was ready, willing and able to follow those orders.

TWO

How does one wake up the morning after your child has been found murdered? That thought kept churning and churning in Reba's head. Her doctor and Rex had made sure that she was well supplied with the right sedatives. But the basic challenge remained. How could she keep living? Lying in her bed, Reba opened her eyes and noticed Rex was not on the other side of it. Trying to get oriented, she heard a sound and could tell that it was coming from the bathroom. The Idaho senator was sniffling. Reba put her hands to her eyes and rubbed as hard as she could, in the hope that it would somehow also help to clear her mind.

Reba found herself drowning in the memories of Amy's life. Even with her eyes closed, she continued to see a kaleidoscope of images of her daughter at all stages of her life. Amy always had an independent streak. As a baby, she did not want any help while she learned to walk. Or, when she was learning to ride a bike. That independence followed her throughout her life.

As independent and confident as she was, Amy also grappled with immense insecurities. Much of it had to do with the attention given to Kyle. Amy felt unloved and neglected and found comfort by using drugs and running with the wrong crowd. Thinking back on those days and overcome with guilt, Reba aggressively shook her head. Fortunately, a caring teacher at Amy's high school had helped her turn her life around. But it was Amy who did the hard work of getting herself off of drugs, going to counseling and forcing herself to refocus. By the time she was enrolled at American University, Amy was a poised, beautiful, and energetic woman ready to take on the world. Reba was so proud of her and found it hard to believe that Amy's life was taken from her just as she was beginning to blossom.

Laying there, still lost in a host of thoughts, Reba reflected on how the night unfolded. When she had spoken with her daughter just an hour or so before the dinner, she sounded happier than ever. Amy even told her mom she might have a surprise for her. Was she talking about her and the professor? If so, how could that lead to Amy being murdered less than two hours later by him? Something did not feel right about the whole thing. Then, on top of it all, she had to find out with those two business bozos, Steve and Bill, at her home. Thinking of them, especially Steve Mills, gave Reba the creeps. Was it a coincidence that they may have been the last ones to see Amy alive? Reba began shaking her head and sobbing.

Rex heard her and rushed back into the bedroom. "Oh, sweetie, I am so sorry."

"I know, Rex. But, at least I feel I still have a reason to live," she said, wiping her eyes with her fingers. "We need to find out the full story behind Amy's death. I am going to get to the truth, I just need you there beside me."

"Absolutely, my love. We are in this together."

By 10 am the morning after Amy Duncan's murder, the cable channels had decided that Jackson Lowery had an obsessive, deadly crush on his young student. There was even a nerdy, bespectacled young man who said he took one of Jackson's classes in which Amy was also enrolled. In interview after interview, the young man said that he would frequently catch Jackson leering at Amy. He even thought that he saw him blow her a kiss once. The former prosecutor was being convicted in absentia.

At the same time, Livermore reassembled his team. Impressed by Mason, he went to him directly.

"Mason, any new theories on where Lowery went, assuming he landed at the Potomac Avenue Metro?"

Confidently, Mason stood up and said, "Yes sir, we sure do." Mason then motioned to a couple of his teammates who began organizing the backup for Mason's response.

"Boss," he began, "we now know that Jackson Lowery was, in fact, on the 30 south bus that ended at Potomac Avenue. We even have a photo - poor quality - but it is unquestionably him. He was the last person off the bus."

Mason paused for effect. Livermore waved his hand encouraging Mason to continue.

"Unfortunately, we did not find any good footage of him stepping onto another bus. We then checked all the end points for buses transferring to northeast and southeast D.C. Once again, we did not see him get off any of the buses landing east of the Anacostia River."

At this point, the excitement felt by Livermore when Mason first began his report, was beginning to wane. "Did you find any sign of him," he asked.

Here, Mason perked up again. "Maybe. We think so, but here is what we have." Mason nodded to one of his team members, who clicked the computer mouse so that a giant photo appeared on the screen.

"While we could not find any definitive evidence of Lowery, we examined all of the cameras on the streets with a six block radius of the various bus drop off points. Take a look at this photo from the convenience store on the corner of Minnesota and Benning Road, just a few blocks from the Minnesota

Avenue Metro. As you can see, the picture shows a cab at the top of the screen, facing us. The cab is sitting just below the front door to the store, unseen in this photo. No camera gives us that view. Look very carefully. You can see the boot of the man entering the back of the cab." You could hear a pin drop in the room. Everyone was craning to see the blurry boot image.

Nodding to his team member again, Mason says, "Now look at the CVS photo of Jackson, which is far clearer." Mason nods again. "Now, look at the enhanced CVS photo showing the same boot." One more nod. "Here are both enhanced boot pictures side by side. The Minnesota Avenue quality is not good, but we feel there is a good chance that this is the same boot worn by the same man, Jackson Lowery. As you can see, though we cannot see any images inside, the cabbie's D.C. tag number is clearly visible. If you all agree, we think that cab driver can tell us where he dropped off Jackson Lowery. We have posted the cabbie's name and address on the screen." Having finished with a flourish, Mason sat down. A couple of the techs started to clap, but quickly stopped when Livermore jerked his head in their direction. Still, this was big news. They had a lead.

In part looking to put the focus back on himself, Livermore did not waste time deciding on next steps. "That is superior work by you and your team, Mason." Glancing snidely at a couple of his ground team, Livermore said, "You think you boys can take it from here, with no mistakes?"

Four of his men, two who had happened to serve with him at Desert Storm, quickly stood up. "Yes, sir!" they said in unison.

"Well, we shall see. Keep in mind the big plan. The world thinks this black college professor is a nut case. None of us can pull the trigger. Once we identify where he is, law enforcement will make sure that our friends are among those who arrive on the scene. Lowery will go out in a blaze of glory. R.J., you have the gun?"

"Sure do, boss," R.J. replied, referring to the handgun that he had wrapped Jackson's hands around while he was unconscious.

Smiling for the first time in ten hours, Livermore raised both hands and said, "Well, happy hunting, boys!"

THREE

Jackson had followed Ronnie's instructions and easily found the dangling cord hanging near the passenger side window of the Volvo. He got out of the car, walked around to where the cord was hanging and gave it a firm tug. Right in front of him, an automatic door opener began to open a mechanical door. The opening door was not wide enough for a car to pass through. Leaving the car out front, Jackson walked in, entering into a big, open room. The smell of fresh coffee hit him like manna from heaven. He realized that he had not eaten anything or had anything to drink since yesterday. He hadn't even thought about it. It felt at that moment that he had been running for weeks. He was tired, thirsty, hungry, and emotionally spent.

On the right side of the room was a large sofa and a couple of side chairs. They were facing a wall that had a large seventy-two inch television flanked by six thirty-two inch televisions, three positioned on either side of the big one. Just right of the stack of televisions was a long work table. On it were what looked to be a couple of hard drives, computer screens, and other technology pieces. *Security*, Jackson thought.

To the left, was a kitchen area, which included a kitchen table set up for four. Straight ahead was a long hallway with doors to other rooms on both sides. Way down at the far end of the hall was still a larger, heavier door. Jackson surmised that Ronnie would return through that door.

Jackson saw a red button next to the door he had just entered and pushed it, which led to the automatic opener closing the door behind him.

Jackson walked to the kitchen, grabbed the coffee pot and poured himself a cup. Ronnie had left two cups on the kitchen counter along with some cream. Jackson liked a touch of cream in his coffee, while Ronnie liked his black. Of course, Ronnie would remember that.

Jackson grabbed his cup of coffee, took a satisfying sip and headed for the sofa. He could feel his body relaxing, which for some reason scared him. He still did not feel totally safe. There was an end table on the right side of the sofa. Several remote controls were on top of the table. Since he was not completely sure which was which, he started to turn them all on, one by one, and sat on the sofa. As the seven television screens came to life, he quickly noticed that his image was on four of the screens. A fifth screen showed the distraught Senator Duncan in front of his home. Jackson thought he was going to be sick. He decided that he was not ready for the news coverage on his life. He turned off all of the TV's.

He sat drinking his coffee, trying hard to relax and clear his mind. He and Ronnie had a lot to talk about. Jackson stretched out of the sofa and reached into his pocket, grabbing the New Yorker article Ronnie had given him. Before long, he was fast asleep.

Rutherford Sims had been driving a cab in D.C. for nearly forty years. Things sure have changed during that time. Fights with the politicians at the D.C. Taxicab Commission, the battle over meter versus zone rates, and probably the biggest of all: Uber and Lyft. With the new amateurs taking over, most of his customers were the reliable seniors he regularly picked up for doctor appointments, senior luncheons, and grocery runs. "Well, that's life," he said to himself.

With it nearing noon, Rutherford decided to grab some lunch. Since he had skipped breakfast and was, as usual, near the Minnesota Avenue/Benning Road corridor, he decided to go to the Denny's near the Shrimp Boat, an old D.C. landmark. Sims had been sitting there for ten minutes when two white cops, one younger and one older came over to his booth and sat across from him. Both were smiling that "I am your cop friend" smile.

Still wanting to enjoy his eggs while they were hot, Sims broke off a piece with his fork and put it in his mouth.

"How can I help you officers?" he said, savoring his omelet.

"Howdy, Mr. Sims," said the older cop, who was actually R.J., Livermore's second in command. R.J. had come personally on this assignment to make sure that this critical lead was not lost. "Sorry to interrupt your lunch. Oh, and we are not cops, but we are here on a matter of national security," R.J. said with a smile.

Sims looked them up and down as he chewed on his white toast. Yes, the white toast he promised his wife he would stop eating. "How much does it pay," he said, smiling back at R.J.

Already anxious to be involved in the conversation, John, who Sims viewed as the young cop, could not contain himself. "Look here, sir, this is not some minor matter in which you are going to get some payoff. This is a matter of national security. Lives are at stake and this matter rises all the way up to the President of the United States."

John's voice rose at the end, prompting the other patrons at nearby tables to look in his direction.

Sims was now emboldened. "You saying President Coleman's involved?" He was getting loud now, loving the fact that he knew the packed restaurant was on his side. "Sheettt! Y'all can arrest me right now, I ain't doing a mother fucking thing for Barry Coleman!"

Some of the patrons started to clap. Others issued a few 'Amens'. The inexperienced John had made the wrong move.

R.J. looked sharply at him and saved the day. In order to gain Sims' trust back, R.J. had to embarrass the kid in front of everyone. The kid wouldn't understand at first, but this would be a coachable moment for him.

"John, that is not the way to talk to Mr. Sims. Take your butt back to the car and wait for me there. Right now!"

Looking confused and uncertain, the young cop stood up and walked toward the restaurant door. On the way out, he was heckled a bit, but most people just let him off the hook. Through it all, Sims was finishing up his eggs and now slurping on some coffee, feeling pretty good about making a cop give him respect -- especially in front of so many people. Word got out quick in this neighborhood and Sims knew he would be able to embellish the story without refute.

Looking at Sims, R.J. saw that his ruse was working. He added to it.

"Mr. Sims, fuck the kid. He is young, arrogant and doesn't know his ass from a hole in the wall, but I have a job to do and you can help me. Around 11:30 pm last night, you picked up a fare from the convenience store on Minnesota Avenue and Benning Road. The man you picked up is a wanted man. A very bad man. He has hurt a lot of people. I need to find him before he hurts someone else."

While R.J. was talking, Sims was weighing his options, all while keeping a poker face. First, he conveyed a look like he was trying to remember the man, then a look as if he was trying to remember the drop off. From the time the cop started talking, however, Sims knew exactly who he was talking about. He distinctly remembered the man in the convenience store offering $100 to the first man who could give him a ride. Sims had hop-skipped past his friend Jimbo and grabbed the honeybee. First, the man said to take him to Baltimore. Then the New Carrollton Metro. Then, finally, the man had him drop him off on Sheriff Road in a residential area. By the time R.J. had finished, Sims knew exactly how to play it.

Nodding his head as if he had made a decision, Sims said, "Look, man. I don't know you or your partner and I sure don't want to know you. I also don't believe that bullshit about national security. But, yeah, I remember the man. Remember him well. At first, he acted like he could not pay all the fare, but he came up with it. I don't like the hustlers out here getting in my cab and chiseling me out of my money. Got no loyalty to the likes of that." Sims then leaned forward, looked around and spoke in a whisper. As is the natural thing to do, R.J. leaned forward as well, listening closely to Sims' every word.

Sims continued. "Man, you got your job to do and I got mine. I can tell you exactly where I dropped him off, for $200, non-negotiable." Sims crossed his arms over his ample belly and leaned back in his chair, staring at R.J.

R.J. thought hard before responding. He wanted to negotiate, but he believed that this old coot was serious. He should dock the money from the kid's pay. Still, he wanted to get something more in return.

"If I pay you the money, will you show me exactly the spot?"

"Now, man, you done lost your mind. First of all, that is not my offer. I got clients to pick up this afternoon. But, more than that, once I tell you where it is, you won't need me to show you. You can just go there."

Sighing loudly, R.J. agreed. "Okay, Mr. Sims. We have a deal. He reached in his pocket, pulled out a couple of hundred dollar bills and started to reach across and hand them to Sims, who held out his hand in a stop motion.

"How about a ten as well, for my lunch you boys interrupted?" Sims said with a sly grin.

By now, R.J. wanted to take the money and smash it in the old guy's face. He was beginning to feel that familiar feeling he felt when he wanted to hurt someone; his demons were never too far away. But he stayed on task, smiling sweetly. "Of course, Mr. Sims. Here you are," giving him the $210.

"Where did you drop him off?"

"That's easy, my friend. I dropped him off at the New Carrollton Metro station. He made sure that I did not take him all the way to the station and had me drop him off a block and half before we got there."

"Smiling, R.J. stood up and patted Sims on the shoulder. "Thanks so much, sir," while heading to the door.

Sims held his money in the light and said loudly, "Nice doing business with ya." Then yelling at his waitress, he said, "Hey, baby, how about a fresh cup of coffee. Also, bring me over the dessert menu."

Steve Mills and Bill Merchant decided to meet for lunch at the Hay Adams the day after Amy Duncan's murder. There was a decided tone of nervousness in the air as they discussed all that had transpired over the previous eighteen hours.

"So, are we in the middle of a shit-storm or what?" Merchant said, looking around.

"Things are not good, I will give you that, Bill. But, honestly, the way things unfolded, was there any other way to handle things? I didn't think we had any other options under the circumstances. Tell me, what could we have done differently?"

"Do not take this the wrong way, but for one, you did not have to talk so specifically and graphically in the senator's home! You have always been the one urging discretion, Steve. The timing of your candor got us in a hell of a mess." It was obvious the pressure was getting to Merchant.

Mills tried to be contrite. "Alright. You made that point last night and I was dead wrong. We still are positioned to get things back on track. I think..."

Merchant cut him off. "Are we, Steve? It has been over fifteen hours and our former navy seals, black op experts have no idea where a non-military college professor could have gone. No frickin' idea! How does that happen? Do you know all the strings we have had to pull to gain access to satellites, local authorities' data and the like? Yet, today we have a civilian out there somewhere who could destroy something we have been planning for years and Livermore can't tell us where he is. Really, Steve? I know you received some of the same communications that I did from some of the others in the group. Roger is on the move. I can feel it. You know how he is ready to go full-blown militant at any time. The next forty-eight hours are going to be critical. Steve, you and I have helped shape this thing from the beginning. I am telling you as a friend, we have got to find the right way to get things back on track."

Mills did not immediately respond. He just looked as his friend while rubbing his forefinger on his chin stubble. The honesty of Merchant's words stung, especially the way in which they were delivered. Mills has largely been the more outspoken of the two and Merchant has gladly accepted a quieter role. For Merchant to assert himself now in this way suggested how bad things were. It also suggested that the others in the group were questioning Mills' leadership. Mills didn't doubt Merchant's loyalty to him. But his friend was sending him another subtle and direct message: these folks were not to be played with and friend or not, he would not be able to help him if they started looking for a sacrificial lamb.

Still watching Merchant picking over his steak salad, Mills could not help but reflect on their history together. The two of them had met many years ago at a New York fundraiser for Rudy Giuliani's failed senate run against Hillary Clinton. The event was at the Waldorf Astoria and they both happened to be sitting at the hotel bar watching a television interview of a local black politician who had sponsored legislation to decriminalize marijuana. As the politician stumbled over his words, Merchant said, "It would be nice if we could understand what the fuck he is trying to say." He then caught himself and said, "Sorry, I have had too much to drink."

Mills immediately chimed in. "No need to apologize, my friend. He is probably doing the best he can." He then extended his hand. "Steve Mills, nice to meet you."

Smiling, Merchant grabbed Mills hand and said, "Same here. Bill Merchant."

From that initial meeting, they learned how much they had in common regarding their shared views on the inferiority of ethnic minorities. Mills had been raised in Nassau County, New York by a working class father who had been eased out of his manufacturing job by an incompetent black colleague benefiting from affirmative action. As a result, the Mills family continued to struggle financially. At least that is how Mills' father saw it. At an early age, Mills had vowed to become financially successful. He was also determined not to be victimized by incompetent minorities.

Merchant, however, was raised in a well-to-do New Haven, Connecticut household. His parents were both college educated. His father owned the most successful insurance company in the state, while his mother taught at Yale. Even though both parents hid their unpopular views on race, their thinking was passed on to their only child. Merchant grew up believing in the inherent intellectual superiority of white people.

Merchant also introduced Mills to *The Turner Diaries*, a book depicting a violent revolution in the United States which leads to the overthrow of the federal government, nuclear war, and, ultimately, a race war. In the book, all groups opposed by white supremacists, such as Jews, gays, and non-whites, are exterminated. *The Turner Diaries* is the Bible of the white supremacist movement.

Before long, Mills and Merchant secretly explored ways in which they could support a white supremacy movement. Initially, they covertly funded hate groups in Montana, Idaho, Wyoming and the Dakotas. They soon settled on the fact that indirect, clandestine social disruption activities were far more effective than the aggressively violent actions employed by hate groups. They began to feel out rich friends on the far right to see if others shared their views. Though years in the making, their efforts were on the verge of yielding results far beyond their initial expectations. Mills knew that his overexcitement threatened to destroy all that they had built over the years.

"Look Bill, I fucked up. And I cannot overstate how appreciative I am of our friendship and your support. But our cause is too strong for us to turn back now. I promise you, we will claw our way back from all of this. I am leaning hard on Livermore. He thinks he has a new solid lead. Let's stay connected. That is the only way we can make it through, Bill."

Merchant bit his bottom lip and nodded. "Yes, we must stick together. I will try to keep the others at bay, but there will be a face-to-face soon. I hope to God this is all done before that meeting."

"Me too," Mills said. "Me too."

———

Jackson did not know how long he had been asleep when he awoke with a start. He must have jumped up as soon as he heard Ronnie come in through the back door. As Ronnie sauntered in, Jackson was rubbing his eyes. "I was hoping you were able to fall asleep. Good for you. Even better that my coming through the door woke you up, because I was quiet coming in. It shows that your sense are still on full alert. You're gonna need that. You still with me, buddy?"

Ronnie could tell that Jackson was still reeling from the trauma of the last several hours. Ronnie knew the look well, having seen it on fellow troops in combat and even on the faces of some of the best black op agents he had ever seen in the field. *We all bleed,* Ronnie thought.

"Yeah, I am getting there, Ronnie. Was having a cup of coffee - thanks, by the way - and then turned on the televisions. It made me feel sick, so I didn't watch long. I pulled out your article and fell asleep while reading it." He was glancing at Ronnie's fishing attire, rounded out by a fishing hat with hooks in it.

"I figured you would turn on the TV. You needed to see what is out there. Sorry, I was gone longer than I thought. There was another boat of fishermen on the river. Had to play it out. Any thoughts on the article?"

Jackson smiled a little before answering. It came back to him how much Ronnie liked word games and puzzle solving. Even with his penchant for the grassroots side of the military, Ronnie was stimulated by strategy. Jackson remembered how much Ronnie used to drill his son, Ronnie, Jr. with mind games. Rose always thought Ronnie pushed Ronnie, Jr. too hard. Of course, that did not change Ronnie's approach one bit.

"I read most of it. Ended up dreaming about it. It says a lot about where we are that rich people are so fearful of the masses losing control that they are now building these secret underground bunkers. It seems like with the money all of them are making, they could easily join together and put policies in place to help level the playing field more. But they want to run and still be exclusive while doing so. Reading it reminded me of those zombie movies. It is hard to believe that we have gotten to this place. Why did you want me to read it, Ronnie?"

By now, Ronnie had taken off his coat, gotten his coffee and sat in one of the side chairs while Jackson was still lying prone on the sofa, leaning back on his hands held together by his crossed fingers.

"Jack, when I saw you on that screen, I knew you had stumbled into something beyond your wildest imagination, even with your experience as a federal prosecutor. A lot has happened in the years since we've talked, my friend. The article is right about our system creating this unhealthy tension between the elites and the rest of the population. But what the article did not point out are two things that I am sure the author didn't get. One, there are probably ten, maybe twenty times as many bunkers out here than he thinks and those bunkers were not built by zillionaires. Not at all. They have been built by people like me. Law enforcement, military, and espionage types who see another tension that could be worse than that between rich and poor."

"What tension is that, Ronnie?" asked Jackson, now fully interested.

"The tension between the people and the government, not over the economy, but the government's potential to start ruling with an iron fist. We rail about Hitler, Saddam Hussein, Castro, and Kim Jong-un in North Korea. We say it could never happen to us. Well, for those of us who have seen how these things start and ultimately end in other countries, we look at the old US of A and say, 'wait, I have been in this movie'. That is why more and more of us are taking our precautions. At its core, survivalism is about preparing for the breakdown of society. While I did not believe it to be possible years ago, it could happen Jack, sooner than we think."

Jackson was taking a lot in. "Okay, let's say that premise is true. How does that relate to Amy? How does it relate to my situation?"

Ronnie put his coffee down and leaned forward putting his forearms on his knees. "This is it, Jack. Whatever led these guys to kill the daughter of our next possible president and drag a respected former prosecutor through the mud is big beyond belief. Whatever it is, it must have the potential impact to help destabilize all of our systems. The chaos created by that instability is what leads to another Hitler or Kim Jong-un. I know it without knowing anything more than what I have seen on the networks. As soon as I got the gist of what was happening, I sent Rose and Ronnie to our bunker." Ronnie then lifted his hands spreading them wide. "This here is just a secure hideaway. Not a bunker for the long term. Like those mentioned in the article, we have a bunker that is fully sustainable for years, if need be."

Jackson was slowly shaking his head. "How do Rose and Ronnie, Jr. feel about this?"

"They understand. Hell," he laughs out loud. "They live with me! Truth is, I told them this is just temporary. We all were praying that you would call me and then make it here. Rose always liked you, Jack. She said, 'I trust Jackson to do the right thing while you both save us from whatever this madness is'. That's high praise, my brother."

Rose's words warmed Jackson. Jackson's ex wife, Pam and Ronnie were first cousins. Both of their parents were born and raised in Marietta. When Jackson first got married, they spent a lot of time going back and forth from D.C. to Ohio. They spent a lot of time with Ronnie and Rose. That was a good time period for Jackson.

"Yes, it is, Ronnie." Jackson now stood up, still processing all that Ronnie had said. Factoring all that he knew, which Ronnie did not, made everything Ronnie had just said pretty remarkable and scary.

Ronnie was not finished. "There is one other thing that sealed my thinking, Jack."

Curious, Jackson asked, "What was that?"

"Remember my undercover days in Montana? Well, I was getting closer and closer to the real food chain, I heard some of the local leaders talk about the money folks. The name Steve Bills came up a few times. When the bust went down, we sent a bunch to jail, but that white nationalist crowd is a pretty loyal, close-mouthed bunch. We could never find a Bills or Bill or even Stevens that made sense. We ended up thinking it was some code name. When the first report came out about Amy Duncan, the news said that the senator and his wife were hosting a dinner at their home with guests Steve Mills and Bill Merchant. In the statement from the senator's office, which was read on all the stations, Duncan and his wife thanked 'Steve and Bill for their understanding and support during this troubled time'. Then, it really hit me. All this time, our Montana team had been thinking about one main money guy, that was our focus. What if Steve Bill was Steve and Bill, two high powered, wealthy Republican donors who were angling to improve their influence? Jack, I do not believe in coincidences. I need to know more about these guys. It feels like there is something to this."

Inside, Jackson was marveling at his friend's sense of intuition. Jackson was also feeding off of Ronnie's sense of purpose. He could feel himself moving from a place of grief to a place of action.

"All I can say is that all of your instincts are dead on, Ronnie. Now, it's my turn. Let me tell you all that I know. Then, let's do what Rose expects us to do and fight this madness." Jackson then preceded to tell him everything. From the very beginning.

———————

After getting the needed information, the bird drone returned to the two men in the fishing boat on the Ohio River. The men who had been fishing within fifty yards of Ronnie Thomas.

While at first glance they looked like a father and son, Dick Strother and Russ McNair were actually two of the best clandestine operatives in the country. When it became clear that Jackson had lasted through the night, with no leads from the Livermore led team, Steve Mills and Bill Merchant's co-conspirators decided that enough was enough and they independently secured the best. The fact that they did so without the knowledge of Mills and Merchant spoke volumes.

Prior to last night's debacle, major doubts existed about the competency of Livermore and his team. But to allow an untrained, black college professor go undetected for twelve hours, without any clues as to his whereabouts, was the last straw.

Within an hour of being hired by Roger Tyler, Strother and McNair had dispatched five active teams to surveil folks from Jackson's past, like his former college roommate who had been a navy seal, and the prosecutor who was part of Jackson's orientation class at the U.S. Attorney's office who later became an active CIA field agent in Romania. But more importantly, the most obvious target of all was Jackson's ex-wife's first cousin, Ronnie Thomas, the former Marine and black ops expert--a force to be reckoned with in his own right. For Livermore to not even know about Thomas was unforgivable and was a direct indictment against the leadership of Mills and Merchant.

That morning, the new contractors caught up with Thomas as he was pulling his Ford truck into his favorite fishing dock on the Ohio River. While the occupants in both boats faked their interest in fishing, a satellite was set in place to lock in on and monitor Thomas.

Once the satellite was in place, Strother and McNair pulled anchor and left the area - but only so far. The bird drone they controlled via smartphone hovered until Ronnie pulled ashore on the West Virginia side of the Ohio. From there, the drone video captured Ronnie's trek through the woods, as well as his uncovering of his hideaway. Once Ronnie was secure inside, Dick Strother uttered his first word of the day, "Bingo!"

———————

Steve Mills has always had a problem with Roger Tyler. Actually, more than one. Sure, the man has connections.

What Hampton-Powell chairman wouldn't? But the man is a bit self-righteous, if not just plain arrogant. Mills has always thought that was an all too common trait found in people who come from money, a luxury Mills did not have. Mills had to work for everything he ever got and no one handed him anything.

To those who know them both, the biggest contrast between the two men was stylistic. Mills wanted to be in charge, anyone around him could tell that. Tyler was the type that would be in charge with no one knowing that he was.

Needless to say, Mills did not smile when he saw that Tyler was calling him.

"Hello, Roger," Mills said, devoid of emotion.

"Hi, Steve. I am sorry for all you have been through the last several hours," he said.

"Thanks. We think we are close to getting things back on track. We got a lead that the man we are looking for may have been dropped off at a suburban Maryland metro station. Liver...." Tyler cut him off.

"Sorry to interrupt, Steve, but Livermore is incompetent. We can talk more about that later, but I took the liberty of securing a contractor to help us out."

Mills was livid. He really wanted to give Tyler a piece of his mind. He held his tongue largely because he knew that his own carelessness had led to the mess.

"Well, that may be been a bit rash, Roger. This new lead has reliability written all over it."

Roger Tyler sighed. That self-righteous, arrogant sigh that Mills hates.

"Steve, that lead means nothing. Our contractor has been on the job just a couple hours and thinks he knows where our guy is. We can talk about all of this in detail later. In fact, we all need to meet. In the meantime, tell Livermore to stand down for now. The contractor will come to see him, so that we all can get integrated. For now, the contractor is in charge."

Mills wanted to push back, but was stunned when Tyler said that the contractor had already found Lowery. If that is true, Livermore has some answering to do.

He asked, "Is the contractor who I think it is?"

"The very same, Steve. He is expensive, but he gets the job done."

"Fine, Roger. I will let Livermore know. Hopefully, this will all be stabilized soon."

"That is my hope as well, Steve. It truly is. Oh, before I forgot, there is one more important thing. We are no longer looking to damage the target's reputation. We are now well beyond that." he hesitated.

Mills hesitated as well. For once, however, he found total agreement with Tyler's way of thinking.

"Good," Mills replied. "No loose ends."

"Agreed, Steve." Tyler said.

Ronnie had listened patiently as Jackson told his story. While Jackson was talking, Ronnie did take the time to whip up some eggs and fried potatoes, southern style. Ronnie also heated up some honey and biscuits. It was all washed down with two bottled waters each and a fresh pot of coffee. Ronnie had made sure to flip a couple of switches to vent the air and minimize the smell from the food. The two friends sat at the table and enjoyed their meal when Ronnie finally commented on all that Jackson had said.

"Well, of course, as you know, it all fits, Jack. I am sorry about Amy. She sounded special," he said sincerely.

"Thanks, Ronnie. She was, though I really did not know her very well. Funny, we both obviously had this attraction for each other for some time, but, as usual, I was stuck in my head."

"For good reason," Ronnie said. "It is not a good practice to fraternize with your students."

"No, I get that. And I agree. I guess what I am saying, Ronnie, is that I really liked her." Jackson was looking to change the subject. He had been, after all, married to Ronnie's first cousin.

"I know, man. And again, I am sorry. Right now, we need to do two things. First, we need to decide if we go on offense or defense. I can tell you right now, that going on offense puts both of us more at risk, but probably paints a straighter line to the truth."

"Is that even a question? I pick offense. So that's two votes," he said with a smile.

Ronnie smiled back. "Okay. I will come back to that. The second thing is that we really need to talk through the meaning behind what Amy heard. How do you exterminate or severely cripple an entire generation of black and brown folks? We need to talk about how who is in the White House could impact on all of that."

"I know. I was thinking about it a lot while driving here." He then told Ronnie about his who, what, when, where, why, and how approach to investigating cases while practicing law. "But let's take a step back. Let's not think in terms of eliminating a 'certain' group of people. Maybe we should start by discussing generally how you eliminate wholesale amounts of people, period, irrespective of race."

Ronnie scratched his head. Jackson's point resonated with him. "Gotcha, Jack, I see where you are coming from. Let's go backwards from there. List the ways."

"A virus? Disease? Contaminated food, air, water?"

Ronnie chimed in. "Some form of weaponry? Poisonous gas? Fires? It has to be one of these things."

"Right," Jackson said. "Now, let's look at how you can target a certain group or groups and limit the collateral damage. By the way, for something like this to work, the traitorous bastards are okay with some collateral damage. But what is the best way to minimize it?"

"Looking at it that way, Jack, you cannot control a virus or disease, once they get out of control. They see no color. Same with poisonous gas. I also am skeptical about putting anything toxic in the air. Hard to target."

Both men went quiet. Jackson spoke next. "Water?"

"We have to consider it. Look at what happened in Flint, Michigan in 2016. Let's say you pick the water supply for the twenty-five or fifty most populous black cities. That could be devastating."

"Alright," Jackson said. "So how do you do it? Especially for quick maximum effect. Flint was about lead poisoning. The results were tragic, but it just feels like these guys are looking to have folks drop dead."

Ronnie was nodding. Both men had left the table by now. Ronnie was sitting in the chair and Jackson was back on the couch. They were looking at each other.

"Food," Jackson said.

"Yep, it's gotta be," Ronnie agreed. "So, we are knocking down your list of questions. Who, what..." Jackson cut him off.

"Wait, Ronnie. Hold it a minute. If it's definitely the food, let's look at the food sources in the hood. Plus remember what Amy said, 'able to exterminate a generation of black and brown babies'. Outside of church, where are we the most segregated?"

Ronnie didn't hesitate. "Schools," he said.

Jackson snapped his fingers. "That's right! And intensely so. Not long ago, I heard a speech at AU by a former D.C. Councilman, who has since gotten into the education reform movement. He shared a statistic that shocked me. Did you know that there are over 13,000 school districts in America?"

Ronnie kind of twisted his face. "I really never thought about it."

"I know, right? But hear me out. The Councilman was making one point of how segregated our schools were, but he was making another point that because so many black and brown kids are highly concentrated in the same school districts, we should be able to target them and fix them. Guess how many of the 13,000 school districts host most of our kids of color? 500! Most black and brown kids in America - well over 50% he said - are found in just 500 school districts. What if you controlled that food supply?"

Jackson was flush with excitement.

Ronnie, understanding the logic, confirmed Jackson's excitement. "You know, you may be onto something, Jack. That would be such a sick but brilliant plan. We need to keep brainstorming this."

Just then a faint warning siren came from Ronnie's long work table to the right of his televisions. Ronnie was on full alert. "Damn it! We have been compromised, Jack! They are on to us. Shit, I knew those guys on the boat weren't from around here. I should have caught on when they never said a word to each other."

"How do you know they're after me?"

"Ronnie pointed to a computer screen on the table, pushed a couple of buttons on a keypad, which converted the screen to a satellite imaging map. Pointing to one part of the screen, he said, "There are the two guys I am betting were on the boat near me. They docked their boat near mine and are headed near my door. See up top here?" he said, pointing to the far end of the screen. "There are two, no three cars headed down the road near where I let you in. They waited until I was comfortable, thinking they would catch me with the element of surprise. What they don't know, what I didn't tell you is that there is a third way out. Grab your things, I have a bag all ready to go. Looks like going on offense is going to have to wait. We are playing total defense right now, Jack!"

FOUR

General Michael Brock felt bad. Just horrible. How could this have happened? His best friend's daughter is dead and somehow he played a role in her death? He did not know Steve Mills well, but had heard about his ego. Brock was glad that Roger Tyler was stepping in to manage things. A steady hand was what was needed most at this time.

But Brock's thoughts kept going back to Rex and Reba. When he spoke to his old friend, he could hear the faraway pain in his voice. They had met at Harvard, two mountain state conservative eighteen year olds among a sea of liberal egotists. Both were raised on large, successful farms owned and managed by their fathers. They bonded quickly. As the Harvard years passed, they grew closer and closer. Brock smiled at the memory of some of their debating team successes. Some of those damned east coast liberals had no idea that an Idahoan and a Montanan could out-compete them.

As both men continued to matriculate, it became clear that Brock's views became far more strident. He came to believe that power surpasses all, so the end game was to be in charge. But there was another, darker side to Brock's political philosophy, one he never discussed openly. Brock had a fixated hierarchical view of society. According to that view, whites were superior to other races in every way and were more equipped to lead the nation and the world. Brock recognized the political incorrectness of his thinking, but his review of history only reinforced his views. Many of his initial thoughts came from his father, a Montana farmer who did not believe in race-mixing of any kind. Brock grew up hearing legendary tales about his own grandfather's westward expansion journey. Fixated between his father and grandfather's stories was a John Wayne cowboy image that was unshakeable in the Brock household. Indians, Mexicans, and Blacks were all subservient to whites. As unpopular as that belief sounds, Brock believed it to his core.

Brock's military experience only served to deepen his views. Yes, the military is known for its diversity, but again, from Brock's vantage point the strategic and critical thinking needed during a time of crisis was always found among the white men in leadership. Sadly, however, America's desire to please everyone politically has gotten in the way of its effectiveness. Diversity has lowered all of the standards that had made us great, according to Brock's way of thinking. Unless we radically changed our direction as a nation, he believed, we would perish.

As he grew in rank and prestige, Brock was able to disguise his radical views on race. It helped that his best friend was the compassionate conservative, Rex Duncan. Brock's conversations with Rex on this issue were far more open than they were with his late wife. Bless her heart. Maggie was the love of his life until cancer took her from him five years ago. As much as they loved each other, however, he could never get her to his side on matters of race. She had been hog-washed by that damn Lutheran preacher father of hers. Despite it all, he still loved her.

Fortunately, near the time of her death, Brock met Roger Tyler at a dinner. After several after-dinner scotches, Brock saw that his views were not as isolated as he thought. Brock learned about Tyler's history. It was well known that he came from wealth. But most people did not know that much of that wealth started on the southern plantations owned by his mother's ancestors. Tyler's great-great grandfather served as a Confederate general under Stonewall Jackson during the Civil War. Tyler grew up believing that people of color were inferior to whites and it galled him to see the demographic population shifts in America. These shifts were first brought to his attention by his mother, who was a teacher. One day, she came home from a teachers' meeting complaining about the population growth in the colored schools. "The way those negroes keep having babies," she said at the dinner table, "one day there will be more of them in this county than there are of us."

Tyler told Brock that he was reminded of his mother's words when his company's marketing team once told him that within twenty years, whites would be a distinct minority. They had said that people of color would be in the majority by 2044. Then, Tyler saw demographers on a PBS program say that people of color would be in the majority by 2025. American schools were already majority minority.

Tyler could not stomach the thought of white people holding a subservient role in America. The only way to stop these trends was to radically stem the rapid reproduction of black and brown kids. Tyler told Brock that something bold and unthinkable had to be done to help save America.

Tyler introduced him to others who thought like him: prominent, well-respected figures who passionately believed in the separation of the races, but had no solid idea on how to reverse the current trends. That is, until they all got together. Before long, the plan emerged. Diabolical yet ingenious at the same time, once implemented, a rightful pecking order would return to America. We are at the dawn of a new day in America, Brock believed.

I will go see Rex and Reba tonight, he thought. Brock knew all too well that Amy Duncan could not be brought back. Brock also knew, however, that the plan would not be derailed and that Rex was key to the plan, an unwitting pawn in the plan to save America. "We all have to get past this," he muttered to himself. Brock would support his friend, and then get him refocused. For our future. He then grabbed the phone to inform his staff that he would be visiting Senator Duncan that night.

While he had made meticulous and diligent plans for any eventuality, Ronnie was caught off guard by the quick discovery of his hideaway. *These can't be the same guys who had been chasing Jackson*, he thought. *No way these guys would have let him get out of D.C., much less Maryland or beyond.*

Ronnie put these thoughts aside as he grabbed two big duffel bags from behind the shelving holding the computer equipment, tossing one bag to Jackson. He then grabbed a smaller duffel, unzipped it a bit, reached in and then tossed a gun to Jackson. "Still know how to use these things, Jack?"

"Yes."

"Good."

Ronnie then went down the hall past the kitchen, motioning for Jackson to follow him. He opened the first door to the left, giving way to a small bedroom containing a twin bed and small dresser. Ronnie pushed the dresser aside, reached down and pulled up a trap door. "Go down first, Jack. Toss the duffel bag

104

and hold your arms in tight like a downhill skier. You will break an arm if you extend it too much. As soon as you hit the bottom, open the duffel bag and grab the black jumpsuit. Put it on. It will block the heat from your body from giving up satellite images. Hear me?"

Jackson nodded and looked down the trap door. He saw a cylinder slide similar to those seen at amusement parks, which plop their riders into the water below. Strangely, Jackson was not nervous. He was in his own form of game mode.

Ronnie acknowledged Jackson's nod. "Good. I am right behind you," Ronnie said.

Jackson threw in the duffel bag first, then followed feet first, hugging himself with his arms. It felt as though he went steeply downhill at first, then it mostly straightened out laterally near the end. When he stopped, he quickly followed Ronnie's instructions and climbed into the jump suit.

Ronnie's duffel bags followed a few seconds later, then Ronnie. Ronnie put on his suit, reached into the small duffel and pulled out a phone.

Jackson had been so focused on following orders that he did not pay as much attention to his environment. They were clearly outside, but in the thick of the forest. It was a bright, sunny, cool fall day. He could hear the mighty Ohio River not far ahead. If his bearings were right, he and Ronnie probably slid to the left of and slightly underneath the two fisherman who were approaching form the river side.

Ronnie held up a finger to his lips and led Jackson toward the left. Jackson could tell that they were headed just beyond the shoreline parallel to the river. After about one hundred yards, Ronnie stopped, walked to a certain spot and removed some foliage, revealing a plastic tarp cover. He quickly pulled it apart. Jackson could see the shape of a small motorcycle. Ronnie climbed on, while Jackson climbed on in back of him.

Before starting it up, Ronnie made a call. Jackson could only hear Ronnie's end of the call.

"You where I need you? Good. How is traffic? Okay. Will have to do. Be there in seven minutes for the switch."

Ronnie then started the motorcycle and shot off. Almost immediately after the motorcycle started, shooting came in their direction. Ronnie, while navigating on the narrow pathway, pushed in a few numbers on his phone and the next thing Ronnie heard was a loud explosion coming from a direction behind the hideaway. He then heard a man howl in pain.

The gunfire got more and more distant. If it were the guys in the boat from earlier today, Jackson thought, they were on foot. *No way they could catch us*. Jackson then heard another explosion. He knew then that the hideaway was destroyed.

Ronnie kept his pedal to the metal and a few minutes later they were approaching a bridge underpass. There seemed to be a fair amount of traffic on the bridge heading it both directions: West Virginia and Ohio. Then the beauty of the escape hit Jackson. Just before the bridge underpass, there was what appeared to be a motorcycle/dirt bike riding area. Several bikers were doing jumps and stunt moves. As they were nearing the stunt area, four bikers raced toward them and turned their bikes around so that they all could approach the bridge together. Ronnie had slowed down considerably to allow them to all be in sync. Just as they got to the underpass, the five bikers, including Ronnie, all weaved back and forth between each other. At the underpass, each bike stopped. They were under the bridge, hidden from the cars or foot traffic above. It was at that time that Jackson noticed one other biker had a passenger. That passenger got off of the bike it was on and ran to the one that contained Ronnie and Jackson. Ronnie jumped off, holding the handlebars for the passenger from the other bike. Jackson had already gotten off the bike and was waiting to follow Ronnie's lead. Ronnie gave Jackson a quick, approving look, then walked away from the bridge, along the shoreline, close to the woods. Jackson followed, but also turned to see all the bikers maneuver the five bikes onto the bridge, whereupon, they scattered in different directions.

Ronnie slipped into the woods and after they had walked another couple of miles or so - this time away from the river - Jackson saw an old farmhouse. By now, the duffel bag was weighing Jackson down some, but he did not dare complain. Next to the house was a dark blue Ford Explorer. The house appeared to be empty, but Ronnie showed no hesitation as he pointed to the passenger side of the car while entering on the driver's side himself, throwing his gear in the back. He then started the car, put it in drive and took off. When they turned onto the main road, Ronnie turned to Jackson and said, "You did damn good, Jack. Would've loved to have had you in my unit. Let's go play some offense."

He then plunged the Explorer deeper into the state of West Virginia.

———————

Like most Americans, the news about Senator Rex Duncan's daughter hit Joe Charles pretty hard, both personally and professionally. Personally, he had, over time and quite unexpectedly, developed a friendship with the senator, socializing with him on many occasions. As a result, he had seen the young and beautiful Amy Duncan quite often. Shaking his head and thinking about it all, Charles could not help but focus on one of the saddest aspects of this tragedy: the once troubled Amy had turned her life around, personally and between herself and her parents. How sad. With two daughters of his own, he could only imagine what the senator and his wife, Reba are going through. When he got the news about Amy, Joe Charles was unsure about what to do. He wanted to call his friend, but that did not feel right to him. Instead, he called Rex's chief of staff to offer his condolences, who promised Charles that she would deliver the message.

A media darling, Joe Charles is a prominent figure in a new wave of Black businessmen and entrepreneurs. He is the CEO of Bartlett Foods, a food service company based in Chicago. Joe's grandfather founded the company and he is very proud of his family roots. Originally a small catering company on Chicago's south side, Charles began expanding the company's services ten years ago to provide breakfast and lunch services to school districts. His biggest boost was in winning the highly lucrative Chicago Public Schools lunch services contract. He then won six more urban school district contracts before his progress stalled. A big believer in minority empowerment, Charles has made it known that he wants to be the face of food in underserved communities. His innovative and creative approach includes offering cooking classes for parents and students as well as job opportunities for folks in the neighborhood. In every school where he has contracts, he has an unlimited amount of fruit, vegetables and juices available for kids to snack on throughout the day. There are no sodas or candy bars given to kids who receive food from Bartlett Foods.

Finally, as a way to further encourage sound, smart, and nutritious eating, Bartlett Foods also supports and oversees the implementation of community gardens for students and nearby residents to maintain. Joe Charles has made sure that his company takes a whole different approach to the food delivery business. In doing so, he has directly challenged the food service big boys, who control most of the food service contracts in school districts across America.

Charles' main competitors are the three other companies who have controlled the major food service contracts in school districts across America. These companies operate in essentially the same way they have for the last forty to fifty years. In reality, the nutritional needs of the students take a back seat to cheap, mass production food processing that can be delivered quickly and efficiently. Charles naively believed that his innovative and caring approach would allow him to cut more deeply into the big boys' footprint. Instead, each of the big three doubled down by investing more in their infrastructure. Hedge funds were willing to invest in these large food corporations because they had come to believe that food service contracts were a secure and lucrative option.

Charles, however, struggled to keep pace with competitive bids as new opportunities popped up. Plus, Charles had also begun to get death threats as his profile had grown. All the threats were overtly racist, but they did not deter Charles' efforts. His vision included bidding to provide lunch and meals on wheels type services in a handful of Native American nations in Arizona, New Mexico, and the Dakotas. His future plans included expanding further and bidding on small community college and historically black college and university food service contracts. For any of this to occur, however, he needed more political support. Yes, minority policies had been helpful. But, Charles believed that his friendship with the powerful Rex Duncan had helped him more. He knew, however, that the hedge funds were trying to leverage their various access points to the senator and push him away from Charles.

So, yes, professionally, Charles needed the senator now more than ever. Even though he hated to be selfish in his thinking at a time like this, Joe Charles knew that the powerful senator's friendship was great for business. With all that had happened, how distracted would the senator be? Would he still be as engaged day-to-day? What about the presidency? Was that a non-starter, now? More practically, how much energy would the senator have in the short term to help Charles, the most critical time for his business?

These questions and more had plagued Charles ever since he got the news about Amy Duncan's death. Charles had a meeting set with the senator later that week. Feeling guilty, Charles was still hoping that the meeting would not be canceled.

"How many were on the bike?" Strother asked.

"I just couldn't tell, Dick. My vision was totally blocked," McNair said.

Strother said nothing. They were about to force open the riverside door to Ronnie Thomas' hideaway when they heard the motorcycle crank up. Instinctively, they both backed away from the door and McNair pulled out his gun and fired in the direction of the sound. Moments later, they heard the first explosion, which was accompanied by screams. Strother and McNair looked at each other. Six of their men were looking for another entrance. Knowing that they could never catch the bike on foot, they were rushing to the screams they heard.

Fortunately for them, following the source of the screams pulled a little further from the known hideaway entrance, and the site of the second explosion. It was much closer and knocked both Strother and McNair to the ground. If they had been any closer, they would have been goners for sure. The hideaway was destroyed.

"You okay?" Strother asked his colleague.

"I will be alright. Looks like I got some kind of puncture wound on my arm, maybe from a tree branch. But I will be fine. We need to check on the others."

They scrambled up and continued in the direction of the initial screams. Soon, they saw the three dark SUVs, but two of them were upside down. They could only see three of their guys. One was leaning on the only upright car, his head was a bloody mess, but he seemed to be alright. The other two did not appear to be injured, but were kneeling on the ground near one of the upturned cars. As Strother and McNair got closer, they could tell that the two men kneeling on the ground were trying to administer to two of their injured brethren. One of the uninjured men, Todd Brown saw them approaching and stood up. Brown happened to be the leader of this team.

"Dick, Russ. Glad you are okay. Let me give you a quick report. While slowly traveling on the main road, we were on the lookout for any side dirt roads that may be partially covered. That is when we found this road." Pointing to the ground at one of the injured, he said, "Jim Link and I were in the lead vehicle. We got out and started walking down the trail. Jim was hanging a bit behind me. That is when the road erupted behind us, flipping the other two cars. Being closer to the explosion, Jim was thrown to the ground. Looks like he has a broken leg. I then heard gunfire, which I am assuming was you guys, right?"

Strother nodded.

"Right. Anyway, we then got the second explosion right over there," he said, lifting a finger in the direction of the now demolished hideaway.

McNair then asked, "How are the other two men?"

"That's the bad news, sir. Doc Gillis is dead. Jonesy is in bad shape. His guts are hanging out. Byron is over there doing what he can."

"You called medical?" Strother asked.

"On their way, sir. I am assuming Thomas is in the wind. Was the subject with him?"

McNair responded, answering both questions. "Yes, he is and we don't know if he was alone or not. I'm guessing that the subject is with him." Looking at Strother, he said, "I am going to get the satellite guys on the horn." Strother just nodded.

As they stood there, sirens could be heard in the background. Strother looked at Brown, who said, "We are covered. We have the proper sign-off by the authorities. As far as the locals are concerned, this is a matter of national security." Strother nodded.

While Strother and Brown looked on, McNair spoke with their satellite team. After a brief conversation with them, he hung up, turned to his colleagues, dramatically arched his eyebrows and said, "Here is the bottom line. No satellite or heat imaging.

They must have put on some heat blocking suits once they left the hideaway. I asked about the motorcycle or any engine movement coming from this spot. Get this. Apparently, when the motorcycle was about four or five miles away from here, it joined up with at least four other motorcycles. There is a motorcycle stunt park up the river shoreline near the next bridge into Ohio. The bikes all rotated among themselves for a short while before making their way onto the bridge and scattering in different directions. Our satellite folks did not know which one to follow."

All three men looked at each other. Each had been in the mercenary business for a long time. They had done ungodly deeds all over the world, but always ended up standing. Rarely did they run into a challenge that left them feeling like they may have met their match. Silent thoughts permeated the air around them. Brown spoke first. "This guy is good."

McNair nodded his head.

Strother, the grizzled leader refused to budge. "Maybe. But there are more of us than there are of him. Plus, the lawyer is an anchor on his neck. We will find them and we will kill them both."

After driving south on the back roads of West Virginia for about an hour, Ronnie felt comfortable enough to talk. "Those guys were not your usual white nationalist militia. Those guys are among the best. You stoked a real beehive this time, Jack."

"Looks like it, man. Hey, thank you, Ronnie. It was something to see you work. Sorry about the hideaway."

Ronnie shrugged. "No sweat, Jack. I have been trained for this. While you were learning the law books, I was learning how to surveil and survive. As for the hideaway, it served its purpose. By now, those guys have probably been all over my home in Marietta. Rose and I have been prepared for this for years. We always thought that white nationalist sympathizers or relatives of one of the guys I put away would find me, so things in Marietta have been bare bones for a while. We have another place further down south in addition to the bunker."

Jackson had his face in his hands and began rubbing his eyes, still trying to sort everything out. "Speaking of Rose, you sure she and Ronnie, Jr. are safe? Are we headed to your bunker?"

"They are fine, Jack. And we are not headed to the bunker, which, by the way, may or may not be in West Virginia. I will say that it is either in Kentucky, Ohio, West Virginia or Tennessee," he said smiling.

"Well, I am glad they are okay. I am worried about Pam and Eddie too. It seems to me that these guys are now looking to do more than set me up. They want me out of the way. What do you think?"

"I agree, Jack. When we stop, I will call a friend I trust in the D.C. area to get them both. I had given Pam a heads up while waiting for you. Plus, she knows my friend."

Curious, Jackson asked, "What did you say to her?" He leaned forward a bit in his seat.

"I just told her that I may need to get her somewhere safe. Pam knows you are innocent, Jack. She and Eddie both do. They also know these folks are dangerous. I mean, they killed Senator Duncan's daughter!"

"Okay. Thanks," Jackson said, leaning back in his passenger seat. "What now?"

"I am going to pull into this diner I know that is a few miles up the road, off the beaten path. I will call about Pam and Eddie and then call my friend in Atlanta."

"Atlanta? Is that where we are going?" Jackson asked.

"Yep. Or near there. Time for some serious offense, Jack. Atlanta gets us going. We are going to use your approach with the six questions. Atlanta may help us with the 'how'. My friend trained with me at Quantico. She was a great marine, but really got into the chemical weapon stuff. She is now with the Centers for Disease Control (CDC) in Atlanta. I trust her with my life."

"Mine too?" Jackson asked with a smirk on his face.

"I think we are both in good hands, my friend. Seriously, Jenny will be able to give us some valuable information quickly. That will help us with our next moves."

"Cool," Jackson said. He paused for a beat and then asked, "One question about the hideaway, Ronnie."

Ronnie, whose hands were gripping the steering wheel tightly, relaxed them a bit and looked quizzically over at his friend. "Sure," he said. "What gives?"

"Having the hideaway so close to the stunt bike area was a nice touch. We could not have made it out without that distraction. I guess that it is fair to assume, that you anticipate all possible scenarios in your work, right?"

Ronnie laughed. "You have to. You have to look at possible scenarios that could lead to both death and survival. Yes, the motorcycle park worked perfectly.

Of course, I had a couple of dry runs with my accomplices."

"Accomplices, who, of course, will go nameless?"

"Yes sir. We may need to call them again before all this is done."

Ronnie was not laughing when he said it.

Dick Strother had a hard time stomaching amateurs. Not only were they bad for business, they could also get you killed. With that thought, he rubbed the back part of his head, three inches above the neckline. Though hidden from view by his hair, Strother had a noticeable bump protruding from his skull. He got the bump because of an amateur mistake made by a so-called colleague back in the Sudan in the nineties.

A certain government hired Strother and another team to take out one of the ethnic cleansing war lords. Strother hated the idea, preferring to work with people he could trust to have his back. The client insisted, and also vouched for the other contractor's competence. The two teams met and divided up responsibilities for their clandestine assault. The amateurs were to secure the perimeter of the property before Strother came in to do the deed and exit quickly. The only thing was that the amateurs did not secure the perimeter. As they were exiting, Strother and his four team members were attacked by the war lord's security. The amateurs were nowhere to be found. They had left their posts.

As a result, One of Strother's team members was shot in the chest, but survived thanks to the bullet resistant vest he was wearing. Strother took a bullet in the back of his head. While it was a grazing shot, it chipped a piece of Strother's skull, leaving an unevenness on the surface of his head.

Thinking back on that assignment, Strother would have accepted it more if the other team had just double-crossed him or sold him out. But it galled him to know that his head had nearly been blown off because of incompetence. He hated amateurs.

Strother knew little about Livermore, but had no doubt that he was an amateur. McNair had spoken to the guy's number two man, R.J., who seemed competent enough, but too trusting of his boss's leadership. Not only did they not look at Lowery's family ties, they also failed to check the bus lines until it was too late, and missed some money Lowery had stashed in his apartment. Strother started shaking his head to himself.

Strother would soon be landing at the Reston airport on the plane provided by his client. From the local airport, he and his team would go to the command post Livermore had set up. While Livermore may be incompetent, this Ronnie Thomas guy was the opposite. After leaving the scene, Strother and McNair went to Thomas' Marietta home. Clean as a whistle. This guy had been ready to leave at the drop of a hat for a while. Seeing how Thomas' home was laid out confirmed what appeared obvious after they experienced the motorcycle park escape routine: Ronnie Thomas was a worthy and disciplined adversary. Strother was determined to take him out as soon as possible.

As Strother, McNair, and Todd Brown walked into the makeshift Fairfax command center, they were greeted by both Livermore and R.J.

"Hello, gentlemen," Livermore said. "We have been expecting you and look forward to working with you to bring this to a quick conclusion. If you like, we can address the group together to lay out the next steps." Livermore was swallowing his pride somewhat, having heard of Strother's reputation.

After his call with Steve Mills, he decided to be as accommodating as possible. Mills had sounded more vulnerable than he ever had. *Could that mean that Mills was on his way out?* Livermore knew he had to play his cards right. He wanted to remain a part of the new future once the plan was implemented.

Strother just looked blankly at Livermore, then half nodded to McNair, who then commented,

"We do not believe in group announcements or discussions. We give out assignments and people do their jobs. In the next half hour, we will give you the things we need done and you make sure they are given to the right folks. If anyone fucks up, they are out of here, hopefully still with their lives. No second chances." He then pulled out a map of the United States and laid it out on a nearby table.

Pointing south from Marietta, Ohio, McNair said, "From where we lost Thomas and Lowery here in Marietta, there are, of course, four directions they could go. We do not see any value in them heading north. There doesn't appear to be any asset help in Columbus or Cleveland, plus they would be a bit more boxed in. The same is true, to a lesser degree, with the westward travel option. It doesn't get them any closer to the truth or immediate help."

McNair then folded the map, covering up much of the western section.

"Logic tells us they are headed back to this area, if not now, at least eventually. Thomas has significant asset help in this region and Lowery is probably pressing to get some answers based on what the

Duncan girl told him. For him to avenge her death, he will likely have to get back to D.C. at some point."

Livermore chimed in with a question, trying to make himself appear useful. "Do we know for sure that Lowery is with Thomas? We were told that visual confirmation was never confirmed."

McNair answered. "There has not been any visual confirmation. However, from the debris found after the hideaway explosion, we saw breakfast dishes for two that had not been cleaned or cleared from the table. We also found two coffee mugs. In essence, they were having breakfast when some warning device alerted them as to our presence. We think they are together."

Livermore just nodded his head.

McNair summarized the group's objective. "We now are at a place where we need to find the targets before they make it back to D.C. We need to make sure that they do not gain access to the senator or his wife. We no longer need to bother worrying about staging any kind of set up. This is all about containment now. We need to get to Lowery and Thomas first, period. We can then cover up what needs to be covered up from there. Understood?"

Everyone nodded in agreement.

FIVE

By now, the public sentiment was that Jackson Lowery was obsessed with his pretty white student, that he periodically stalked her, and that he somehow lost it when they met on that fateful night. CNN, FOX, MSNBC and others continue to characterize him as a person of interest, but deep down, the popular belief was that Jackson killed the senator's daughter. This sentiment worked perfectly from the vantage point of Tyler, Mills, Merchant, the General and their co-conspirators. But increasingly, Mills was concerned that a change in this widely held perception could be devastating. He said as much to Bill Merchant while Strother, Livermore, and others were meeting in Fairfax.

Reaching Merchant on the phone, he said, "Bill, what if the public changes its mind and sees love? That could send things in a whole different direction, don't you think?"

"I do, Steve. But that is why I feel better having the contractor on board. They will make quick work of this and our problems will be solved."

"But what if they don't? What if, somehow, this stretches out for a few more days and a believable love story emerges?"

Merchant had to think through that one. Ever since Roger Tyler had become more assertive, Merchant felt more at ease. As much as he loved his friend Mills, Merchant believed that Tyler's steadiness was best suited for this crisis. "This is what I think, Steve. We should circle back with Roger, the contractor, and others about that issue and reach an

121

understanding on how to quash any facts or other sources that change that perception."

Mills liked what he was hearing. Being proactive was always the best approach. "Makes sense, Bill. Can you bring up these points to the others?" Mills asked, rightly sensing that the issue would be more favorably received from Merchant than from him.

"Yep, I will. Right away."

———————

Georgetown University junior John Finnegan drove for Uber part time. Like many Uber drivers, he made it work for himself based on his schedule on any given week. Finnegan was fortunate that the Georgetown area was one of the most popular destinations on the east coast and that finding parking in the area was a perennial nightmare.

Generally, Finnegan, a music major, worked three to four days a week, depending on his class and practice schedule. Finnegan played the flute. He had been playing since he was six years old and wanted to teach kids when he got done with school. Finnegan loved working with kids. He gave free lessons to elementary school kids at the Holy Trinity School near Georgetown's campus and was super excited to be chosen to work with kids at the Kennedy Center Thelonious Monk Jazz Ensemble.

Finnegan was blessed with an outgoing personality. Slightly overweight physically, Finnegan was not one to bite his tongue or suffer fools. If he was thinking something, he'd say it. Last Friday night, Finnegan had just finished practicing and decided he would accept a few Uber rides. He had an hour to kill and one of the benefits of being an Uber driver was that it allowed him to meet and talk with new people, something he loved.

As soon as he drove off the Georgetown campus, he accepted an Uber request from Amy Duncan, who was either at the Tombs or 1789 restaurant. He wasn't certain which, because both restaurants had the same address. Finnegan arrived within a few minutes of the call and saw an attractive couple walking across the street away from the restaurant. On seeing this, Finnegan smiled, because he knew what was going on. Following dinner at the Tombs or 1789, many couples stroll across the street to view the Exorcist steps. He had waited on many a fare who did the same thing. If he was in a hurry, he would blow his horn or pull up next to the fare and identify himself so he could get going.

But on that night, Finnegan was enthralled by the chemistry between this couple. The woman was a knock-out. The guy was obviously much older and this was probably early in their dating history, but the energy between them was powerful. Sitting there, in his silver Hyundai, Finnegan did not believe that he had ever seen two people seem so happy together. The feeling surprised him, so he kept watching.

As predicted, the couple walked to the famous site and the man pointed down the steps. He was clearly in rare form and was more the tour guide of the two of them. Then, he turned to face her, cupped her face with his hands and kissed her. Finnegan felt as though he was watching a movie, an old Hollywood love story. He kept thinking to himself, "I want that."

The kiss lasted a long time. After a bit, Finnegan was feeling a little creepy, so he gently honked his horn. Startled, the couple looked up, saw him and smiled happy smiles. Finnegan waved and smiled back. The couple held hands as he walked her to the car. She got in the car and Finnegan drove off. Looking at the girl in his rearview mirror, he noticed that she had turned completely around and had both elbows on the back dashboard obviously savoring whatever lasting look she could get from her date.

When she turned around and sat facing forward in her seat, she said, "Hi!"

"Hiya doing? Well, you two seem happy," Finnegan said smiling.

Giggling, she responded, "I am the happiest I have ever been in my life. I am in love."

It went much like that for most of the rest of the ten minute ride. Finnegan and Amy talked about chemistry, attraction and love. When she got out of his car, Finnegan once again thought, *I want that!*

On Tuesday afternoon, following class, John Finnegan walked into the Georgetown student lounge with his lifelong friend and roommate Joe Sweeney to unwind a bit before dinner. The television was on, tuned to CNN. Wolf Blitzer was talking to a group of panelists who, as he said, either knew or worked with Jackson Lowery. One panelist was a former prosecutor, another an AU history professor and the third, a law firm partner. The caption on the screen said, "Murder in Georgetown." Normally, these kinds of stories did not interest Finnegan, but as he kept looking at the picture above the name, Jackson Lowery, he knew where he had seen the face. He pointed at the television and screamed, "No way!"

"What are you getting all bent out of shape about, Finn?" Sweeney asked.

"Look at the screen, no way that guy is a murderer!"

Just then, Amy Duncan's picture hit the screen next to Jackson's. Blitzer mentioned that there was a manhunt for Jackson, who may have been responsible for Amy's strangulation.

On seeing this, Finnegan put his hands on his head and kept shaking his head. "No freakin' way he killed her! You hear me, Joe? No freakin' way. I am telling you, those two were in love."

"Wait a minute, is this the couple you have been blabbering about all weekend? The 'epitome of love' couple that you kept going on and on about? And he killed her?"

Finnegan looked like his friend had just slapped him. "Do not say that, Joe. This guy did not kill her. I don't know what is going on, but two people that much in love on a Friday night don't end up in a place where one of them kills the other by Monday night. No fucking way!"

Sweeney just shook his head, trying to take it all in. Finn was acting like he really knew this couple.

Now glued to the screen, the two friends watched the telecast as Blitzer shifted to an earlier press conference held by Idaho Senator Rex Duncan, Amy's father.

"See, see! Do you see that, Joe! There is the connection. That's the answer. Amy's death has something to do with her father running for president and these bastards are trying to pin it on Lowery. You, of all people, have to understand that!"

Well, Finn had him there, Sweeney thought. Plus, that bit of information did shed a different light on things. "Touché on that one, Finn! You may actually have something there, especially since you saw how they were with each other. And, of course, I do know how the government can be."

Joe Sweeney was a techie genius. Going back to age nine or ten, Sweeney was a wonder with computers. He could hack into any system, any time, any place. As he got into high school, his skills improved and so did his mischief. He hacked into school records, DMV sites, and potential girlfriends' computers. Once, he accessed a major bank site, and when he saw how easy it was, he got scared and signed off. Trying to be responsible, his parents enrolled him in a program for highly gifted young techies.

In truth, the program was setup by the government to find those kids with skills like Sweeney's so they could squash them. Sweeney now knew that there were approximately two hundred young people like him on the east coast, more in other parts of the country. They got paid a hefty stipend not to be on their computers. They were heavily monitored and constantly watched. Some did work for the government. Others, like Sweeney, did not. Sweeney was an English major at Georgetown. He picked a field as far away from computers as possible so as not to draw scrutiny. After years of dealing with government regulators, monitors, and secret agent types, Sweeney's inescapable conclusion was that the government was full of pricks.

"What are you going to do, Finn? I know you too well. You are going to do something."

"I am calling MPD, the local police. Maybe even the senator's office. I must report what I know to save Jackson. The real murderers are getting away while they go after the guy who loved Amy."

Again, Sweeney was struck by how Finn talked about the two of them like they were old friends. Whatever the truth, there was no denying that seeing them together left a lasting impression.

"That could be dangerous, pal. What about the blowback? If it is the government, these folks could easily turn on you."

"True. But I gotta do something. Help me think!"

The two friends sat silently for a bit, learning more about both Jackson and Amy from CNN.

Finally, Sweeney offered a suggestion. "How about this? You talk to the local cops who patrol near our campus. Get one of the Georgetown Security cops to go with you. Tell them what you know and ask them to at least talk with their desk sergeant about whether to take it further up the food chain. I am with you, it feels better to sound this out with local folks first, before going full bore with the Feds."

"Love it," Finnegan replied. I am going to do this now before I practice. Thanks, partner!"

One hour later, Finnegan had a brief, straightforward conversation with two young MPD police officers and one of the best on the Georgetown Security team. The officers took the information without any strong opinion or expression. They did promise, however, to talk with their sergeant, as Finnegan requested.

Later that night, Finnegan had finished practicing at the Davis Performing Arts Center at the edge of the Georgetown Campus, not far from the corner to 37th and O streets in D.C. On nights when he had his most thorough practice sessions, he walked right across the walking path to Healy Hall. Finnegan volunteered at the Kennedy Institute of Ethics, which was located in Healy Hall. When he practiced late, afterwards, Finnegan would drop by the Institute to finish whatever administrative assignments that were left for him. Once done, he would walk the couple of flights down the black concrete stairs located between Healy and Gaston Halls to the main floor, then out of the building.

Finnegan had followed the same routine week in and week out for three years, without incident. On this night, Finnegan was starting to walk down the steps with his flute case in hand and his backpack over his right shoulder. Deep in thought, Finnegan was still reeling a bit thinking about. the Jackson/Amy tragedy. I guess, he surmised, sometimes, life is not fair. At that same moment, having stepped down onto the first step, a strong, unseen hand pushed him at the top of his back, sending him headfirst down the stairs.

For Finnegan that night, life was not fair. He landed on his head, breaking his neck and instantly killing him. The man with the unseen hand scuttled quickly past Finnegan's body and headed out of the building.

———————

Steve Mills was feeling somewhat vindicated. Just earlier that day, he shared with Bill Merchant his concern about someone coming forward and suggesting that Lowery and the Duncan girl were in love. Merchant saw his point and passed on the concern to Tyler and the contractor. Lo and behold, not long after that, some chubby Georgetown student doubling as an Uber driver told the local D.C. police about picking up Amy Duncan, who talked about being 'madly in love' with Lowery. This was exactly the type of thing that Mills warned could happen. Fortunately, the kid had an 'accident' and all was back on track. Mills felt good about his foresight, which could not have come at a better time. Tyler got the group together as soon as the mess was officially cleaned up. Mills had to get back on good graces with his group. He could feel that Tyler was trying to edge him out. But as his most recent insight made evident, Mills was still a valuable asset, and he thought that as long as he remained patient, he would be able to work himself back into the group's leadership.

SIX

Jackson and Ronnie were on their way to meet Ronnie's former marine bud, Jenny Roberts. Throughout the day, they had been traveling partially on I-77 south, but primarily through the back roads and woods of West Virginia. They went through Beckley and near Bluefield, West Virginia. They skirted along parts of I-81 southwest and the Great Smoky Mountains heading in the direction of Knoxville, Tennessee, when they decided to stop at a diner in Newport, Tennessee. Still almost four hours outside of Atlanta, they had plenty of time to kill.

To her credit, Jenny offered to drive part of the way to meet them. Like Ronnie, she was wary of the technology found in major cities. Plus, whoever they were dealing with could easily choose Atlanta as a target to watch. Jenny would meet them later in the night in a hotel room just south of Asheville, North Carolina, where they would hear her thoughts and switch cars.

In the meantime, Jackson and Ronnie put their thinking caps on over a light meal. Ronnie had a cheeseburger, while Jackson has a plain salad with tomato soup. The waitress, sporting a name tag that read, 'Doris', looked at him strangely when he said that was all he wanted. Ronnie shook his head, waited until she left and said, "We have gone undetected all day until you draw attention to yourself by eating like a Yankee!" He was smiling when he said it, but only partially. Years of undercover work and training had taught Ronnie that the number one rule to live by when hiding was to do whatever you could to blend in.

Ordering a plain salad and tomato soup in Newport, Tennessee was not how to go unnoticed in that town.

"My bad," Jackson said. "Let's go back to some of the stuff we have been talking about off and on while on the road. We both feel like this is some kind of assault on the food supply that will disproportionately impact people of color, right?"

"Yep, agreed."

"Ok. And let's go back to the school district idea. You would need access to a bunch of these school districts to have any kind of meaningful impact. So, we are talking about food service providers, right?"

"Again, agreed, Jack. That is why I briefed Jenny a little bit on the phone. She is going to research these contractors and the politics of the whole school lunch program."

"That's good. Real good. But, why is Senator Duncan so important to all of this? He really cannot help deliver these contracts. It would be hard for him to be that heavy-handed without being noticed. We are missing something, Ronnie. Why would his presidency matter to this plan?"

"That, my friend, is the sixty-four thousand dollar question. There has got to be another aspect to all of this that we just cannot see. Why would it be so important to have a guy in the White House who is unaware of your plan, but critical to the plan's success?"

Jackson smiled. "I think I just said the same thing. Either way, understanding that question helps connect the dots big time."

" Jenny will certainly help. I figure once we spend some time with her, we can get some shut-eye before getting back on the road. All soldiers know that you eat and sleep when you can. In the heat of battle, you may need to go a long time without either one."

Nodding, Jackson commented, "Then what, Ronnie? Back to D.C.? What is our plan?"

"We do have to get back to the D.C. area. I see it as the only way to clear your name. These assassins expect it too, so we are walking on eggshells here. But you know, Jack, your question about Rex Duncan is key. We need to have a sit down with him and also his wife."

"I agree, but don't see how these guys will let this happen."

"I am not sure I know yet, either. But the answers are all in the D.C. area. Sorry, Jack, but we gotta go right into the mouth of the lion, my friend."

"I get it. And I know that we are dealing with an incredibly massive undertaking. If these guys come close to pulling this off, millions could be affected. We have got to get to the source of all of this."

"We will. By the way, Jenny will have info on Steve Mills and Bill Merchant for us as well. We may need to pay them a visit when we go back to D.C."

Jackson was staring out the window. Now completely dark, the quiet southern town was beginning to feel very sleepy. "Let me ask you something, Ronnie. It is hard for me to accept or even understand this level of hate. How was it for you being undercover around all that hate day in and day out? It had to be awful."

Now, Ronnie was looking out the same window as Jackson, seeming to call up and suppress some of those memories at the same time. "Here's the thing, Jack, day to day, you do not feel you are around hate. At least not all the time. You get to know the people. Their hopes, dreams, aspirations for their family. You get to know their loves, likes, strengths and weaknesses. You see, for so many of them, they are hungering for something to believe in. Something, for the most part, they did not get at home. They wanted to belong and often got swept up by their environment. Then, the bad group-think mentality kicks in with steroids. And trust me, having spent years in the military, too much group-think is not a good thing."

"I guess I never looked at it like that," Jackson said. "In my experience, especially while doing criminal law, I saw that some folks were just plain evil. They were the scariest kind."

"I know what you mean, Jack. Those types are still there and must be dealt with. My only point is that the face of evil can be deceptive because it can often appear so normal. Also, good people can do bad things. Never forget that."

"That is so true, my friend."

———————

Joe Sweeney was sad and distraught. Sweeney knew that his best friend had been murdered. He just could not prove it. They had said that Finn had slipped and fell on the steps between Healy and Gaston Hall, which led to him breaking his neck. But Sweeney knew the truth. His friend had been killed. Based on all that had happened in the last twenty-four hours, Sweeney also knew that Jackson Lowery was innocent; that he was not the man being caricatured on all the news outlets. There was some big conspiracy taking place with Senator Duncan at the center of it all. Yet, the senator wasn't a direct part of it. Sweeney needed to do something. But what? Just by going to the local D.C. authorities, Finn ended up dead. *What should he do?*

In Sweeney's mind, it all came back to the senator. He had to talk with him, something virtually impossible with all the added security. *What about his wife?* Sweeney thought. If he could plant the seed with her, it could generate some real movement on behalf of her husband. Whatever he did, Sweeney knew it would have to be done soon. He was going to violate his deal with the government and do some research on the senator and his wife.

General Brock was in his full dress uniform when he visited Rex and Reba Duncan that evening. Upon seeing his longtime friend, the senator nearly broke down. "Thanks for coming, Michael. This is the toughest thing that I have ever had to deal with. Nothing else compares." Brock hugged his old friend, while motioning for Reba to join. There stood the three of them, held close together in the spacious front foyer.

Reba grabbed each man by the hand and led them into the living room. The Duncan's sat on a sofa while Brock got comfortable in an easy chair he always seemed to find during his visits to the Duncan home.

"Any updates from the authorities, Rex?"

"There is the nationwide manhunt still going on. Everyone says it is just a matter of time before they find this guy. It is all so hard to believe, Michael. None of it makes any sense."

It was at moments like these when Brock found it was most important to bite his tongue. His internal views were so strong that he generally had to rein himself in before speaking his mind.

"One thing is for sure, Rex," Brock said, looking at Reba. "This will work itself out. The answers you seek will come. They may not be pretty or tied up in a neat bow, but it will all come out. Trust in knowing how special Amy was and how magnificent her growth was on this short journey. You all should be very proud of how much all of you hung in there to experience her maturity. As tough as it is to swallow that she is gone, you have to give yourselves time to celebrate her life. The other stuff will work itself out. That's about the best advice I can give tonight."

Reba worked up a smile through her tears eyes. "That is about the nicest thing we have heard all day, Michael. Leave it to you to know what to say and how to say it." She squeezed her husband's hand.

"No speechifying here, Reba girl. Love you both too much. Every now and then, I have to say what comes from right here," He says, pointing to his heart. No way to fake anything at a time like this."

The three friends sat and talked for the next hour and a half. Reba got up a couple of times to make sure that the General had his favorite glass of scotch by his side. Rex and Reba joined him by having some red wine. By the end of the night, all of them felt better if not good. As they walked Brock to the door, Reba found herself thinking about her doubts around Steve Mills and Bill Merchant. Earlier in the evening, she started to share those thoughts with the General, but decided to hold her tongue. She made the same choice as he walked out the door. Alone with her husband, she said, "I love Michael, but like I told you earlier, Rex, I am not looking for the authorities to tell me what they think I want to hear."

Rex knew what it meant when his wife was this determined. "I know that, my love. But, I am glad that you did not say anything to Michael about your concerns. We need to figure out how to navigate this on our own, for now."

"I agree with you about that. But starting tomorrow, I am going to start asking some questions."

"Okay, sweetie. But, please let's be careful. At least, let me know where you plan on asking before you start. Maybe I can give you some thoughts that could help."

Reba pondered that one. "Alright, Rex. That makes sense. But, I am determined to get the truth."

Ronnie and Jackson were about to leave the money for their meal on the table, when Jackson noticed the waitress, Doris, looking in their direction while taking with another waitress near the cash register. Trying to act nonchalant, Jackson said to Ronnie, "Is it me or have we been made by my friend Doris?"

"You have been made. She said something to the cook a couple of minutes ago, who tried to ease back into the kitchen. My guess is that he called the local Sheriff. Go ahead and leave the money, then wait for me in the car. I am going to ask them about hotels in Knoxville before heading out."

Jackson rushed by the cashier toward the front door nodding at Doris and her waitress friend. They looked at him like he was Jack the Ripper. As he was walking out, he heard Ronnie say, "Is there a Holiday Inn on this road sometime before we get to Knoxville?"

Doris seemed eager to help, though in truth it meant that she would have updated information to share with the local Sheriff.

"Oh yes, keep on this road another forty-five minutes or so and you can't miss it. Y'all drive safe."

In the car, Jackson could see the two waitresses and the cook looking at them from the window. Ronnie gunned the Explorer and took off on state road 411 toward Knoxville. After a mile or so, he doubled back on a side road, drove for about three miles, then got back on I-40 south away from Knoxville, headed toward Asheville. He then picked up his phone and called Jenny.

"How far are you from Asheville?" Jackson heard him ask her. Jenny gave an answer that Jackson could not hear.

"That's good. You are ahead of us. We just got made so we will need to ditch the car. Be sure to check in and meet us ten miles outside the city. We will be on the highway access road. Thanks, Jen."

Jenny had already worked out a plan of action. First, she would check into a hotel under an assumed name with different identification. Immediately thereafter, the three of them would get together to get rid of the car and then go back to the hotel. Jenny would park in the back, right by the room she secured. Jackson and Ronnie would then use the key she gives them to enter the hotel from the back door, just steps from the room.

By then, Jenny will have disabled any cameras facing that part of the hotel. Then she would walk all the way to the front of the hotel, go in through the front door, and head straight for the room. Once they've debriefed, she would take a cab to the Asheville airport, where she will have a flight reserved under another assumed name. Ronnie and Jackson will then take the car she has left for them and get back on the road the next day.

"At least," Ronnie said while finishing laying out Jenny's suggested next steps, "that is the plan. We shall see how the night goes since the folks after us will be nearby. Hotel sweeps are not out of the question."

"Then what will we do?" Jackson asked.

"We will figure it out. Having new wheels buys us some time. We need to try hard to hide this car to keep them further away from us."

Jackson took a deep breath and settled back into his seat. Something told him that this was going to be a long night.

———

"We have a hit," Livermore said to Strother and McNair. He spoke almost without expression, a sign that Strother's quiet, almost wordless, leadership had already begun to filter down. Livermore's techie crew, led by Mason, were given the assignment of monitoring information that popped up from local law enforcement. Just a few minutes prior, a waitress from a hole in the wall diner in Newport, Tennessee called the local sheriff to report serving tomato soup to the 'colored man who killed the white girl in D.C.'. The waitress also said that the killer was with another man and that she heard them talking about hotels in Knoxville. A host of authorities, including the F.B.I. would be descending on Newport and its surrounding town within the hour. Livermore watched as Strother, McNair, and Todd Brown contemplated the situation. To Livermore, it seemed as though each was waiting for the other to act. R.J., who was also in the area, was obviously thinking the same thing. He looked at Livermore and silently shrugged.

Finally, Strother spoke. Looking at no one in particular, he said, "Find out specifically what was said about Knoxville, and how it came up. I think it is a distraction play. What is the next big city going in the opposite direction?"

R.J. had the map ready. He laid it on the table, saying, "Asheville is a little over an hour away. Greenville, South Carolina, two hours."

Strother rubbed the gray stubble on his chin. He had this perpetual look of a weather-beaten fisherman who never shaved, but also never had a completely full beard.

"Focus on Asheville," he said. "We don't have the manpower to go door to door. Suggest to our friends at the bureau that they do that. What we can do," he started, motioning to Livermore's techies, "is look at all the film from the hotel cameras within a ten mile radius of Asheville starting from now until morning. Todd, you monitor things here with Livermore. Russ, let's you and I go to Asheville. Now."

Everyone nodded, fully aware of their roles and responsibilities.

Joe Sweeney had done his research. He knew almost all there was to know about Rex Duncan and his family. One opportunity popped right out at him. The Duncan's oldest son, Kyle, was born with cerebral palsy. Understandably, the disease has become the primary source of philanthropy for the family. Each year, for the last ten years, Rex and Reba Duncan had served as co-chairs of the National Foundation for Cerebral Palsy Research (NFCPR) annual dinner. This year, for the first time, Any Duncan was also listed as a co-chair. The dinner would be held tomorrow night at the Four Seasons in Georgetown. Looking at his computer screen, Sweeney was betting that the Duncans would still go to the dinner as a way of honoring their daughter. *If so, this could work perfectly,* Sweeney thought. An uncle of one of Sweeney's classmates ran the valet parking garage at the Four Seasons. Once in a while, when the uncle was short staffed for big dinners, Sweeney had helped with the valet parking. The tips were always great. Sweeney was going to call his friend to see if he could work the NFCPR dinner tomorrow night.

If the Duncans showed up, he would find a way to talk to them. But, how? Sweeney knew he had to give it some thought. In the meantime, he jumped up from his dorm room desk to track down Yesus, his friend. Sweeney was determined to be part of tomorrow night's valet parking team at the Four Seasons Hotel.

Ronnie and Jackson were facing a dilemma. As they got closer to the rendezvous spot with Jenny, they needed to decide whether they could risk spending the night in the hotel room she had set up for them. The more Ronnie thought about his diversionary conversation with Doris, the more he believed that it would not work. "The guys who found my hideaway are mercenaries," he said. "They will smell the Knoxville conversation out right away. I would bet anything that they are headed to Asheville."

Jackson agreed, but he too was unsure of the right move. These decisions were a lot more magnified when they meant life or death.

"Let's look at the options," Jackson said. "We could stay in the Asheville hotel, get Jenny to drive us further away - with me staying in the trunk, if need be, or we can go back to the Newport area and hide in plain sight."

Ronnie squirmed a bit in the driver's seat. They were now parked on a back road near a lake about five miles in from the interstate. Jenny would be there any minute now. "Well, it is true that regular law enforcement and the Feds probably don't know about me. At least, they didn't. Doris has probably changed that. What do you mean by hiding in plain sight in the Newport area?"

"We could have Jenny stay at the hotel in Asheville, just in case there is a room by room check. What if we went back to Newport, broke into the restaurant and stayed there until early morning? Jenny could pick us up and bring us back to the hotel. By morning, everyone will have thought that we are long gone."

Ronnie was giving Jackson's idea some deep thought. He smiled. "Did you notice that the diner was positioned right in front of some woods? Those woods stretched back for at least a couple of miles. We could hang out there. But, if law enforcement has dogs like they do with prison escapes, we are cooked."

"We have talked about going on offense, Ronnie." Jackson said. "What is the aggressive play?"

Ronnie did not hesitate. "Hiding in the woods. It is also suicidal. Crazy. But it could work." Ronnie shook his head. "Jack, I am gonna make a black ops guy out of you, yet."

Jackson lightly pounded his knees with his hands. "Not quite yet, my friend. I still see myself as a college history professor." Even as he was saying it, however, Jackson felt like that part of his world was years ago.

Ronnie smirked a reply. "Jack Ryan, college professor," he said, referencing the famous Tom Clancy character.

Both men then had their attention diverted to the car lights they could see coming in their direction. "That would be Jenny," Ronnie said. "Let's get this show on the road."

Jenny Roberts pulled up in a used white Jeep Grand Cherokee, fully loaded. Jackson was struck by the car's classy look. He expected something more discreet. Following Ronnie's lead, Jackson got out of the Explorer, pulled his duffel bag from the back seat and walked over to the Grand Cherokee. Ronnie opened the passenger side and got in. Jackson opened the rear door behind Ronnie and got in that way.

Once inside, he looked at Jenny behind the steering wheel up front. He could tell that she was an attractive woman, with a slim build. Her jet black hair was shoulder length and she wore black pants, a black turtleneck, and leather black jacket that matched her hair. When she looked at Jackson to smile a hello, he noticed the bluest eyes he may have ever seen.

Despite her warmth, however, Jackson could tell she was all business. "Hi, Jackson. Nice to meet you. Sorry it is under these circumstances and sorry about your student, Amy."

"Thanks, Jenny. I can't tell you how much I appreciate you going out of your way like this. Thanks so much."

Jenny looked at Ronnie and said, "That is what we do, right, Ronnie?"

Ronnie was ready to talk business. "As you know, Jen, things have changed. Jackson and I have talked through some options and we need your thoughts." Ronnie then went through all of the options that they had discussed, asking her not only her thoughts, but whether she could think of any other options.

Jenny was now fully focused on the mission herself as well. "Let's do this," she said. "First, lets' dump your car so that we can be done with that. The last thing we need is for some local yokel to come down this road and recognize the Explorer. Then we can come back to this spot and I can update you on my research. Things are moving fast, but my knowledge needs to be your knowledge, especially as you decide the next steps. I was going to do the briefing in the hotel room, but that may not work. Once you hear all that I have to say, we can go through those options."

The two men nodded, with Ronnie miming an exaggerated salute. Looking at Jackson, he said, "Can you imagine having to work for her in the field, Jack? Recruits were terrified to be trained by her, until it was done. Then they all bragged about it."

Jenny just said, "Let's go, guys."

Ronnie and Jackson had found a boat launch out of sight from the main road. It took about a minute to ease the Explorer into gear and then push it into the water. The biggest fear that the three of them had was whether the entire car would submerge in the lake. All three watched patiently from the shore to see the car go deeper and deeper into the water. Finally, the roof of the car disappeared completely from the surface.

"Okay," Jenny said. "Let's go talk."

Once back into the car, Jenny launched right in. "Let me first talk with you about Steve Mills and Bill Merchant, the two men that Amy overheard at her parents' house. The two have been close for some time. They are very conservative Republicans and donate to just about the same candidates. Merchant is the softer of the two and is a management whiz. That is how he rose to the ranks of CFO at ITM. Needless to say, he is worth millions. Never married, no kids. Rumored to be gay. Mills, on the other hand, is a highly successful hedge fund manager, one of the most successful in the world. His net worth is in the billions. But, he is not nearly as likable as Merchant. He is a known egotist who will do anything if you stroke his ego the right way.

"In fact, among philanthropic circles in New York, the word is that if you found a way to elaborately honor Steve Mills, he would personally give you six figures or more. Groups from the arts, education and other charities have been stepping over themselves the last few years to feed his ego. Some even started to coordinate their efforts. Mills' ego blinds him to their brazen plotting for his money. He is divorced with a grown son, who doesn't speak to him."

"What about their ties to white nationalism?" Jackson asked.

"There is no paper trail or public comments on any of that. They have obviously covered themselves well on that front."

Jackson and Ronnie then went over in greater detail their theory about the food service industry being the launching point for a conspiracy to poison kids of color.

Jenny was ready for the conversation. "If it could be pulled off, it is a realistic plan. But the coordination is key. You are right, there are 13,000 school districts in America and it makes sense that only 500 or so have most of the black and brown kids in them. Of those 13,000 school districts, less than twenty percent outsource their food service responsibilities. That translates to about 2,000 contracts, nationwide. Not surprisingly, most of these contracts are with the big cities, the larger school districts. The big three contracts in this space are Claremark, Jawer Foods, and Honeyberg Industries. Claremark is the big boy. They have been doing this for almost fifty years and have 700 school district contracts. They have major quality issues, but they also have strong, longstanding political relationships. Jawer Foods and Honeyberg have about 300 contracts each. For many years, Honeyberg was viewed as a potential direct threat to Claremark, but then they ran into management and infrastructure challenges. Plus, it has been a while since they have won a new contract."

"What about the rest of the school districts? That still leaves a lot out there," Jackson said.

"True," Jenny replied. "The rest of the contracts are a lot of one-offs or mom and pop operations. None of them have more than a handful of contracts, nor are they looking to grow their footprint, except for one. Have you heard of Joseph Charles?"

"The name is familiar," Jackson said.

"Yes, I know who he is," Ronnie added, snapping his fingers. "He is the food service king out of Chicago. Has a nice rep and wants to get our folks in the community to eat healthy and organic."

"Right. There is not much bad to say about Joe Charles. He seems to be a good guy, all around. His grandfather founded Bartlett Foods, a catering company that catered to black churches and community groups many years ago. Charles jumped into the school district contracting wars when he won the Chicago public schools food service contract a few years back. Folks there love him. He gives cooking classes and has trained community members in the 'hood. He has even talked about bidding on food service contracts at small colleges and community colleges that cater to minorities.

"After the buzz surrounding his work in Chicago, he won nine straight bids on school district contracts. People in the industry project that he will be able to take on the big boys soon. Interestingly, nearly seven hundred of those contracts will be up for bid in the next eighteen months. Recently, however, Charles lost the New York public schools contract, one that everyone thought he would win.

"Now check this out: the word is that certain hedge fund money has jumped in to help Claremark. They got their New York contract renewed even though the Post kept running stories about kids eating moldy food. The word is that key hedge fund players cut a deal with the Claremark CEO. Millions of dollars are involved based on the upcoming contracts. Also, and this is not public, but Charles has been getting death threats. Interesting, huh?"

Jenny paused for effect.

"Are you saying, Jenny, that it is possible that Mills, Merchant, and their crew are propping Claremark up? Is that what's going on?" Jackson asked.

"We have no evidence of that, but that is what I am saying. Based on what Amy heard, they are looking to infect the food supply of kids in a big way. One other thing. As you know, I work at the CDC and deal with mass poison theories all the time. In order for the right kind of poison to work, you need widespread distribution at the same time. That is what makes the food service contractor idea brilliant. But you also need a singular distribution source. That way you can make sure that the poison is in the food that is loaded into every truck that leaves the food making facility. Of the four we have discussed, Claremark and Jawer control their own food making facilities. With the others, they have contracts with other food companies, who may also service other clients. The cleanest way to do this is if you control everything, from soup to nuts."

"We need to look at the ownership of Claremark and Jawer," Ronnie said.

"I have started on that and will do more research on them tomorrow," Jenny said.

"Very helpful, Jen," Ronnie said. "But how does this all relate to the senator? We know he chairs the agriculture committee in the Senate. But there has got to be something more to it than that."

"I agree, though I haven't figured that out yet, either. Obviously, there is some aspect to Duncan being president that makes this plan work. It may not be him, per se, but rather, who comes with him once he is elected."

Jackson and Ronnie looked at each other. "That has got to be the key," Jackson said. "Mills, Merchant, and their crew need Duncan in the White House because someone who is sure to be in the administration is essential to them pulling this whole thing off."

"Alright, boys," Jenny jumped in. "Once you make it through the night, what are your next steps?"

"We both feel that we need to get back to D.C. We need to confront Mills and also find a way to get to the senator," Ronnie said. "We need more answers."

Jenny was thinking it all through. "Here's what I think," she began. "As crazy as it sounds, I like Jackson's idea of hanging in the woods by the diner. If you can break in and steal a couple hours of sleep, all

148

the better. I kept the ID I used for the room, so I will go back there and spend the night. We are only fifteen minutes away from there, so you can drop me off nearby. My bags are in the room." She then lifted up the room key holder with a number written on it. "If it makes sense to go to the room in the morning, here is the key and room number. Be sure to use the back door. The camera is disabled and the room is right by the door."

"What about D.C., Jen?" Ronnie asked.

Jenny's response was quieter, more hesitant. "Ronnie, I just don't know. Something else has got to give. It feels like you are fighting with an arm tied behind your backs, with no room for error." She then lifted up an envelope and demonstrably handed it to Ronnie. "Like you, my friend, I have my own version of hideaways out there. Here are the directions and access to my place in Bryce Mountain, near Basye, Virginia in the Shenandoah Mountain range area. It is about six hours from here, but less than two hours from D.C. I feel like the roads may be too hot and heavy tonight, but during the day tomorrow, it could be easier. Go there first and regroup. I don't like the idea of you guys being so loose on the street. You need a safe place. Use this one."

Ronnie nodded. "This helps a lot, Jen. Thanks."

"I don't know what to say, Jenny," Jackson muttered, looking down.

"Fuck that," Jenny said. "Just go save the world."
They all laughed.

Strother and McNair landed in Asheville, North Carolina around 10 pm that evening. By now, roadblocks had been set up within a two-hour radius from Newport, Tennessee. The Feds were also checking hotels and motels in and around Knoxville, Asheville, and even Greenville, South Carolina. Strother, as was his nature, liked to work backwards. Once he and McNair got into their rented SUV, he told McNair where to go. "Take me to the diner," he said.

McNair nodded and headed up I-40 north toward Newport.

Jackson and Ronnie dropped off Jenny within a ten minute walk from her hotel. They made sure to pick a spot where there were no people or cameras watching. They agreed to check in with her in the morning.

On the way from Asheville to Newport, Jackson and Ronnie saw several police cars headed opposite from them, many with their flashing lights on. They did not see one police car headed in their direction. Once they got near the town of Newport, Ronnie navigated to the back roads. He instinctively knew where the diner was and was looking for the right place to park the Grand Cherokee, so as to not draw attention. Although he did not say anything, Jackson once again wondered why Jenny picked such a showy car. You don't see many Jeep Grand Cherokee's in this part of Tennessee. It also did not help that the car was white. Ronnie must have been thinking the same thing, because he said, "to be honest, I did not think as much about where we park this car, Jack. This could be a problem."

"I know. This car is making me more and more nervous," Jackson said.

By then, Ronnie was traveling on the street that ran parallel to the street where the diner was located. There was about a mile and a half between the two streets. Out of nowhere, Ronnie pulled over and stopped. Then he smiled.

"What?" Jackson said.

"Look around you," he said, smiling.

Jackson looked around, noticing that they were in a light industrial area. There were a handful of beige, bland looking buildings, all with loading docks attached to them. There was also a tractor dealer and a hardware store. Then, Jackson saw it. A used car dealership. Although it mainly consisted of trucks, there were a smattering of SUVs on the lot, including a few Grand Cherokees.

"Nice!" Jackson exclaimed.

The men then pulled onto the lot and parked their Grand Cherokee next to the other ones. Taking care to look around, they unloaded their gear and walked across the street toward the woods. If Ronnie's memory was correct, the back of the diner should be at the end of the woods, within a mile away. They began their short walk.

"So, what is Jenny's story," Jackson asked as they walked through the woods. "Does she have family?"

"Jenny is a hard case, Jack. She had a tough, abusive childhood. She had one major relationship, but he could not handle her independence and strength. That is about all I can say, Jack. She is a good woman, who cares about her country, but who has been given the short end of a lot of sticks. There is no one better in the trenches, though."

"Obviously," Jackson said. "I sure hope she finds her peace."

"Yeah. And, I hope we find this diner. I am ready to take a load off," Ronnie said.

Soon thereafter, they could see the edge of the woods and the roof of the diner.

Once at the end of the woods, they stayed hidden while looking in all directions. Ronnie then held his hand out for Jackson to stay back, while he ambled toward the diner's back door. Jackson saw him turn the back door knob, easily opening the door. Ronnie looked back at Jackson, shrugged his shoulders, smiled broadly, then motioned for Jackson to come forward.

Once inside, the two men laid their duffel bags behind the counter and went back into the kitchen. The diner was a vintage southern diner, with about eight booths and a counter seating area with ten swivel chairs.

Jackson reached into the kitchen refrigerator to grab two bottles of orange juice. He sure wished he could make some coffee and maybe fry a couple of eggs, but he suspected that would not be advisable under the circumstances.

As Jackson closed the door to the refrigerator, Ronnie held his finger to his lips and pointed down the street. A dark SUV was driving slowly down the street, heading towards the diner. Both Ronnie and Jackson scrambled to get behind the counter. Once positioned, Ronnie whispered, "Did you lock the back door?"

Jackson paused for a minute, then nodded his head vigorously. In response, Ronnie reached into his duffel bag and grabbed two guns, handing one to Jackson.

They could hear the SUV pull into the diner's gravel parking lot. Then, they heard two doors open and slam. Someone was definitely checking back at the last place the two of them were seen. Jackson could tell that Ronnie suspected it was the same guys he saw fishing on the Ohio River, what now seemed to Jackson like it was a lifetime ago. Ronnie and Jackson held their breath as they strained to hear where their new visitors were headed.

Jenny walked confidently into the front door of the Red Roof Inn outside of Asheville, as if she didn't have a care in the world. She purposely wanted to exude that 'successful business woman after a long day' look, a practiced visage she had used over years in many countries. The young registration desk clerk waved politely at her as she walked down the hall, made a quick right and went straight to her room. After tossing her leather jacket on the bed, Jenny turned on her secure computer and began looking up more information about Senator Duncan. What would his presidency bring to Washington beside the barrel chested Idaho native? Jenny decided to dig a little deeper and learn as much as she could about the senator and his affiliations. Half an hour into her research, Jenny was interrupted by a firm knock on her door. She quietly went to the door and saw two men in dark suits. Feds, she thought. Jenny then opened the door.

"Excuse us, ma'am. I am John Polley and this is my partner, Jim Hurtable. We are with the F.B.I."

Both men showed their badges. They were legit, Jenny observed.

"Again, we are sorry to disturb you, but unfortunately, we are in the middle of an investigation and are asking people in the area, specifically this hotel, if they have seen this man." Polley then held up a picture of Jackson Lowery.

Jenny took a serious look at the picture and then said, "No, I have not seen him other than on CNN recently. Is he in this area? Am I in danger?" She hugged herself while asking the last question.

"No, not at all, ma'am. We are not concerned about anyone's safety. You are fine. We are just being as thorough as possible in our search. I hope you understand."

"Well, okay. So, what do you need from me?"

"Ma'am, if you do not mind, my partner and I would like to walk through your room, peek into the bathroom, and then leave."

"You think I am hiding this man?" Jenny said as if insulted and repulsed by the thought.

"Ma'am, no we don't. But we are taking a look in every room in the hotel, just to be on the safe side. We sure hope that you understand."

Jenny just nodded her head and backed away from the door to let the agents in. They did as promised quickly and walked back out the door. She watched them walk down the hall. Once back in her room, she looked out her window at the parking lot, which was crawling with agents. They were checking the license plates of every car. Jenny closed the window curtain, shaking her head at the same time. *Good call, Jackson*, she thought. Jackson and Ronnie were much safer holed up in that old diner than they would have been had they come with her to the hotel.

———————

Strother and McNair walked to the front door of the diner and tried to look inside. The place was pitch black. Strother leaned his head on his two cupped hands that were pressed against the window, hoping to get a clearer view of the inside. He saw an old school counter, with a bunch of round swivel chairs attached to it. This place will be crawling with people by 6 am, he thought. He then tried the front door, which was locked. McNair had gone around to the back, where he was looking in as well. He tried to open the back door, but it too was locked. Strother joined him in the back as he was working the door.

"Shall I open it?" McNair asked. It is pretty easy to pick without leaving any real damage."

Strother said, "No need. You know how I am. I like to feel the people I am up against, get a real sense of them." McNair just nodded, remembering how Strother walked around the charred remains of Ronnie Thomas' hideaway while McNair and Todd Brown waited.

"Like I said," McNair offered, "I can easily get us in and out."

"No. We have taken enough time here. I don't know where they are, but something tells me they are not that far. Let's go back to Asheville and see if our folks in D.C. have any more information. There is no doubt in my mind that the targets are coming our way."

"I agree, Dick. Let's go."

With that, they got back in the SUV and headed back to Asheville, North Carolina.

"Did you see them?" Jackson asked.

"From behind," Ronnie said. "They are the same guys fishing on the Ohio. The mercenaries."

"These guys are on it. Man! What would make them come back here?"

"Being thorough. Leaving no stone unturned. They think there's a chance we didn't go far."

"Should we leave now, Ronnie? If we got on the road within the hour, we could make it to Jenny's hideaway by morning. What do you think?"

"I think we keep just barely dodging bullets with these guys, so we really have to make sure we are making the right moves."

"You feel comfortable calling Jenny?" Jackson asked. "It feels like we should check in with her."

Ronnie looked at his watch. It was just past midnight. "It can't hurt," he said.

He made the call.

Jenny picked up right away. "All good?" she asked.

Ronnie then told her about their visitors. In turn, Jenny told them about hers. Ronnie made an exaggerated whistle sound when she recounted seeing hordes of F.B.I. agents in the parking lot.

Ronnie had put Jenny on speaker, so Jackson could hear and participate in the call.

"Jenny," Jackson said, "do you think that the roads are safe? If we left soon, we could make Virginia by morning."

Jenny's response was quick and to the point.

"Negative. Absolutely not. Think about it. If the F.B.I. had at least ten agents knocking on every door and shaking down the parking lot at THIS hotel alone, you better believe they have some roadblocks in place between here and D.C. You guys need to wait it out and leave during the day tomorrow. Grab some shut-eye, but be sure to be out of that place by 5 am. I also think that you are good to come here in the morning. I will get some breakfast buffet food and leave it in the room. Remember, park in the back. I gotta go back down south for a day or so, but will catch up with you in D.C."

Ronnie chuckled. "Guess you are on the team now, huh, Jen?'

"You guys would be lost without me!"

WEDNESDAY

ONE

Joe Charles was sitting in Senator Duncan's office first thing Wednesday morning. He had expected that the meeting would be canceled, but the senator's office confirmed that the meeting was still on when Charles called the office late Tuesday afternoon.

As was usually the case, Charles did not have to wait long. The senator strode confidently into the office and greeted Charles with his usual gripping handshake, followed by a bear hug.

"Senator, I am so very sorry about Amy. I just don't have the words, sir."

"No one does, Joe. Trust me. This is the hardest thing I have ever faced, but I have to keep moving. The more I sit and think about the reality of what happened to her, well, it..." The senator looked as though he was about to get choked up.

"I do understand, senator," Charles said. "I really do. I strongly believe that you and Reba must do whatever you must to find peace." Charles felt he needed to change the subject and not take too much of this grieving man's time.

"Let me get out of your hair, senator. As you know, I have a strong vision about nutrition and wellness in poor, minority communities. Chicago has become our flagship contract and the people love my approach. I think that I can make a difference and in the process save millions down the road in health care costs by changing the eating habits of low income individuals and families."

The senator was absorbed and focused on Charles' vision, which was exactly why he had come back to work – to be distracted from his grief by the work he most enjoyed doing. "Joe, you know I know your vision well. That is why I have always supported you. And I always talk you up to whatever governor, mayor, or food regulator I can. You also know that I cannot get involved in your contracts or the bidding process. That is not my style."

"Yes, of course, senator! And, I have never asked you to get involved in that way. But you may know that I had won nine contracts in a row fair and square before I lost the big one in New York recently. Other big ones are coming up in places like Los Angeles, Houston, Miami, Philadelphia, and Denver. We now know that my biggest competitors are getting an infusion of hedge fund money to help them buy these bids. Sorry, senator, but I do not know how else to put it."

"Understood, Joe. I had gotten wind of that as well. Let's say it is all true. How do you think I can help?"

Charles leaned forward in his chair. "I have one simple request, senator. You know these hedge fund guys. Many of them are supporting you to be our next president as, by the way, I am as well. You can talk to them in ways I cannot. I am asking you to talk to some of the key hedge fund leaders and ask them to back off. I know that it is a big ask, sir, but I can compete with these guys on merit. There are over thirty major school district contracts coming up next year. In addition, I am close to this deal with several historically black colleges and universities. But, I cannot and will not pay folks off as we go state by state like these guys are doing with all the money that is coming to them."

Rex stood up from his chair and walked to his big picture window overlooking the D.C. Mall. Rex could see the reflecting pool and the Washington Monument directly in front of him. He then clapped his hands together and turned to Charles, pointing downward to Charles in a way reminiscent of the 36th president, Lyndon Baines Johnson.

"Tell you what, Joe. I am going to do this for you because I think that it is the right thing to do. Give me a couple of weeks. I need to get through this funeral and make some other decisions about my future. But I need you to do something for me."

"Of course, senator. Name it."

"If my wife approves, I will run for president, but I will be damned if I do it the typical Republican way. I need you to help introduce me to the right groups, the right leaders, city by city for conversations. That is it. Just conversations. I want to be as inclusive as I can. I also want to make sure that I get a diverse group of folks on my team that reflect different points of view. Because of the circles you move in, you are better suited than anyone I know who I trust to help me achieve this. That is what I need from you, Joe."

Charles was blown away. He had always liked and respected Senator Duncan, but those few words demonstrated to Charles a level of depth and growth that, frankly, Charles never knew the senator had in him. As he stood up to meet the senator eye to eye with his response, Charles was struck by one powerful thought: *this man was ready to be the next President of the United States.*

Charles reached out his hand to the senator. "I would be honored to help in the way you described and beyond, senator. Hearing your thoughts today confirms what I have suspected for some time. Our nation needs your leadership. I am at your disposal."

Both men smiled, shook hands one more time, and Joe Charles left the senator's office.

Rex went back to gazing at the Washington Monument from his senate window.

Jackson and Ronnie left the diner around 5:05 am and scrambled into the woods to go get their car. They realized how close they had cut it when they heard tires on the diner gravel driveway. They were only thirty yards into the woods. They stopped, hid behind the foliage, and looked to see who had just pulled up. They both recognized the cook, whom they had seen the day before. Jackson and Ronnie looked at each other, shook their heads and trudged on.

The Grand Cherokee was parked exactly where they had left it the night before in the used car lot. Ronnie started it up, exited the lot, and headed back toward Asheville. When they got to Jenny's hotel, they went to the back, parked the car and used her key to enter the building and then her hotel room, close to the back entrance.

As promised, Jenny had a couple plates of food under napkins on cafeteria trays lying on the bed. The food was still somewhat warm meaning that Jenny had not been gone too long. Jackson and Ronnie were starving and devoured the food quickly. They then savored the coffee that she had left as well.

Ronnie suggested that they take turns in the shower and then catch a couple more hours of sleep. They agreed to leave around 10 am, before the 11 am checkout, for Bryce Mountain. While Ronnie was showering, Jackson sat on one of the beds thinking about how much his life had changed over the last three days. Looking at his watch, he realized that normally on Wednesdays he would be teaching a world history class to freshmen. It then hit Jackson that he never called the school to let them know he needed a few days off. *Duh*, he thought. I don't think they were expecting me to show up after watching my face on CNN all night. Jackson then thought about his son, Eddie. Ronnie had called Eddie and Pam, who were safe with Ronnie's old D.C. friend. Pam even sounded supportive, offering encouragement to them both.

Yes, Jackson's life had changed overnight. It's funny how you can be going along at such a regular, consistent pace only to have your world permanently changed in the blink of an eye. Lying on that hotel bed in Asheville, North Carolina, Jackson knew that his life had been radically changed and that no matter what happened, it would never be the same. To find out what the next phase of his life would look like required that Jackson stay alive. He found himself thinking about how to stay alive as he drifted off to sleep.

———————

That morning, after finding out that he would be able to work valet parking at the Cerebral Palsy event, Joe Sweeney was trying to figure out how he would approach Reba Duncan. He had also considered saying something to the senator, but that would be much harder. Having been a valet attendant at a few of these Four Seasons events in the past, usually the spouse of a famous person stands alone while the celebrity is chatted up by others waiting for their cars. Sweeney remembered seeing the Tonight Show host, Jimmy Fallon, waiting with his wife for their limo at the Four Seasons entrance. Although it was just a couple of minutes, several people came over to Fallon. The entire time, his wife was standing alone, occasionally smiling when someone noticed that she was with Fallon.

But even if he could get Reba Duncan's attention for a couple of minutes, what would he say? How could he convey all that needed to be conveyed in the short amount of time he may have? Sweeney pondered these and other questions and settled on a different tactic. He decided to write a short letter and place it in her hand. *That could work,* he thought. He would just have to make sure he said something provocative to her as he handed her the note. Provocative, but not creepy. He had to strike the right balance. Sweeney sat at his desk and started writing.

Joe Sweeney had rehearsed his introductory lines several times during the day. He also looked time and again at the short note that he planned to slip into Reba Duncan's hand. As he paced up and down in his Georgetown dorm room, he knew that his nervousness was consuming him. It did not help that Finn's family was coming to get his stuff tomorrow. It was all so surreal. Sweeney's own parents talked with him seriously about dropping out and coming back home to Boston. "You can easily get into BU with your transcript, Joe. We feel it is much safer for you here," they told him.

That was probably right. But Sweeney felt a sense of purpose and responsibility that he had never felt before. He knew that his friend had been murdered and he knew why he was murdered. But he could not prove it, nor could he talk with anyone about it. If he did, there was a strong chance that he would be murdered as well. So, Sweeney had to avenge his best friend's death quietly, until he had some credible help. Clearly, Reba Duncan represented credible help, but he had to make sure he did not scare her off. If she said something to the police or even someone on her husband's staff, it would certainly mean trouble for Sweeney. Still, he felt a sense of power unlike he had ever felt before in his life. He was taking ownership of a problem, fighting through a solution, and seeing it through to the end. Just thinking about it in that way helped Sweeney gain the courage to do what he needed to do.

Sweeney had tapped into the senator's calendar and was able to confirm that the senator and his wife would get to the hotel around 7:15. They would both speak briefly about their ongoing support of Cerebral Palsy research and then leave by 7:50. Sweeney was also able to confirm that the senator was not bringing staff to the event, so only he and his wife would be in the car. Sweeney looked at his watch. 10 am. He had a Psych class in twenty minutes. *I should go to class,* he thought. It would help him understand why he was doing this crazy James Bond stuff on his own. But, Sweeney was going to skip the class. He decided that he was going to spend the day hanging in the gym. Long, lean, with bright red hair, Sweeney was not much of an athlete, but he loved sports. He would play some basketball with the noon crowd at the Yates Field House, then grab a late lunch before getting ready for the evening. More and more, he felt like the superstar athlete getting ready for the big game.

While Sweeney was preparing for the Cerebral Palsy dinner, Strother was bringing together his group at the Fairfax command center. Sitting around the table were Strother, McNair, Todd Brown, Livermore, and R.J. Strother began by posing a question.

"Let's say you are this guy, Lowery, a former prosecutor, who has had his life turn topsy-turvy on him and finds himself on the run after being publicly accused of murder. What would be your primary objective?"

"Prove you are innocent," Livermore quickly said, still eager to please.

"That's right," Strother said. "Again, now we are thinking like Lowery. So, after everything that has happened the past few days, what are you thinking that your next step would need to be to prove your innocence?" Strother looked around the table.

"I want to hear from everyone," he said flatly.

Todd Brown raised his hand and started talking. "I would want to get to the Duncans. Part of it would be to convince them that I didn't kill their daughter, but I would also think that if I could convince them, they could help clear me."

"Okay," Strother said, nodding his head.

"I agree," R.J. said. "But I think that I would like to get to Reba Duncan alone. If I am Lowery, I am thinking that she could tell I loved her daughter and has the power to lean on her husband."

Here, McNair jumped in. "All of that makes sense, but Lowery has Thomas with him. Thomas comes from our world. If Lowery hasn't already thought much about it, Thomas is probably pushing him to go after Mills and Merchant. Thomas is thinking that this doesn't end until the big picture is exposed. I think their next move is to go after one of them.

Strother leaned forward, more animated than usual. "Which one would you target?" he asked.

McNair responded, "Thomas will want Mills. They have probably done some research and view him as the leader. They want to break him down."

Livermore added the most insight he had offered since the crisis began. "I am thinking that they will go after Merchant. He is the weakest link. If they have done their research, they know that Merchant takes a back seat to Mills. They will be thinking that once they get Merchant alone, they can easily break him down."

The others at the table looked around at each other. Strother seemed pleased by the responses. "Any other thoughts?" he asked.

Silence.

"Let me ask this. Mills has his hedge fund in New York, but spends most of his time here in D.C., as does Merchant, who is based in ITM's Tyson's Corner office, right?"

Livermore nodded yes.

"Okay, we need to watch all of them. Let's make sure they both are in the D.C. area for the next few days."

"So, we are using them as bait?" Livermore asked.

"In essence, yes," Strother said.

McNair then said, "I am assuming that we will just keep an eye on the senator and his wife without their knowledge. Do we let Mills and Merchant know we are keeping an eye on them?"

Strother pondered the question, then replied. "I don't think they should know. I want them to appear natural and unconcerned as they go about their day. Thomas, in particular, will be able to sense any tension or unease in them when he scopes them out."

"Makes sense," Brown said.

Strother then slapped both hands on the table as he stood up. "Good. We have an understanding. R.J., I would like you to keep an eye on Mrs. Duncan; Todd, you have Merchant; Livermore, you watch Mills. We could get others on the team to do this, but I want our best folks around when Thomas and Lowery show up."

Looking around, McNair asked, "What about the senator? You want me to watch him?"

"He is the toughest one for them to access right now. We can reconvene in twenty-four hours, but for now, let's focus on the others. I have something else I need you to do, Russ."

Waiting for everyone to clear the room, Strother sat back down. When they were alone, he looked at McNair. "I have been in touch with Tyler and the group. They are really uneasy about Mills and Merchant, but if anything happens to them, it would raise too many questions, potentially draw too much attention to other things. Everything is dependent on getting Lowery and Thomas out of the way. They must be getting some help from someone else. Livermore's a Neanderthal, but his tech guys are good. Let's dig deep on Thomas' relationships. Drill down on internet inquiries about Mills, Merchant, anything else that could help. We need to find out who is helping them so that we can set our own trap. Use the techies to find out who this person or persons is."

McNair had been thinking through everything Strother was saying as he was speaking. When Strother finished, he said, "I am on it, Dick," as he walked to the techie table with Mason and his team.

TWO

Jackson and Ronnie left the Red Roof Inn Asheville West shortly before 11 am. They felt refreshed and ready to go. It was decided that Jackson would sit all the way in the back of the Grand Cherokee on the bench seat. They were both glad that the SUV had tinted windows from the back seat and beyond. Ronnie planned on driving north on I-26 to I-81. He would then head northeast on I-81 past Staunton, Lynchburg, and Roanoke before getting to Bryce Mountain resort.

Both men were a bit antsy about the trip. I-81 was one of the most traveled interstates on the east coast. It was always full of trucks, cars, and police. Ronnie tried to keep his eyes as far down the road as possible. If he saw any sign of a backup, which could mean a possible roadblock, he would immediately get off the interstate and meander his way along the various mountain roads. There was a good argument for using back roads all the way to Bryce, but both Ronnie and Jackson felt the need to get there as quickly as possible.

Well into the ride, the two men talked about what to do when they got to D.C. and when to do it. With Jackson way in the back of the SUV, Ronnie felt like he was yelling at a kid sitting away from the adults on a road trip. When he told Jackson what he was thinking, both men laughed. Humor sure helped in the midst of ongoing tension.

Fortunately, the ride went well and was uneventful. When Ronnie stopped for gas outside of Lynchburg, he grabbed a couple of sandwiches - tuna for Jackson, ham and cheese for himself. They got to Bryce just after 5 pm. By then, Jackson had moved to the front seat and had in his hand the envelope Jenny had given them with the complicated instructions to her hideaway. Jackson navigated while Ronnie deftly maneuvered along the mountain roads up to the site. Once settled, they planned on checking in with Jenny as they prepared to go to D.C.

It had taken most of the day, but Mason, Chang, and the rest of the techie crew proved their mettle once again. Early that evening, they told McNair they had something to report to him. McNair went to get Strother so they could receive the information at the same time. During the course of the day, Strother had been monitoring the surveillance activities of the rest of the team. Livermore and Todd Brown had actually been in the same area for a couple of hours. Mills and Merchant had lunch together at the Hay Adams, seemingly a frequent lunch spot for the two of them. They both then returned to their offices.

Reba Duncan stayed in her house all day. She had pretty much been incognito since the death of her daughter. The team did learn that she and the senator would make a brief appearance that evening at an annual Cerebral Palsy dinner at the Four Seasons. R.J. would be there watching.

McNair found Strother sitting in the small conference room looking at a large map spread out on the table. He looked up at McNair as soon as he walked in. "So where do you think they are, Russ? Where would you be hiding?" he said.

"Dick, they could be anywhere. But this Thomas guy is good. Between him and his network, I would not be surprised if he has various hideaways in assorted hills all over. If I had to bet, I would guess he is bunkered down in the hills."

"Hmmm," Strother said, nodding his head, still looking at the map.

"But we may be moving closer to an answer. Livermore's techies have something to report. I figured we could learn what they know at the same time."

This news energized Strother. "Let's go hear it!" he exclaimed, beating McNair to the door.

Mason and Chang were ready for Strother and McNair. As usual, Mason took the lead. "Sirs," he began, "after talking with Mr. McNair earlier, I dispatched our team to track down internet searches regarding the Duncans, Jackson Lowery as well as Mr. Mills and Mr. Merchant. As you might imagine, with all of the news coverage there were millions of hits. We then took the liberty of adding other names and concepts. I will not bore you with all of them, but we tried to be as expansive as possible. One phrase we included was 'food service contracts'. Taking that phrase alone with the other names led to a lot of search activity coming from the Atlanta area."

It was at this point that Mason had the full attention of both Strother and McNair.

"In particular, detailed searches from the same Atlanta computer focused on the Duncan family, Mills, Merchant, and food service contractors Claremark, Jawer Foods, and Honeyberg Industries. In addition, that same computer did extensive research on Bartlett Food and their CEO Joseph Charles.

Strother and McNair both looked at each other with wide eyes. As much as they needed to know this information, this was not good news. Their employers could slide swiftly into panic mode if they got any notion that Jackson and Thomas, or another party, were too close.

Mason, sensing the uneasiness, stopped talking to let the two men digest what they had just been told.

McNair said, "Go ahead, Mason. Continue."

"Anyway, we could not identify the ownership of the computer other than it was registered to the Centers for Disease Control in Atlanta. All of the computer activity came from the CDC headquarters in the downtown area."

"So, you don't know who was using it," Strother asked.

Here, Chang chimed in. "No, we are not saying that, sir. We just wanted to make sure to walk you through our steps. Mr. McNair also asked us to do a deeper cross-reference on Ronnie Thomas and his government allies. As you know, he has been pretty much a lone wolf since leaving the marines and doing clandestine work for the government. His background has been a blank page for the most part. There have been a handful of people who he has kept in touch with periodically since all of them have been in training together in the marines. One of them is this woman, Jenny Roberts." At that point, Chang nodded to a techie, who then put Jenny's image on a nearby computer screen.

Strother and McNair looked at the attractive woman in the picture, understanding that looks aside, this woman was probably as lethal as one could get.

Chang then proceeded to tell them about Jenny's background and her expertise and interest in infectious diseases.

"So, you are saying," McNair asked, "that she gave up her clandestine career to do chemical and infectious disease research?"

"Exactly," Chang said. "She still works closely with counter terrorism groups. Her known forte is dealing with chemical weapons."

Strother put his hands on top of his head, lacing them together.

"So once Jackson told Thomas what the Duncan girl told him, they started to put two and two together. Then, Thomas called his old colleague who has some expertise in all of this and boom, these three have connected the dots. Whew!"

"Where is Roberts now, guys?" McNair asks.

"Right as we speak, she is in her office. At least that is where we think she is. But guess where she was last night?" Mason asks.

Strother answered right away. "Don't tell me she was in Asheville?"

"Yes, she was," Mason confirmed, "Look here." He then described how they matched her photo against digital images from hotel cameras in and around the Asheville area last night. He showed them a grainy image of a tall, lean woman strolling through the lobby of the Red Roof Inn Asheville West dressed in all black. Though she was adept at keeping her head away from the camera, at one point she slightly lifted her head to return the wave of the receptionist clerk. Mason froze the image of her face and placed it side by side next to the file photo of Jenny Roberts. It was unmistakably the same person.

Chang continued. "Roberts checked in under the name of Emma Jones for two nights. We do not know when she left, but we have seen her enter the CDC headquarters today from police cameras in downtown Atlanta."

Strother decided to sit in a nearby chair. Looking at McNair, he said, "It looks like we need to go to Atlanta."

Mason then spoke. "Maybe not, sir. When Mr. McNair went to find you, we noticed that Jenny Roberts booked a plane ticket for tomorrow."

"To where," McNair asked anxiously.

Mason smiled. "She booked a direct flight from Atlanta to D.C. Reagan airport. Jenny Roberts will be in D.C. tomorrow morning."

———————

Joe Sweeney arrived early at the Four Seasons, something that pleased Yesus' uncle. "Glad you are here early, Joe. Many VIPs will be here and since Senator Duncan is coming, some people have even come early to hang out in the lounge and wait."

Sweeney knew exactly what Yesus' uncle was referring to. The Four Seasons lounge is a famous hang out spot for people watching. All dinner guests going to the main ballroom in the basement have to pass right by the lounge to get downstairs. With all of the publicity around the death of Amy Duncan, many must have come to the lounge just to see the senator and his wife walk by. Sweeney was also sure that there were a few members of the press hanging out in the lounge.

One thing Sweeney liked about parking cars was that doing it definitely helped time move fast. He had just come back from dropping off a car when there was a palpable stirring in the atrium area right outside the hotel. Sweeney quickly looked down at his watch and could not believe that it was almost 7:30. Just then, a beige Cadillac pulled up and just like that, Senator Rex Duncan climbed out of the driver's seat. Sweeney was on the same side as the senator, who was handing the keys to one of Sweeney's colleagues.

As was the case with many VIPs, the valet team would not take the senator's car to their usual parking spot a couple blocks away. Rather, they would park it right up front in one of the eight spaces that could be used for these occasions. Sweeney had factored this in as part of his plan. While one of the valet workers had the car and drove it in a circle through the street and then back through the main entrance, Sweeney was sure that some folks would start chatting up the senator. He would then slyly approach Reba Duncan. He would have about thirty seconds to do so.

Sweeney watched as Reba Duncan got out of the passenger side, aided somewhat by her husband, who had hustled around to her side. While the senator looked elegant in his standard black tuxedo, Reba Duncan looked absolutely magnificent in her silver sequined gown with a fox wrap covering her shoulders. She was a beautiful woman, and had a palpably sad energy following her. Sweeney felt instantly saddened as she and the senator walked into the hotel.

Sweeney parked a few more cars when Yesus' uncle announced that the senator was leaving. He said, "Senator Duncan and his wife are on their way up here. Jonah," he said, tossing the keys to one of the hotel's fulltime valet workers, "Go get their car and pull around front so they won't have to wait long."

Stuck in his own head, Sweeney was beginning to panic. He looked around expecting that everyone would be looking at him, as if they were all aware of his plan. Instead, he noticed that everyone in that little atrium area outside of the Four Seasons entrance was looking in the direction of the door and waiting for the senator and his lovely, sad wife. He had to have just a few seconds with Mrs. Duncan. He positioned himself near where the car would end up so he could open the passenger door for her. He would then slip the note in her hand. Sweeney's heart was beating a mile a minute. Jonah then pulled the car up front at nearly the exact same time that the senator and Mrs. Duncan came through the main hotel doors.

Sweeney had walked right up to the passenger side of their car and was reaching down to open it. *Stay cool and calm*, he thought. He looked to the other side of the car, where Jonah was holding the driver's door open with the senator's keys in his hand. Jonah threw him a smile as if to say, "nice touch."

Then, Sweeney got a break. As he had hoped, the senator was deluged by several onlookers. Hotel security was with him, but at least ten people began to mill around the senator and follow him like a herd to his car. Sweeney noticed that the senator's wife, seeing the mad rush of people, looked a little unnerved. She looked toward the car and relief showed on her face when she saw Sweeney standing there smiling with the passenger door open. She rushed toward the car. *Here we go,* Sweeney thought.

Holding the car door with his right hand, Sweeney stepped toward Reba Duncan as she positioned herself to get into the car. He then gently grabbed her right hand with his left as if to help her into the car. In his left hand was the note he had been working on all morning. Reba Duncan had a shocked look on her face as she could tell that he was handing her something. While nudging her into the car, Sweeney had forgotten the lines he had obsessed over.

His anxiety began to overwhelm him. He thrust the note in her hand and simply said, "Mrs. Duncan, please read this note and do not tell anyone. Please." With that, he shut the door behind her, never taking his eyes from hers. Reba Duncan had her mouth wide open, but did not break the stare between them. By then, Rex Duncan had made it into the car and quickly started the car and pulled out of the driveway. Jonah looked over at Sweeney saying, "Way to step up, Sweeney. She was not having those crowds."

"Thanks," Sweeney said, nodding back toward his fellow valet worker.

On the sidewalk, just twenty-five yards away, R.J. studied Sweeney intently, wondering why some snot-nosed kid valet would go out of his way to place a piece of paper in Reba Duncan's hand.

Ronnie had to hand it to Jenny. The entrance to her Bryce Mountain hideaway was as elaborate as any he had seen. *Jenny was always a cut above the rest of us,* he thought to himself. To gain access to Jenny's place, you first had to go to a log cabin located at the top of a winding road on which a host of other cabins were located. As instructed, Ronnie drove into the entrance of the cabin and followed a driveway that led downhill to the back of the cabin. Not visible to the street was a small one-car garage. Again, as instructed, Ronnie pulled the Grand Cherokee into the garage, whereupon he and Jackson exited the car with their duffel bags in tow, closing the garage door behind them. Jenny had noted that the log cabin was a rental property, but that it was unoccupied at the time. Ronnie and Jackson then walked to the back of the garage where they faced a dense set of woods. Since this property was near the top of a hill, there were no other cabins in site.

Walking about twenty yards into the woods, they ran into a shed-like structure. Using the key she had given them, they opened the shed and saw piles of chopped wood stacked inside on several shelves. Jackson, who was still holding the instructions, walked to the very back of the shed, reached with his hand to the top shelf, then searched for a button on the back part of the shelf. Finding it, he pushed it three times.

Suddenly, the wall opened up behind the shelves. Jackson and Ronnie walked behind the shelves and saw a circular staircase leading downward. They entered the staircase, but before walking down the stairs, Jackson found another hidden button on wall beside a light switch. He turned the switch on and pushed the button three times which resulted in the wall closing behind them. They walked down the staircase about three levels down, ending up in a rustic living area. As they walked around they found two bedrooms, one with a queen bed and one with two twin beds. They also found a fully stocked kitchen, a kitchen table with four chairs and a living room with a couch, two easy chairs, and one big screen television. There was also a computer desk and chair in the corner of the living room.

The last part of the note Jenny left in the envelope suggested that they go through the trap door found in the bedroom with the queen bed. She wanted to make sure that they were familiar with the exit, should a quick escape be necessary. It was here that the genius of the hideaway was most evident. The trap door exit led to and escape hatch carved inside of a big tree. The side of the tree opened up in the middle of some woods, which were only about seventy-five yards to the Stony Creek River. Right by the exit was a small boat. There was no way anyone who knew the entrance to the hideaway could even fathom the exit area. Even with Ronnie's superior sense of direction, he was sure that the exit door would lead them to the base of the mountain near the road where they began to climb to get to the log cabin. Instead, they ended up in a place that was almost two roads over from where they started. Both men looked at each other, amazed.

"Pretty fucking unbelievable," Ronnie said. "This is the best emergency exit setup I have seen."

Nodding, Jackson agreed. "It is pretty amazing. I still must admit, however, the motorcycle park thing was a darn impressive stunt."

They went back inside and had an extremely tough time making it up the escape hatch. When they were finally secure in the hideaway, Ronnie started to prepare some food. After they ate, he was going to call Jenny. D.C. was within their reach.

Reba Duncan had a lot of swirling thoughts in her head when the young man handed her the note. At first, she thought it was some crazy activist play, possibly a way to get some political point of view to her husband. She was then haunted by the look in the young man's eyes. She felt his authentic desperation. Reba looked at her right hand. In it, she held the note given to her by the young red-headed boy. She was eager to read it, but afraid to at the same time. Reba sensed that the note's contents would confirm all of her suspicions: that her daughter was murdered for some crazy political reason. She also knew, however, that the note could help her avenge her daughter's death. She was more than ready for that.

"What was that boy talking to you about, dear?" Rex asked her as he drove them home. "He looked

181

like he had something important he wanted to share."

Reba felt as if her thoughts were interrupted. "Oh, nothing. He said he was sorry for my loss. It kind of hit me strange. So many people know about our situation, yet we know nothing about theirs. Anyway, he was trying to be nice."

Rex looked at his wife and tilted his head slightly as if he understood her point. "Well, I hope you are glad we came, sweetie. Amy would have been proud. You were terrific, by the way." His eyes sparkled thinking about his wife's brief, but heartfelt remarks.

Reba was genuinely flattered. Even after all of these years, Rex could say a certain thing in a certain way that would get her flustered. She smiled at him. "Yes, I am glad we went too. Amy would have been proud. I am proud also of who she was in her life. She was an amazing woman, Rex."

"That she was, Reba. She was just like her mother."

The two smiled at each other warmly as Rex pulled into their driveway.

Once inside, Rex went to the bar to fix himself a drink. He also said that he needed to make a couple of calls to his office about his schedule tomorrow. Neither of them were looking forward to the services for their daughter which would be in Boise next week.

Reba walked upstairs and sat on the stool in her dressing area. As she began to take off her jewelry, she opened the note that was still crumpled in her right hand. It read:

Dear Mrs. Duncan. Last Friday, my roommate John Finnegan picked up your daughter following her date with professor Lowery. When he drove her home,

Amy kept saying that she was in love. All weekend, Finn kept talking about the two of them. He told me that he wanted that kind of love. On Tuesday, when we saw the CNN broadcast about your daughter's death and the manhunt for professor Lowery, Finn was adamant that there was no way Lowery would kill Amy. He decided to go to the local police to tell his story and that he believed Lowery was not the killer. That night, he was dead. I think he was murdered. If you want to talk more, meet me at Booeymonger on Prospect Street tomorrow morning at 10 am. Please come. Joe Sweeney.

Reba read the note several more times. As she removed her make up, the immediate question Reba had to face was whether she would tell her husband about this new development. Her instinct was to do so, but she was worried about Rex's safety as well. She was growing increasingly certain that those assholes Steve Mills and Bill Merchant were the reason her precious daughter was dead. *How far would they go? Would they kill her? And Rex?*

She was sure that under the right circumstances, they would do whatever they needed to do. Still, she did not know what motivated them. *Why did they think they needed Rex so much, yet still let his daughter be killed?* Reba fought back tears during her thinking. She resolved to talk to this Sweeney boy first, and then go to Rex. While she felt sure that he was legitimate, she would have a better sense of things after spending some time with him. She would tell Rex about it later.

Just then, she heard her husband coming up the stairs. *He was such a good man,* she thought. She now had to protect him from these awful people who killed their child. Looking at herself in the mirror, she gave a weak smile. All of that could wait until tomorrow. Tonight, she believed, something else was more important. She stood from the dressing area, letting her sequin dress fall to the floor. She was going to make love to her husband.

Things were happening fast. It was all coming to a head. Strother could feel it. The techies had come through big time about the Roberts woman. A decision had to be made about when, where, and how to confront her. Or should they let her lead them directly to Jackson and Thomas so they could take them all down at once? He would work through that decision soon.

Strother also had to deal with the story he got from R.J. Apparently, while following and watching the Duncans at the charity that evening, a young, white valet parking attendant handed Reba Duncan a note. *Who the hell was this young man and what was that all about?* Strother was juggling a lot of balls, but loose ends were the worst.

If this kid were in any way connected, he would need to be eliminated. Quickly. Strother would meet with his team at 9 am to discuss all these matters and their options. Strother also had to update Tyler on all of this, especially the Roberts woman and her research. Tomorrow would be another busy day, but is also could be the day of resolution. At least, Strother hoped so. Indeed, one could only hope.

THREE

Sweeney was hoping that Reba Duncan would show up. Deep down, he suspected that she would, but you could never be sure about these things. When they locked eyes, however, he did not see fear in her face. Rather, he saw determination. She was looking for answers too.

All night long, Sweeney thought through how they should proceed. He played over various scenarios in his mind, finally landing on an idea that he thought could work. Once Mrs. Duncan heard his idea, he hoped that she would agree with him. She was the key to making it work.

Sweeney was thinking about all of this as he walked down Prospect Street toward Booeymongers. He was only a block away, but could see that several of the outside table and chairs were still available. *Great*, he thought. He could have a much more private conversation with her outside as opposed to inside the cafe.

As Sweeney crossed over 32nd Street, right in front of Booeymongers, he noticed someone waving to him off to the left of the Cafe. Sitting at one of the outside tables was a woman with a baseball cap pulled down and sunglasses covering her eyes. She was wearing a stylish dark blue sweater. Reba Duncan. She still looked stunning, but in a different kind of way from the night before.

Sweeney waved back and walked straight to the table instead of going into the cafe.

"I bought a coffee for you," she said, holding it up. "Also, a pastry. Here is the cream and sugar."

Sweeney's eyes lit up. "Thanks. This is all good."

Smiling, she said, "I remember the appetite of college boys. I also figured you were not at the age yet where you started drinking your coffee black. You probably will, someday."

By that time, Sweeney was already digging in. The pastry tasted perfect to him.

Having gotten over the shock from the night before, Reba had decided that she was driving the conversation. "So, young man. Tell me everything. About you. Your roommate. Your story. If we are going to work together, I need to know about you and trust you." She folded her hands together under her chin and leaned forward on them.

Sweeney nodded several times, still chewing. "First, Mrs. Duncan, I am so, so glad you came. I wasn't sure where to go or who to talk to and I rehearsed our meeting so many times." Suddenly, Sweeney got emotional. He was thinking of Finn and the entire mess, finding himself getting choked up. He stopped talking in order to pull himself together.

Reba reached out and held his hand. "That's alright, Joe. You know I understand. This has been a lot for you to hold onto by yourself." She continued, "I am on your team now, you can trust me."

Sweeney smiled back, regaining his composure. He then told her everything. He told her about himself, about Finn, and their friendship. He then went into greater detail about the way Finn reacted to Amy and the professor. He said that the two of them debated all weekend the meaning of true love. This part of the conversation provoked a teary-eyed response from Reba.

When he finished, she said, "Thank you. Now, is that all I need to know about you?"

Sweeney looked at her. He wasn't sure if she knew his story with the government or not, but he went ahead and told her.

Reba just nodded her head. "Okay, Joe. It seems to me that we should be able to use your skills to help us get to the bottom of all of this. Do you have any ideas?"

Sweeney perked up. "I have been up all night thinking about it. Listen, who would we both like to talk to as a way to get a handle on all of this?"

"Jackson Lowery" she said, without hesitation.

"Right. But, he is on the run and the bad guys want him dead too. But, he is the key. Amy told him whatever she knew that led to her death. All night, I have been thinking about the best way to draw him out, but in a way that he feels safe reaching out."

Reba arched an eyebrow. "And?" she said.

"Hear me out. What if we send him a message that is coded and wrapped in the form of a reward announcement from you?"

She looked confused. "How do we do that?" she asked.

Sweeney was beyond animated now. He held his hands out flat, pushing them down as if to say hold on.

"Later today, you could release a statement announcing a private hotline for information leading to the arrest and capture of your daughter's murder. Make the award say, $100,000. I can monitor all the calls and messages. And trust me, the bad guys will not have anyone on their team who can hack into my security setup to track the calls we receive."

Still confused, Reba asked, "But what in the message will make it likely that Professor Lowery will call?"

"It will be the hotline number itself. Finn picked Amy up at 1789 Restaurant, right down the street from here. We could put 1789 in the number. Something like 1-800-123-1789. Get it?"

Reba was deep in thought. "The idea makes sense." She paused, and then said, "Let's adjust the number a bit. How about 1-800-AMY-1789? That would get his attention."

Sweeney smiled broadly. "Even better," he said. "Much better."

"Now, tell me how we set this up." Reba replied.

———————

Strother hung up the phone after getting an updated report from R.J. Strother was mystified by what was going on between this college kid and Reba Duncan. He got the techies to check the valet work schedule at the Four Seasons in order to get the kids name. Soon, he would also have his profile.

Walking back into the conference room in Fairfax, he continued the meeting that had been interrupted by R.J.'s call. In the room were Livermore, McNair, and Todd Brown. "As I was saying before I got R.J.'s call, we are pulling the surveillance today because there are some action items we need to take care of. Russ, you, Todd, and two of the younger team members are on this Roberts woman. Latch on to her at the airport and follow her until she connects with Lowery and Thomas. Then take them all out. Quickly and efficiently. Livermore, I may need you as back-up for R.J. if we decide to take out this Sweeney kid. Once

I get more information on him, I will ask our bosses' opinions."

Mason then poked his head in the room. "Excuse me sirs, we know who the Four Seasons valet is."

"And?" McNair said.

"He was the Uber driver Finnegan's roommate."

Livermore groaned audibly.

Tyler had set up a quick conference call with General Brock and two other powerful members of their group, perhaps the most powerful. While Mills and Merchant planted the seeds that got the group together, Jim and Susan Carr were the ones who made the philosophy seem real to the group. In his quiet way, Jim helped General Brock understand the difference between white nationalism and white supremacy. Jim Carr also introduced General Brock to the teachings of various eugenicists like Henry Fairfield Osborn.

As Carr simply explained, "White nationalism is the belief that national identity should be built around white ethnicity, and that white people should be in control to protect our interests and our ethnic pride. White supremacy is the profound understanding that white people are genetically and intellectually superior to darker skinned races, including the Jews. We know it and deep down they know it, too. For those of us who are so enlightened, we must do all we can to maintain the purity of the white breed and keep the darker skinned people of the world in a subservient role. If we fail to do so, our republic is forever doomed."

The Carrs ran one of the largest food supplier companies in the country. Yes, the big boys like Claremark, Jawer, and Honeyberg had the contracts and each of them ran their own food distribution divisions, but their quality control suffered. Companies like the Carr Company specialized exclusively in preparing, packaging and distributing quality food in bulk. Although, they had ten warehouses located across the country, the Carrs did not have any direct food service contracts with school districts. Recently, however, they had entered that space as a subcontractor. The Carrs had just signed an exclusive agreement with one of the major food supplier companies to supply them with certain foods on every new contract. Like Mills, Merchant, Tyler, and Brock, they too were part of the secret white supremacy group. But, they were a critical part since they were the ones funding the research on the poison and also supplying the food.

The Carrs had been working closely with the scientists in Pennsylvania, trying to find a way to disseminate the poison expeditiously. For months, their collective thinking was to insert the poison in the food or as part of the preparation process. Recently, however, the scientists began to look at packaging. They were examining whether food wrapped in plastic packaging saturated by poison would absorb the toxicity necessary for the plan's implementation. Preliminary results were encouraging.

The Carrs were able to deflect attention away from themselves politically by appearing left wing. They extolled the virtues of organic, plant based, non-GMO healthy foods, and they were publicly apolitical. The Carrs had been made aware of the drama at the Duncan household earlier this week, but neither Carr liked to get their hands dirty. Tyler, however, thought it was time to bring them into the fold and get their input.

After bringing everyone up to date, especially regarding the Sweeney-Reba Duncan connection, Tyler asked if anyone had any thoughts. The General piped in first. "What a goddamn cluster fuck. That damn Mills is a royal fuck up. Before this Sweeney kid got to Reba, we had been talking about containment. Now, we are in a position where everything can be exposed and our opportunities lost."

Tyler responded. "It is bad, General. There is no doubt about it. But things still may be salvageable. The contractor has a bead on the professor and his helpers. That should be taken care of in a day or so. The question for us right now is how we deal with Mrs. Duncan's mission. She is not going to stop until she gets real answers."

Here, Susan Carr interjected. "She is a mother, for God's sake. What do you expect? Jim and I think it is clear what the only answer is. Isn't it obvious?"

In fact, it was obvious. Steve Mills and possibly even Bill Merchant had to be thrown under the bus. But, it had to be done in a way to deflect from the overall mission of the group. They had to make it look like a business deal had gone bad for Mills. Or something like that. Once all of this had been discussed, Tyler agreed to come up with the story they would use. He was going to involve the contractor in it.

At some point, the General would sit down with his dear friends and tell them what he had unearthed about Steven Mills. Whatever it was, it had to be enough to satisfy Reba Duncan. With that framework of a plan in place, they agreed to reconnect soon and they all hung up. Tyler immediately reached out to Strother to discuss a strategy.

191

FOUR

Jenny sauntered through Terminal B at D.C. Reagan airport after exiting her Delta plane from Atlanta. She was headed to the Enterprise car rental counter so she could pick up her reserved Expedition and rendezvous with Jackson and Ronnie. She was glad they had made it to her hideaway. She had been worried about them all day. Now, she was going to help them with their boldest move yet. Here is where the Expedition would come in handy. Speaking with them late last night, it was clear that they had zeroed in on their target – it was their way to play offense. It was definitely a high risk, high reward plan, but Jenny saw the logic. She believed in high stakes games.

As Jenny settled into her rental, she began to adjust the driver's side mirror. In doing so, the mirror caught a dark haired muscular man looking directly at her. When he saw that his reflection was being caught in the mirror, he awkwardly looked away. *This is not good,* Jenny thought.

Not good at all if I'm already being tracked. Jenny backed out of the parking spot and exited the rental lot. Soon she was on the George Washington Parkway headed toward I-66. She now had a decision to make and needed to alert her colleagues about her tail. She checked her encrypted phone and placed a call.

Jackson picked up right away, pressing the speaker button on the phone. "Hi, Jenny," he said. "We are just about to head your way."

"Change of plans guys. I am just leaving Reagan and I think I am being followed. At least one, I expect more. I bet that they are waiting for us to connect."

Ronnie placed his hands on his hips, looking at the ceiling. "We need to meet somewhere to even the playing field."

Jackson cut in. "But, how did they find you? That's impossible," he said.

Jenny was nonplussed. "Most likely through the internet searches. I am sure their tech guys are savvy enough to narrow down where internet searches have been coming from. They also probably did a thorough background on Ronnie. I know the hotel cameras caught me, but the 'how' doesn't really matter now. Let's focus on what we do."

"How about Luray Caverns?" Jackson asked. "We are closer to it than you are and they don't know what car we are in. When you get close let us know. Go ahead and pay to get inside. We will already be there. What do you think?"

Jenny said nothing.

Ronnie said, "It could work, but this is the real deal, Jack. Make no mistake about it, Jenny is being followed by a hit squad. When we strike back, there is no holding back."

"I read you, Ronnie. Loud and clear. What about our D.C. plan?"

Here, Jenny commented. "They are feeling the squeeze. They may even be watching our target. We have to do this dirty work first. I like the Luray Caverns idea. But Ronnie, tell me what the play is. Remember, I am not packing."

Ronnie responded. "Try to see how many there are. Pull off at a gas station so you can easily see who else gets off the exit. I am thinking that Jackson will go inside and wait for you to pay and enter the exhibit. I will hide outside, see who is following you and neutralize whomever I can. It would help to know how many."

"Sounds good," she said. "I will let you know about the tail."

Steve Mills walked back from lunch and into his spacious Connecticut Avenue office, anxious to get an update on Jackson Lowery. It had now been several days and Mills honestly thought that they would have caught the wily college professor by now. He did not want to admit it, but Mills was beginning to feel the pressure.

As more time passed with Lowery still on the loose, Mills had become increasingly wary about his partners. *You really cannot put anything past them,* he thought. Mills sat behind his large mahogany desk in his leather swivel chair and sighed loudly. Though not yet two o'clock, he needed a drink. He buzzed Sarah, his longtime assistant.

"Sarah, can you please bring me a scotch and water? It has been that kind of day."

He could hear her chuckled reply. "Understood, Mr. Mills. I will mix it for you right away."

Mills laid back in the chair. *It makes a difference,* he thought, *to have competent help.* Again, his mind drifted to Lowery. *Maybe I should send Sarah after him,* he thought, smiling to himself. Through it all, Mills was confident that the plan would still work. It had to.

In his mind, implementing the plan was a final tribute to his father. Arthur Mills was a researcher for legendary eugenic scientist William Shockley. Shockley won the Nobel Prize in 1956 for co-inventing the transistor and ushering in the computer age. But his later work, which trumpeted theories of black inferiority, made him a pariah. Arthur Mills was a true believer and was blackballed for being close to Shockley. As a result, the family always struggled financially. But those circumstances also drove Mills and made him determined to validate his father's work. Mills fervently believed that both his father and William Shockley were right. Whites were superior. America belonged to them.

Five minutes later, Sarah knocked on his door, and then walked in. She was a short, matronly looking woman with a pleasant smile. Mills liked having her around because she had spent many years as a secretary with the CIA in Langley. She knew the espionage world very well.

Smiling, she placed the tray on his desk and handed him his drink. Mills could smell the vintage scotch and was eager to take a sip, which he quickly did.

Sarah walked toward the door, then slowed down. She turned and looked at Mills as he took another big gulp.

At first, Mills smiled at her, but then he felt his throat constrict. Something was not right. All of his senses were put on overload all at once. Though hard to process so quickly, he intuitively knew what was happening. He looked pleadingly at his assistant, who just stood staring at him.

Finally, Sarah walked toward him, placed her hands on his desk, leaned forward and said, "Goodbye, Mr. Mills."

She smiled as Mills drifted to unconsciousness and the glass dropped on the marble floor. Miraculously, the glass did not break.

The assistant then scooped the glass from the floor, picked up the phone on her boss' desk and dialed a number. In response to whoever answered on the other end, she simply said, "It's done," and hung up.

One hour later the afternoon news reported that longtime, successful hedge fund manager Steve Mills had died of a heart attack while working in his northwest D.C. office.

The news regarding Steve Mills' death received surface treatment at best. The big news that afternoon was the statement released by Reba Duncan. Her statement, which was broadcast and read verbatim on countless news programs around the country was as follows:

Our family remains shattered by the horrible, senseless killing of our daughter, Amy. We have decided to open a twenty-four hour, privately funded hotline to receive tips that can help us find her murderer. Any person who provides information on this hotline that leads to a conviction will receive $100,000 from us. While we respect and appreciate the work being done by national and local authorities, we must do what we can to find the truth. Please call 1-800-AMY-1789 anytime day or night.

Bill Merchant had been at an ITM board meeting all day, so for the most part, he had been out of the loop. He was still in the meeting when he received back-to-back CNN alerts about Mills and the Amy Duncan reward on his smartphone. Seeing the news about his friend stopped him in his tracks and sent a chill up his spine. Steve Mills, with all of his faults had been Merchant's best friend. They had known each other over twenty-five years. They vacationed together, had lunch three or four days each week together, and they had put together the group that created the plan. Now, it was apparent that the group had killed Mills. Was Merchant next? Could it be that they were waiting for his board meeting to end to finish him off?

Merchant felt himself panicking.

He had to gather himself. He still had a couple of hours left with his ITM colleagues, followed by a company dinner. Should he take a break and call Tyler? Maybe he should disappear for a while. Once the plan was implemented, each of the group had their own exit strategy, including hiding spots here and abroad. Merchant could easily get to his hideout in a few hours. That may make sense.

Then, Merchant's mind shifted to the Duncans. *What is that all about?* he thought. *Did the General know that Rex was going to do that? Or was it driven by Reba? How did things get so off-track? A week ago, the team was celebrating the lab results from Pennsylvania, and Rex Duncan looked to be well on his way to be the next president. Everything had been going according to plan. Then one faux pas... well, it was too late for replaying the situation now.*

Merchant knew that now he needed to fully focus on his own survival first and foremost. He never thought he would be thinking like this, but as far as he was concerned, the plan would just have to wait.

———

Luray Caverns is eastern America's largest and most popular caverns. A physical and geological wonder, the caverns possess cathedral-sized rooms with ceilings ten stories high, filled with towering stone columns and crystal-clear pools. Nestled in the scenic and historic Shenandoah Valley, Luray Caverns is one of Virginia's most popular tourist attractions. Nearly daily an assortment of schools take field trips to the caverns.

The drive to Luray Caverns was a relatively short one from Bryce Mountain, around thirty minutes. It would take Jenny three times as long to get there from Reagan airport. While driving there, it hit Jackson about the school field trips.

"Ronnie, I just remembered how popular the caverns are for school field trips. We cannot endanger any kids," he said in a panic.

Ronnie looked at him, then nodded. "Yeah, I agree. Let's see what she says about the tail. Also, since we will be there way ahead of her, let's drive around the area and see if there is another good spot to lie in wait."

Once in the Luray area, they started to drive around. They even drove over to nearby I-66 to see what some of the back roads looked like near that interstate. They knew that Jenny would be coming to them via I-66. Jackson called Jenny when they had worked out a way to trap her pursuers. Jackson told Jenny to take the exit onto state route 17 near Delaplane, Virginia. He told her to then make a right onto Maidstone Road near the small local airport, and gave her the land markings to look for so that she could make a right turn down a winding and dusty dirt road. They would be able to connect with her on that road.

Jenny also confirmed with them that there were two SUVs following her. When she had picked up on the fact that she was being followed, it looked like each car had just two men. But, she had to be sure. She decided to make a big show of stopping at a gas station convenience store without getting gas. She braked hard at the entrance, looked rushed as she walked down the aisles obviously looking for a certain item, found it, then paid for it. The item she paid for was a box of tampons. Once purchased, she went to the ladies room before returning to her car. She hoped that her performance would satisfy her pursuers. More importantly, it allowed her to see how many men were on her tail.

Ronnie and Jackson had found a perfect hiding spot in the woods behind a smattering of oak trees just off the winding dirt road they had described to Jenny. Once Jenny let them know she was about to get off I-66, the two men were going to get out of the car, and with guns in hand lie in wait for Jenny to pass. They would then give her a gun and all three would position themselves at various spots on both sides of the winding dirt road to wait for her followers. Earlier, Jackson said to Ronnie, "So this will be a flat-out ambush, right?"

Ronnie could not tell if Jackson was being sarcastic or just plain naive. "Jack, this is real serious stuff. The big leagues. You know, save the world kind of stuff. You need to put yourself into a different state of mind, buddy. Kill or be killed. These guys only mean us harm. If we get the jump on any of them, we need to take them down. Period."

Jackson got the message. "I know, Ronnie," he said sheepishly. "I am ready. My whole brave new world still takes some getting used to."

Ronnie just smiled and patted him on the back.

While settling in to wait for Jenny, Ronnie flipped on the news station on the radio, which was reporting the headline reports of the Steve Mills heart attack. Jackson spoke first.

"Well there goes our plan!" he said, obviously frustrated. Last night, while talking to Jenny, the three of them agreed that it made the most sense to track down Steve Mills and force him to talk. Jenny had gotten information on his home and office. They had intended to confront him that day.

Ronnie just silently stared out the front car window. He then said, "They are really starting to circle their wagons, now. In situations like this, the bad guys end up settling for less than expected. I wonder how far they have progressed with the big plot. I am getting concerned that their fear of being exposed may force them to move into action earlier than planned."

Jackson had not thought about that. Ronnie's observation started to redirect his thinking. Just then, on the radio, the news channel was going into greater detail about the Duncan reward. The radio news anchor was reading the Duncan statement verbatim. On hearing it, Jackson pounded the dashboard, momentarily stunning Ronnie.

"Whoa, man. You alright?" Ronnie asked.

Jackson turned to his friend with a wild, yet excited look in his eyes. Ronnie had not seen Jackson this excited since they watched the super bowl together many years ago when Jackson was married to his cousin. In fact, since they reconnected several days ago, Ronnie had not seen his friend happy at all. He had forgotten that Jackson Lowery could look happy.

"Ronnie, they know! Don't you see? The Duncans know I am innocent, but they need our help. They want me to reach out to them. They know I did not kill Amy!"

At this point, Ronnie saw that Jackson appeared to be on the verge of tears. He tried to get a handle on what was going on.

"Slow down there, buddy. Just take a couple of deep breaths. Let's back up a bit. What did you just hear in the statement that led you to believe what you just said - that they believe you are innocent and are sending you a coded message to reach out to them?"

"I know it's crazy, but it is right there in the 1-800 number, Ronnie. The last part. 1789. That is the restaurant where I took Amy. That is where we had our one and only date. Somehow, they know that and the bad guys don't. Maybe Amy kept a diary or something, but it is not a coincidence that they would choose the number 1-800-AMY-1789! They want me to call that number!"

Ronnie was not convinced.

"It could also be the opposite, Jack," he said. "They could know about the date and still think that you had an obsession over their daughter."

Jackson was about to reply, but soon realized that he would have to table his thoughts. They had been interrupted by the sound of several cars' racing engines. What followed those sounds was the sound of sub machine fire.

Jackson's phone then rang. They looked at each other, knowing it was Jenny. Jackson picked up the phone, putting it on speaker.

"Jenny," he said. "Are you alright?"

"I've been hit! They opened fire when I got on 17. It's bad. I think I am passing out, but am trying to make it to you. I'm coming in hot. Cover m..."

Another gunshot interrupted Jenny before she could finish. Jackson and Ronnie heard an explosion coming from Jenny's end. Then silence. Seconds later, they could hear a car coming down the winding dirt road. They saw the cloud of smoke before the car was visible.

When the black Expedition came into view it had slowed down considerably, as if it was running out of gas. As Jackson and Ronnie hurried to the car, they saw nothing but blood on the front windshield. Bits and pieces of her phone was scattered all over the dashboard. Jenny was slumped forward with her head on the steering wheel. She looked unconscious.

Jackson opened the driver's side door, while Ronnie reached in carefully trying to see where she had been shot. Blood was coming from her left shoulder. He gently guided her out of the car, handed her to Jackson and said, "Jack, get a towel from my duffel bag and stuff it into the wound on her shoulder. Then lay her in back of the big tree near our car. I am going to the bend to pick them off. Once you set her down, go on the other side of the road opposite me and shoot like hell at anyone who makes it past me. Whatever you do, Jack, shoot to kill!"

––––––––––––

While waiting for Jenny Roberts to land at Reagan airport, McNair had double-parked near the B Terminal and dropped off Byron Beck where he could follow Jenny from the baggage claim to the car rental station. Todd Brown double-parked near the Enterprise car rental exit, since they knew she had reserved a car from that company. John, from Livermore's team, had been assigned to mill around the Enterprise counter to verify the make and model of the car Jenny eventually rented.

When Jenny climbed into the Expedition, John was caught watching her when she adjusted her side door rear view mirror. He quickly moved out of her line of sight, but knew he had been seen, and told Brown when he climbed back into the car. Both sets of cars, Brown and John in one; McNair and Beck in the other, followed Jenny down the George Washington Parkway and west on I-66. Just past Manassas, they noticed that she took an exit and rushed into a gas station convenience store. Watching her through binoculars, Brown could see that she had purchased some tampons. She went back on the road after visiting the bathroom.

As they were getting closer to I-81, McNair got a call from Strother. "You still following the Roberts woman, right?" Strother asked.

"Yes, Todd and John are in the lead car. We are right behind her. She is in our sights."

"Well, Mason and his techies have been able to zero in on her phone signals. They have locked in on where she is making her calls. Lowery and Thomas are less than ten miles from you and we have a satellite on their location," Strother said, hardly restraining his excitement.

"Man," McNair said. "Those techies are good. What do you want us to do?"

"Based on where we think Lowery and Thomas are located, Roberts will probably get off on Road 17. More than likely, they have planned some kind of ambush. When she gets off of I-66, take her out. Then go finish off Lowery and Jackson."

"Will do, Dick. Let me set it up with Todd. I'm out for now."

When Jenny exited onto Road 17, John pulled out his automatic rifle and immediately started firing at Jenny. The first shot hit her on the upper left side of her back, but she was able to gather herself enough to swerve back and forth avoiding most of John's shots. She then turned onto a winding dirt road, kicking up dust and blocking Brown's sight as he tried to follow. McNair then called Brown.

"Todd, stop the car. We have them pretty much trapped. The two of you should get out and circle to the left. We will go to the right. Let's continue on foot and go take them out."

Jackson had stabilized Jenny as best he could. She was starting to come around. She reached out to Jackson. He took her hand and she pushed it away. Then, he got it. Even in her semi-conscious condition, she wanted him to hand her a gun. Seeing her like this made Jackson angry. He was angry at the men who did this to her, who killed Amy, and were trying to kill him. He handed her one of the guns Ronnie had given him. He then grabbed Jenny's face to make sure she was focused, telling her that Ronnie was ahead of them to the right of the road and that he was heading to the left of the road. Jackson patted her on the cheek and crept beyond the tree to his left.

Up ahead, Ronnie was crawling in the woods in the direction of Maidstone Road. On either side of the winding dirt road was a combination of chest-high foliage and dense woods. Anyone crouching down was virtually unseen. Ronnie did not hear any running car engines, which meant that the four gunmen had gotten out of their cars and were planning on circling them in both directions. Tactically, when circling a target, you should go as wide as possible. But Ronnie also knew that in the heat of battle, patience sometimes gets lost.

For those who are young and inexperienced, their circling technique essentially amounts to a slightly wider straight line. Ronnie decided to move little, if at all. He didn't know the experience levels of his pursuers, but knew these guys were good. Still, he was going to let the men come to him. He had been in many a battle, and he had the patience of Job. Ronnie was fine with letting the game come to him.

Jackson was moving through the woods on pure instinct. Following Ronnie's orders, he was not going on a half-cocked chase. Rather, he was going to remain positioned in the foliage, not far from the big tree, waiting for whomever he might see. Plus, he felt uncomfortable moving too far away from Jenny while she was still in a half conscious state. He crouched on one knee, pointing his gun to the left of the winding road. It did not take long before he heard gunfire coming from Ronnie's direction. Two shots, a moan, then silence. Jackson felt sweat rolling down his face. He was determined to keep his hands from shaking.

Ronnie was lying on the ground in a sniper's pose. As he expected, the two men who were circling in his direction were barely twenty yards from the winding road. Ronnie also noticed that they were much too close to each other. From his prone position, Ronnie saw their legs first. He then followed them with the barrel of his gun until they were less than thirty feet away. Both men were so intent on making it to where they believed Jenny's car was that they were not focused on what was immediately in front of them, a mistake that cost them their lives. Ronnie did two quick taps, both head shots and the men dropped. Not missing a beat, Ronnie backpedaled toward the big tree where he had left Jackson and Jenny.

Jackson saw Ronnie backing toward him and breathed a sigh of relief. He stepped forward a bit from out of the foliage, drawing Ronnie's attention. Ronnie then put two fingers to his eyes, then pointed in a sweeping manner to the winding dirt road all the way beyond Jackson back to the big tree. Jackson understood. The other two men were circling now from his side.

Ronnie instinctively believed that the remaining two men were more experienced. Or at least one of them was. He knew they had heard the gunfire, but they did not respond in any audible way. Ronnie could hear the quiet. Like true pros, the remaining mercenaries were riding things out, sticking with the plan. Ronnie had to be careful with these last two. Looking at Jackson, he held his hand down, making sure that Jackson stayed where he was and that he remain alert.

Ronnie then crept back to the big tree and checked on Jenny. Jenny's face had lost most of its color. Still, she was pointing her gun towards the foliage in back of the tree. It then struck Ronnie that she might be safer and less of a target sitting deeper in the woods rather than right against the biggest tree around. Ronnie scooped her up and half dragged her past the Grand Cherokee into the woods. Jenny understood and weakly nodded thanks.

While Ronnie was moving Jenny, Jackson heard a twig snap slightly behind him to his far left, but not as far back as the big tree. He then saw movement. Someone was edging toward the tree. In another couple of seconds, they would have a bead on Ronnie, who was still helping Jenny. Jackson aimed at the figure and fired. Since he had not fired a gun in many years, Jackson had forgotten the force of the kick from a handgun. He almost lost his balance as the kick jerked him backward. A yelping scream followed as the man reached for his knee and fell forward. Ronnie hit the ground and fired two more shots in the direction of where he heard the screams. The screams stopped.

Russ McNair saw Byron Beck grab his knee after he had been shot. He then saw him fall face forward when struck by two more bullets. McNair knew that Thomas and Jackson had taken out Brown and John, thereby leaving him alone. He wished he had gotten the automatic rifle instead of letting John have it. He thought about opening fire toward the big tree, but Beck had been hit from gunfire that had come from both sides of the tree. Whichever direction he fired in would lead to a quick return volley from the other direction. He decided that he would shoot in both places, first to the tree's left, then to its right. He stood to shoot.

Jenny had somewhat come to her senses when she saw Ronnie fire the two shots into the woods past the tree she had laying against. Ronnie had gotten back on the ground and was crawling to the woods. That is when Jenny saw a man stand up and fire to the other side of the tree where Jackson had been positioned. With a bird's eye view at the man's head, Jenny cocked her gun and fired, clipping him in his shoulder. The man dropped the gun, turned and broke out into a run, deeper into the woods. Jenny dropped her gun, exhausted.

Ronnie saw the man run and went to check on Jackson, who had been running back to where Ronnie and Jenny were.

"You guys okay?" Jackson asked.

"Yes, wanted to make sure you were good. Nice work, Jack. I was going to give this last guy a chase, but we have some cleaning up to do. And, we don't want to be here when the police arrive. Put Jenny in the Cherokee and drive it past her Expedition to where the other cars are near Maidstone."

Jackson did as he was told. Jenny had passed out so he gently put her in the back of the Cherokee. He then reached into her Expedition, grabbing her suitcase and purse, making sure that the car was cleaned out. He drove to where the other cars were parked.

Ronnie flagged him down and came to the window. "Jack, the only reason why they shot Jenny is because they knew where we were. I studied satellite tracking quite a bit and can tell you that they found us by tracking the phone number she was calling. They still probably are zeroed in on our body heat. Help me load up the bodies. We are going to put them in one of their SUVs. I know how we can shake them. Can you get us to Luray Caverns from here?"

"Definitely," Jackson replied.

"Good. Once the bodies are in the SUV, I will follow you to Luray. When you get there, let's hope there are still school buses in the parking lot. Park as close to one or more of the buses as possible. Most of those bus drivers leave their engines on. All good for us. I will squeeze in right behind you, then get into the car with you. When the buses leave, we will leave too. Hopefully, the satellite will be thrown off just enough. We can then go back to Jenny's hideaway and patch her up."

Jackson nodded. "Let's do it."

They placed the three bodies in the SUV that had been driven by Todd Brown. Ronnie then grabbed the keys from the SUV they were leaving behind just in case the last wounded man tried to come back for it. Ronnie then started up the SUV, which contained the bodies and followed Jackson on Maidstone Road, then back on I-66.

FIVE

Rex's office had been inundated with calls all day, both about Steve Mills and the Duncan's statement. Rex's staff issued a public statement of condolences regarding Mills, but were otherwise silent on that matter. As to Reba and Rex's reward announcement, the staff said that it was a deeply personal matter and that the family would not rest until their daughter's killer was brought to justice.

In his office, Rex began to think about his wife. Suddenly, she seemed energized in her pursuit of justice for Amy. Even when they made love last night, she exhibited more purpose and passion than she had in years. Was it the grief? It seemed like more than that. She had it in her mind that there was more to Amy's death than they had originally realized and Reba was determined to get to the bottom of it.

Earlier that day when she presented the reward idea to Rex, he had wanted to push back on the idea, but there was no saying no to her. It was almost as if she was working her own plan. Rex loved his wife dearly and hoped that she was telling him everything. He felt as if she was holding something back. He needed to assure her that she could talk to him, that she should let him in.

Just as importantly, he needed to know what she was up to. He did not want her hurt and he also did not want her pursing wild goose chases. His concern was eased somewhat when the secret service decided to provide protection at their home. Staring out his window at the view, he thought about this Jackson Lowery person still at large, out there somewhere. He would feel a whole lot better when Lowery was brought in - for a host of reasons.

After getting the okay from Reba, Sweeney quickly set up the hotline. Of course, his superior technology skills served him well in this effort. He went back to his Georgetown campus dorm to gather some things and reached out to a friend who lived in an apartment just a couple blocks from the main campus. Sweeney would always stay at his friend's house and use his computer when he wanted to go online without the government knowing that he was doing so. He always took care to make his surfing untraceable. Fortunately, Sweeney's friend and his girlfriend were taking the train to NY for the weekend, so Sweeney had the place to himself.

As soon as Sweeney was ensconced in front of his friend's desktop, he went to work. Sweeney set up the reward and put in place the necessary protections to make sure no one could hack into the responses. He had given Reba a safe and secure iPad to take with her so he could communicate with her directly. They had been going back and forth all afternoon regarding the responses. None of them seemed legitimate. As expected, she immediately got thousands of calls from the usual crackpots, conspiracy theorists and crazies. The hotline also received calls from persons who likely had committed other crimes, even other murders. When Sweeney shared some of the taped calls, Reba shivered.

Sweeney found that he had to keep her calm. He could tell that she was getting impatient. When on the phone with her, he could hear her shoes moving across the floor. She was obviously pacing while they talked.

Her impatience jumped when they found out that Steve Mills had died of a heart attack. That news alone convinced Reba that some deep-rooted conspiracy was in place and the cover up was happening. Reba was desperate to talk with Jackson Lowery. They both wondered if the coded message was too obscure. They even discussed changing it. Eventually, they agreed to remain patient. Lowery was on the run, Sweeney kept reminding Reba. "When he can, he will call," he said in an encrypted text message.

"Let's just hope it is soon," she texted back.

Strother started the day beginning to feel as though the loose ends were being cleaned up. His team easily caught up with the Roberts woman at the airport, who then led them directly to Lowery and Thomas. Steve Mills was no longer in the picture, making the Sweeney kid and the senator's wife not as big as a threat, especially if they could get rid of Jackson. Yes, things had been looking up. The day that started with so much promise, however, went south fast. Real fast. Strother had just gotten off the phone with McNair. In all the years they had worked together, he had never heard his friend sound like he did on that call.

"Dick," he had said. "It went bad, real bad. Todd and Byron are dead, as is Livermore's guy, John. I have also been hit. I will make it, but my right arm is shot to hell. I think they got a nerve or something."

"Jesus, Russ. Where are you? What happened?"

"I am in some field off I-66, almost to I-81. What happened was they just caught us. After hanging up with you, we opened fire on the Roberts woman and nicked her, but she made it to Thomas and Lowery. Thomas then killed Todd and John with two clean shots. I think Lowery got Byron while that bitch caught me by surprise as I was about to knock off Thomas. I thought she was done. Son of a bitch."

Strother closed his eyes and took it all in. He then squeezed his forehead repeatedly with his right hand, while holding the phone with his left. *None of this was good,* he thought.

"Okay. I am glad you made it out and I'm sorry about your guys. Give me a better read on where you are and I will send someone to get you. We need to fix you up. Let me see if the techies can get a fix on them via satellite."

Strother then hung up. His head was beginning to hurt. At his core, Strother and his team were guns for hire. They were not white nationalists or white supremacists. They were not Republican or Democrat, capitalists or socialists. They were mercenaries who enjoyed power, control, money, and killing. When not working, they all lived good lives. Strother had fulfilled contracts for new governments, old governments, and soon to be governments all over the world. It had been a long time since he had lost a man. On this contract alone he had lost four, along with having his best man wounded. Was someone trying to tell him something? Had his time come and gone? His head started pounding even harder.

He gathered himself and went back to work, grabbing Livermore and R.J. before heading to the spot where Mason and his crew hung out. He brought everyone up to speed based on his call with McNair. R.J., thinking about John and their meeting with the D.C. cabbie, sadly shook his head.

Strother then addressed Mason. "Mason, you got anything on the satellite read? Where are Lowery and Thomas?"

214

"Well," Mason began, "they ditched the phone they had been using to talk with Roberts. While we were not sure what was going on, we used the infrared heat to follow their movements." Pointing to the screen, he said, "As you can see here, it looks like two cars left the scene and went back on I-66. They went to, of all places, Luray Caverns."

"Luray Caverns?" Livermore said. "Why on earth would they go there?" he asked.

"We wondered that at first too. But if you see their movements, it makes sense. The caverns host a lot of school visits, so there are often buses on the premises. It is the end of the day, so most of the buses were started up, ready to load their students. Now, look at where the two SUVs ended up. They pull in right in the middle of four buses on the Luray Caverns parking lot. There are about fifteen other cars in the area. When you have that much heat from so many buses and other heat sources, with any kind of cloud cover, it can be hard to identify a specific car. I'm betting Thomas knew all this, just like he knew how to use the motorcycles in West Virginia."

Strother could not contain himself. "So, are you saying that this bastard got away again, even with our satellites dead on his ass?"

Everyone put their heads down, unaccustomed to such an outburst from Strother.

Mason, however, was unmoved. "Sir, that is exactly what I am saying. Look here." He pointed to the screen again. "They waited until all the cars and buses were ready to go, then left with them at the same time. See how all these heat sources are blended together? They then took the most common route and scattered. We have no way of telling which car is the car holding Lowery, Thomas, and Roberts. They are gone. One thing, though. If you go back and look at the Luray Caverns parking lot, you will see one car - it looks like an SUV - still on the lot near where the buses were. I bet that they left in one car, leaving that SUV on the lot."

No one said a word for quite a while. Livermore spoke first. 'If I may, I think we should put tails back on Merchant, maybe even Duncan's wife and the college kid."

R.J. nodded in agreement. Hearing Livermore's suggestion reminded Strother of another issue.

"You are probably right, Livermore. By the way, Mason, have you been able to follow the calls to the 1-800 number that the kid set up for Duncan's wife?

Mason lowered his head slightly. "Uh, actually, we have not, sir. It looks like the anti-hacking measures put in are unlike any we have seen. We have not been able to penetrate them so far."

"What? How is that possible?"

"We don't know, sir. But we are working on it."

Strother shook his head, saying, "Well, step it up. Please. Livermore, we know Merchant had an ITM board meeting all day. Try to catch up with him at their dinner tonight. Stick with him. R.J., find Sweeney. I have a call to make to our bosses. Unfortunately, it will not be a fun one."

———

Roger Tyler set up a call with the Carrs and General Brock right after getting the devastating update from Strother. After debriefing with his group, he commented as to where things stood.

"Folks, unfortunately Lowery, with considerable help from Thomas and Roberts, has proven far more formidable than we ever could have dreamed. Also, we now have Reba Duncan hot to trot over this 1-800 reward thing. While I don't have to say it, the longer Lowery is out there with the potential of joining forces with the senator's wife, well, it could serve to destroy all that we have put in place. We need to quickly assess and rethink our timetable."

Tyler was merely voicing all that had been boiling in him since he first heard of Mills' blunder within earshot of Amy Duncan. Before that happened, all that had been put in place had almost been too good to be true. Yes, Mills and Merchant put the group together, but once Tyler helped round it out with the Carrs and the General, they were comprised of six of the most powerful people on the planet. Each of them played a pivotal role in selectively and strategically recruiting key surrogates both inside and outside the government.

By the time the plan was scheduled to be implemented fifteen months from now, they estimated that as many as a thousand people would be working behind the scenes to ensure the plan's success. Increasingly, however, Tyler was questioning whether they would make it another fifteen months before everything imploded. He had to recommend an alternative for the team to discuss.

The General weighed in quickly. "It seems as though we keep thinking that this thing will get better each day and it does not. From my vantage point, we have just a couple of options. One, we can stay the course, hoping that Lowery will be neutralized before connecting with Reba Duncan or anyone else who may be in a position to give his story credibility. I am liking that option less and less. Two, we can move forward with a modest version of what we planned for next year. This option depends on how far our scientists

217

have progressed and how much impact the Carrs feel we can have if we act soon, say next week. If we pick this option, the Carrs will need to go underground for a bit. Roger and I would have to rebuild for a bigger bang once Duncan gets elected. With this option we must, unfortunately, neutralize Bill. It helps to be able to point the blame to Bill and Steve, thus leaving the public unaware of what we are really building over time."

Susan Carr spoke. "General, we are on the same page. Jim and I have been leaning on our scientists. We are close. Honestly, we have worked too hard at this to walk away with nothing. We can get you some real numbers on impact in a day or so, should we need to accelerate things, right honey?"

Jim Carr, normally soft spoken, agreed. "Without question. We will get you the numbers and Susan and I can go underground as long as necessary. We just do not want to leave things undone. If we need to act now, we need to do it. Also, we need to make sure we neutralize Bill the right way. General, maybe you can figure out some way to make it look like he was stopped in the act of this conspiracy or something like that."

"Good point, Jim. There is one other thing," the General said. "This is important, especially since I get the sense from Roger that the contractor has gotten itchy fingers. The Duncans are off the table as targets. Think about it, folks. Our best chance for long term success is for him to be in the White House. The sympathy factor out there for him is huge. He can win this damn thing and she presents well as a First Lady. Serving up Mills and Merchant will satisfy her, trust me. But Roger, make sure your folks leave the

Duncans alone. We don't need any crossfire bullshit, either!"

Susan immediately seconded the General. "We strongly agree," she said.

Tyler quelled their concerns. "I have consistently made that clear to the contractor and will strongly remind him of that fact again. How about we circle back within thirty-six hours to decide on a scaled back implementation date for next week?"

"Sounds good," Brock said. "Keep the pressure on your team, Roger."

Back at Jenny's Bryce Mountain hideaway, Jackson and Ronnie were focused on getting Jenny well. Ronnie suspected that the Luray Caverns diversion worked. If it hadn't, Bryce Mountain would have been crawling with mercenaries by now. One nice touch in Jenny's hideaway was that she had several camera screens reflecting images from the main cabin near the hideaway's entrance as well as images from the streets in and around the mountain.

Ronnie was able to see that Jenny's wound was manageable. The bullet went through the fatty part of her upper arm and lower shoulder area, right near the armpit. Fortunately, they would not have to worry about removing a bullet. It would be painful as hell, though, so Ronnie knew he had to fill her up with pain pills. Jackson found a fully stocked first aid kit under the kitchen sink and Ronnie dressed Jenny's wounds as she drifted in and out of consciousness. He then got Jackson to help him prop her up for a call she had to make. Since they had left her car at the scene, Ronnie needed to have Jenny report the car as stolen to the Enterprise officials. He and Jackson agreed that she should tell them that she had gone into the Fair Oaks Mall for a couple of hours only to come back to the lot to see that her car was missing. It was important that she not be tied to the shoot out. After much effort and even a little rehearsing, they were able to get Jenny to pull off making the call to Enterprise. They then fed her a bunch of pain pills and let her go back to sleep, giving them time to take a breather and deconstruct all that had happened that day.

Ronnie could not help himself. Sprawled on one of the easy chairs, holding a beer from the fridge, he said, "Well, Jack, I never thought I would ever say this to you, but, thanks for saving my life!"

Jackson grinned. "Well, my friend, you kept telling me this was the real deal. I had no idea how real it could get. Seriously though, Ronnie, I had never been in a situation like that. You learn so much about yourself in a life or death experience. While everything is moving fast, it also seems to slow down too. I can see why some people are able to think soundly, while others cannot. It is so different when you know your own life and the lives of others are on the line."

Ronnie lifted his beer to Jackson. "Well said, Jack. But really, you performed well in the heat of battle. I suspected that you would, but you never know for sure. The West Virginia escape showed me a lot. I saw what you had in you."

Jackson, having eased himself into a comparable level of relaxation thanks to Ronnie's current comfortable mood and the security of the hideaway, was stretched out on Jenny's living room sofa. "You were amazing, Ronnie. Thank you. Do you think Jenny will be alright?"

"Yeah, she sure is a tough SOB. She took down that last guy while half way passed out."

"That is why I am asking. She lost a lot of blood," Jackson said.

"She did. But she will be fine. Now, Jack, where do we go from here?"

"I have got to call that 1-800 number, Ronnie. Reba Duncan knows I am innocent. I can feel it. We have to connect with her and meet with her. I want to call her right away."

"Maybe, but we have to be careful. First, how can we be absolutely sure that Reba Duncan believes you are innocent? This could be a trap."

Jackson laced both hands together on the back of his head and leaned back, deep in thought.

"It could be a trap, Ronnie. I give you that. But my instincts tell me it is not. I think I need to respond."

Ronnie relented. "Alright. But again, we have to be especially careful. They got to us because of our calls back and forth with Jenny. You've gotta think, Jack, that the mercenaries and their technical people are monitoring those calls. We need to make the call from a pay phone far away from here."

"Okay. But still how do I talk to her? When we make the call, it will probably lead us to a voice mail. What number do we leave? Do we wait a few minutes at the pay phone hoping to get a quick call back? How do we respond so they know it is me, so we can set up a place to meet?"

Ronnie thought about the dilemma.

"Maybe the best way to respond to her coded message is through a coded response. Let's say you are right and she knows that 1789 was the place where you and Amy had your first date. What if, in some way, you use that knowledge in your response?"

Jackson crossed his legs and gently pounded his right fist into his left hand. He was thinking through the best way to send Reba a coded message. Jackson looked at Ronnie, who he could tell was doing the same thing. They both sat still for a few minutes, deep in their own thoughts. While sitting, they heard a small wail coming from the back bedroom. Ronnie went to check on Jenny.

"She is fine. Resting," he said when he returned. "Out for tonight, I'm sure."

Jackson then jumped up. "Hey," he said. That's it, Ronnie. We do not need a long message. It has to be short and sweet. If she gets it, she will get it. How about I call from a pay phone and leave this exact message? 'First date. Tonight.' and then hang up."

Ronnie contemplated Jackson's suggestion, smiling while rocking his head from side to side. "It could work," he said.

Jackson added to Ronnie's point, "Also, there is no way anyone else could pick up on the meaning or the place of the meeting unless they knew about the 1789 restaurant. I really think that is the way to go, Ronnie. If you are cool with it, I say we drive closer to D.C. tomorrow, find a pay phone near a gas station and let me leave that message. We can then go to the 1789 Restaurant that evening. What do you say?"

"I like it, Jack. I'm in. Now, one other thing, what about the rest of tomorrow? And what about this Bill Merchant guy? Should we try to find him? The mercenaries took out Mills. On that, we can be sure. They may want to take out Merchant, too. Jenny had gotten us his information. We need to consider paying him a visit."

"That is true, Ronnie. But they are also probably thinking about our next move as well. They could be watching Merchant and waiting on us, hoping to trap us."

"All true. Let's sleep on it and hopefully Jenny will be feeling better and can weigh in as well. I am going to prepare some grub. I pulled out some bass that Jenny had in the freezer. It should be thawed by now. How about some fish tonight, Mr. Pescatarian?"

"With rice?" Jackson said smiling.

"Of course, my leader. Fish, rice, and greens. Yep, I am definitely out of the Midwest!"

They both laughed.

As board gatherings go, Bill Merchant had a successful day. He liked the new CEO as well as the longtime ITM board chair. Merchant had known the board chair for years and knew that the man was in his corner. Years ago, when Steve Mills and Merchant were trying to identify potential team members for the group, they considered the ITM board chair. Ultimately, they viewed him as a risky proposition. *It was also a little too close to home,* Merchant thought. Still, he liked the man.

During various breaks throughout the day, Merchant was making plans to escape for a few days to his own get-away. When they began this venture, each of the six of them designed and developed their own private escape site. Some were overseas, some were underground. With each, however, they would be able to get off the grid for an indeterminate amount of time.

Timing being what it was, Merchant had prepared both the board chair and the CEO for his upcoming time off. They both embraced Merchant's need to recharge. What they did not know was that Merchant could be back in a few days, a couple of weeks, or never. That really did not matter to him. He had no wife, no family. The one thing that Merchant did learn over the last few days was that he could not control the fluid nature of things. He was convinced, however, that it was time for him to disappear.

It was not lost on him that Tyler and the others had not been in touch with him since Mills' death. Yes, they knew about his board meeting. But wouldn't they want to reassure him, especially now? No contact at all was certainly not a good thing.

Merchant looked around nervously as he left Morton's Restaurant in Tyson's Corner and walked to his waiting limo. When the driver opened his door, he glared a bit at the man to make sure it was a familiar face, prompting the driver to ask, "Is everything okay, Mr. Merchant?"

"Yes, Julio," Merchant replied. "Everything is great."

Julio then drove Merchant to his Great Falls estate. From there, Merchant planned on finalizing his arrangements for his escape. He hoped to be out of the area by early afternoon the next day.

Careful as he was, he failed to see the spark from the cigarette coming from the dark sedan parked down the street. Inside that car, Livermore watched Merchant intently as he wondered whether his current order to observe would change to an order to kill.

THURSDAY

ONE

It was the scratching sound that woke Jackson up. It seemed like it was coming from the kitchen area. As he slipped out of his bed, the noise grew more pronounced. Jackson snuck down the hall and heard male voices. He was in bare feet and while making his way down the hall, he noticed his feet were wet. Looking down, he saw blood. A lot of it, on the floor, curling between his toes. Jackson bit his knuckles, but kept walking forward toward the kitchen.

He was almost there when he saw to his right a scraggly bearded man with a large knife in his hands. The man was rubbing the knife blade against the wooden kitchen counter top. That was the scratching noise. Was he sharpening the knife?

Jackson started to reach at the man, to try to subdue him. He then looked to his left and saw two other men holding Jenny by the arms. She was covered in blood. Looking beyond Jenny, Jack saw that Ronnie was laid out on the floor, either unconscious or dead.

Jenny looked up at Jackson with pleading eyes. The two men holding her saw Jackson and smiled broadly. On cue, the scraggly bearded man held up the knife, pointed at Jenny and said, "Right on time, Mr. Lowery. We have been expecting you and want you to see this. You think you are a killer? We are going to show you how real killers kill." The man was laughing sadistically while he spoke.

Jackson lunged for bearded man, who sliced at Jackson's chest with the knife, forcing Jackson to back up. Jackson felt the warmth of his own blood flow down to his groin.

The man laughed again. Let's see how much blood squirts from this pretty neck, Mr. Lowery. He then leaned toward Jenny, causing Jackson to scream loudly, "No!" he cried. "God, no!"

Jackson then woke up to Ronnie standing by his bed and shaking him awake. "Jack, snap out of it, man. Wake up!" Ronnie was saying. "Get up, Jack. You were having a nightmare!"

Jackson finally got his bearings, sitting up and shaking his head. "Man, Ronnie. That was so real. They were about to slice Jenny's throat and I thought you were dead." Jackson then grabbed at his chest, looking down to the groin area. "They cut me too. I could feel my own blood."

Ronnie sat down on his own bed, across from Jackson, who, by now, was also sitting up. "Combat nightmare. It always happens after your first deadly battle. You are initiated now, Jack."

For some reason, Jackson did not find that comment funny and stretched back out on the bed. "What the hell are we doing, Ronnie? I am a college professor, not a black ops guy. What am I going to do when this is done? Will I ever be able to get my old life back or is it the case that when you cross certain lines you can never go back?"

Ronnie looked at his friend softly, saying, "Jack, my brother. I really don't know if you will ever go back to your old life. Truth is, after all of this, you may not want to. Your focus right now should be survival, minute by minute, day by day. That is the kind of focus that has kept you alive all week and God willing, it will see you through this thing to the end. Beyond that, take it one day at a time. Just one day at a time."

Jackson closed his eyes, trying to drift back to sleep, hoping that no more vivid nightmares would disturb him in his sleep.

Try as he might, R.J. could not find Joe Sweeney. The kid was not in his dorm room, nor had he been to any of his classes over the last couple of days. R.J. tried to chat up a couple students in Sweeney's dorm building and the student lounge, but college students have no reason to sell out a peer to someone with as obvious a military bearing as R.J. Tough as it was, he had to let Strother know that the kid had vanished.

Strother took it better than expected. "Alright, we will come to the kid later. I need you to get to Merchant's home in Great Falls to help back up Livermore. With Mills gone, we are beginning to think that Lowery and Jackson may try to get some answers from Merchant."

R.J. was happy to get the new assignment. He had been on edge since this whole thing had started and he needed to let out some aggression. It still bothered him that he let the black cabbie off the hook. The psychopath in him was eager to hurt someone, and the racist in him had developed a personal animus toward Jackson Lowery. Up to this point, Lowery and Thomas had been lucky. As he headed to great Falls, R.J. thought about how he wanted nothing more than to settle a score with Lowery, using his own bare hands.

Safely tucked away in his friend's apartment, Joe Sweeney had been checking the reward hotline voicemail most of the night. Just after 7 am, Sweeney recovered a message on the reward hotline that had been left about an hour earlier. Though short and succinct, Sweeney knew it had been left by Jackson Lowery. It simply said, "First Date. Tonight." Sweeney could not contain himself. He immediately texted Reba Duncan on the iPad he had given her.

"Contact made!" said his text. "Let's discuss."

Less than thirty seconds passed before he received her reply. "Calling you now!" His phone buzzed on his computer.

"Hi, Mrs. Duncan. It looks like we are in."

"What did he say, Joe? How can you be sure?"

When he played the message for her, she was convinced. "This is too good to be true, Joe. And you are sure that nobody else can access the message?"

"Trust me, Mrs. Duncan, we are totally clear. Should we meet beforehand?"

"Yes, Joe. Meet me there around 6 pm. We can then get our ducks lined up. I will reserve their Garden Room. It is a private dining room for about fifteen to twenty people. We definitely need to be away from the general public."

"Sounds good to me, Mrs. Duncan. See you then!"

"Joe, before you go, one more thing. This thing is getting more and more dangerous. How far are you from where the restaurant is right now?" Sweeney had told Reba that he was staying at a friend's apartment near the school.

"I am only about five blocks away," he said.

"Good. Promise me that you will stay where you are until tonight. I mean it, Joe. Don't go anywhere. Okay?"

"Gotcha, Mrs. Duncan. They have plenty of food here and with a computer nearby, I am like a kid on a playground."

"Alright. Please sit tight until later. Bye, Joe."

After hanging up the phone, Reba had to face whether or not to tell her husband about the new development. When he came home last night, he asked her to promise that she would keep him apprised of her activities relating to finding Amy's killer. She could tell that he knew she was holding back. But she could not bring herself to come clean.

Should she bring him in now? Reba played over and over in her mind what would happen once she told Rex what she suspected and what she knows. She knew how her husband was wired. His first instinct would be to reach out to some heavy-duty law enforcement types. The F.B.I., maybe even the D.C. Police chief. Those were logical moves to make under the circumstances. But Joe's roommate Finn did the exact same thing and it got him killed.

If there was some crazy conspiracy at play, it went to the highest levels. It had to if Mills and Merchant were both involved. No, Reba reasoned to herself, now was not the time to bring in Rex. She needed to have a tighter package of facts to share with him. Facts that would confirm what Reba suspected and, at the same time, would give Rex pause about seeking help through the traditional channels. Tonight, she would go it alone with Joe, the young college student and her new partner in crime. She picked up the phone to call her husband who by now was almost at his office to let him know that she would be having dinner with some friends in the evening.

Jackson and Ronnie had woken up early in order to drive halfway to D.C. to call the reward hotline. When they left, Jenny was still fast asleep. As a sign of the times, they stopped at a couple of gas stations and convenience stores in Manassas only to find that none of the places had any pay phones nearby. They finally walked into a Denny's, where one of the waitresses said they could use her phone. Jackson was hesitant at first, not wanted to draw her into the line of fire. His hesitancy vanished when she handed him the phone saying, "Make sure your call is on the up and up. That is my boyfriend's phone and he is a Virginia State Trooper." Jackson happily mocked a fake salute.

"Will do," he said to her. After leaving the quick message, he and Ronnie hurried back to Bryce to check on Jenny.

By the time they got back, Jenny was awake and brewing coffee. She looked sort of stunned to see them as if she were still getting her bearings, but then she held out her arms and said, "Group hug!" Jackson and Ronnie readily complied. As they did their post-mortem of the previous day's activities, Jenny kept beating herself up about missing the head shot for the fourth bad guy. "I had his head in my sights. He should be dead."

She admitted, however, that she was surprised that the bad guys were able to trace her computer searches. "I blocked my browser and used all of the security walls that worked well in the past. I also was using a secured phone when I left Reagan airport. Their tech folks are really good. And, I am getting old and rusty in all areas."

Jackson and Ronnie just shook their heads. "You still have a lot of fight left, Jen," Ronnie said.

They then updated her about the reward hotline and Jackson's message. She agreed that the reply message should work. They all thought it would be best to go to the 1789 Restaurant en masse. Since

Jenny said she felt strong enough to be a part of the effort, she was designated to go to the restaurant first to check it out. Other than the bad guys, no one knew that a woman was helping Jackson Lowery, so she would be the best person to run advance at the restaurant.

They also discussed whether they should go find Merchant and lean on him. Jenny liked the idea, but was more intrigued by seeing what the Reba Duncan meeting would bring them. "Let's face it," she said, "if Reba Duncan is on board and is able to bring her husband along with her, he has the resources to get to the bottom of this easier than we could through this Merchant guy."

Jackson was nodding in agreement, but Ronnie voiced opposition. "I understand your point and following the letter of the law in principle, I would agree. But trust me, if you leave me alone in a room with Bill Merchant, I guarantee that I will get all the information we need to know a lot quicker than the senator would using his channels and process."

All Jenny could say was, "Point taken."

Key to all of this was whether there was an imminent threat to the lives and safety of innocent children based on what Amy Duncan had heard. If all of this was still in the planning phase, a few days would not make a difference. But if it was something that could happen sooner rather than later, that was another story. Jackson reminded them that Amy related what she had heard in the context of Mills and Merchant believing that her dad becoming president would help them.

They agreed to wait until the dinner that evening. The weekend was starting, so the earliest anything diabolical could occur would be early next week, which was clearly unlikely. They would process and rethink things after seeing Reba Duncan.

The three sat at Jenny's kitchen table sipping coffee like old friends until the physical toll from yesterday started to grind Jenny down a bit. Jackson could see it in her eyes. She looked "a bit peaked" as his grandmother used to say. She excused herself and went back to bed.

When they heard her door close, Ronnie whispered to Jackson, "Now let's go get that Merchant bastard." He was smiling like a Cheshire Cat.

Jackson soft punched him in the arm. "Man, I ain't messing with Jenny. She won't miss that head shot if it is aimed at me!" They laughed, but later wished that they had followed up on Ronnie's suggestion and visited Bill Merchant that morning. It would have made things a whole lot easier.

———————

Bill Merchant was still planning to go on his indefinite vacation, but had to wait a little longer than he would have liked. He received a call from the airlines indicating that the second leg of his trip to Australia had been canceled and that he could take a couple of more flights in order to get to Sydney, arriving three hours later than originally planned, or he could wait until the next morning and get there even earlier than his original flight would have gotten him there. Reluctantly, he decided to wait. He did not know, of course, that his travel agent had been paid a mighty sum to keep him in the states one more day.

Livermore and R.J. were still positioned on Merchant's block. Since they were in two separate cars, they could alternate between food and bathroom breaks. R.J. was sill eager to hurt someone and he kept asking Livermore if their orders had changed. Livermore assured him that it was just a matter of time.

TWO

Jenny was refreshed and ready to assume her role as the advance person for Jackson's meeting with Reba Duncan. Looking resplendent in her black slacks, thick white turtleneck sweater and black silk-cotton blend jacket, it was hard to believe that she was in the middle of a gun battle just a day earlier. She actually drove the Grand Cherokee from Bryce Mountain to D.C. while Ronnie sat up front with her and Jackson sat in the back seat behind Ronnie. The tinted windows made it almost impossible to see Jackson clearly from outside of the car.

It was understood that Jackson and Ronnie would drop Jenny several blocks from the restaurant while they would park in the lot across the street from Georgetown's Cafe Milano. Ronnie was increasingly suspicious about the meeting, but Jackson was determined to go. As a result of Ronnie's urging, however, they all agreed that Jenny would go to the restaurant first in order to gauge the mood. If she felt comfortable, she would contact Ronnie with the okay. Ronnie had given Jenny a new, clean phone. Jenny would call them when it was time for them to walk into the restaurant.

While Jackson, Ronnie, and Jenny drove to D.C. from the Shenandoah area, Reba Duncan was the first one to arrive at the 1789 Restaurant. She had just been seated in the private dining room, which could accommodate nearly twenty people. The hostess who sat her down asked her how many people she was expecting. Reba, trying to avoid drawing too much attention to herself, quietly said, "Just a few, thank you." The hostess then went back to her station by the front door.

She returned soon thereafter to show Sweeney to the room. Reba greeted Sweeney with a hug and said, "I am nervous. I should have told my husband. What am I doing here? What if this man did kill my Amy?"

Before she could go any further, Sweeney held up his hand and calmly said, "If any that were true, neither one of us would be here. Mrs. Duncan, you are about to meet the man who loved your daughter, the man she loved. However brief that love was, I believe it has kept him alive. You should be happy to get closer to the truth." Sweeney sounded like a wise, mature sage or medicine man, something not lost on Reba.

With arched eyebrows, she said, "You need to think about becoming a shrink, Joe. You could make a lot of money."

Sweeney smiled. The two of them were then surprised when the door opened. They looked expectantly at who entered the room only to be disappointed to see that it was the restaurant chef. "Good evening, Mrs. Duncan. Good evening to you as well, young man. I am the chef at this fine restaurant. They call me Chef Pablo. Welcome!"

Both Reba and Sweeney said hello.

Chef Pablo then closed the door behind him and said in a whisper, "Mrs. Duncan, I saw your name on the reservation list and wanted to be sure to express my condolences to you for your loss. To you and your husband."

Reba bowed her head slightly. "Did you know my daughter?"

Here, Pablo turned to look around the room, even though the door was closed and just the three of them were there. "To be honest, Mrs. Duncan, that is why I wanted to talk with you. I have been the chef here a long time. Jackson Lowery is a long time customer of ours and I consider him to be a friend."

Hearing this prompted Reba to ask, "Did you see him with my daughter?"

"Yes, yes, I did. He and your daughter were here one week ago tonight. It was their first date. I have known Jackson a long time, but I had never seen him like this. He was clearly enamored with your daughter." Pablo then proceeded to tell Reba and Sweeney about the entire evening.

Hearing Pablo speak about their dinner reminded Sweeney of the way Finnegan talked about the chemistry between Amy Duncan and Jackson Lowery. Sweeney found himself wishing he could have seen them together. He looked over at Reba Duncan, who, by now, had tears in her eyes. Pablo handed her a handkerchief from one of the place settings.

"Why haven't you come forward?" she asked.

"Mrs. Duncan, I have been reading all that is going on. It is not good and there is something more happening, like the government is involved. I am from Mexico. I know corrupt governments. I did not want to put myself at risk going to talk to the government. My plan was to talk with Jackson or his attorney when he was back. I do not trust what I am seeing."

Struck by the chef's honesty and similar sense of wrong doing, Reba buried her head in the handkerchief and wept silently. Sweeney patted her left shoulder, while Pablo rested his hand the right one. At that moment, the door inched opened slightly and the hostess poked her head in saying, "Excuse me. There is a lady here who is with your party."

Reba looked at Sweeney, who looked at Pablo. All three looked confused. The hostess stood to the side to allow Jenny Roberts to walk into the room. Jenny waited until the hostess had left and closed the door then smiled and said, "I am here to introduce you to Jackson Lowery."

Pablo guided Jenny to a seat, motioning to Reba and Sweeney to sit as well. He then said, "We may end up filling this room tonight after all."

They all began to talk and get to know each other. Pablo brought out some of his best wine. After about ten minutes, Jenny pulled out her phone to call Ronnie. When he answered, she said, "Time for everyone to meet." Then she hung up. Less than five minutes later, the hostess once again opened the door, poked her head in and said, "Here are two more of your guests."

Ronnie entered the room first, followed by Jackson. Pablo ran to his friend and bear hugged him. Jackson hugged him back, but his eyes were riveted on Reba Duncan. She looks a lot like Amy, he was thinking. Their mannerisms were nearly identical. Reba wiped her eyes and walked slowly to Jackson. The entire room fell silent.

She then opened her arms and said, "Thank you for all you did for my Amy. Thank you for allowing her to feel love." Jackson fell into her arms matching her teary eyes with his own.

He pulled back, looked directly at Reba with tears still in his eyes and said, "I am glad you understood my message."

Reba placed her hands on her hips and said, "I am glad you understood mine!" Everyone laughed. Then they sat down, ate and got acquainted. Pablo left them alone to eat and talk.

When Jackson got around to telling Reba exactly what Amy heard from Mills and Merchant, Reba went ballistic. "Those heartless pigs were sitting in my dining room and eating my food, while at the same time sending vile men to kill you and my daughter! Oh, I think I am going to be sick." She almost was. It took her a few minutes to recover from the knowledge that she had longed to receive from Jackson.

By earlier agreement, Jackson, Ronnie, and Jenny agreed that they would not go into detail about the school district poison theory. While each was convinced that the plot was real, they needed more evidence. It would not be fair to send Senator Duncan on a wild goose chase. They had to corner Bill Merchant. They told Reba that they would be tracking him down as the next step in getting to the truth.

While Reba was glad to hear that Jackson, Ronnie, and Jenny were going to go after Merchant, she was not satisfied. She wanted to ferret out all of the people who were part of the conspiracy. She promised to tell her husband everything, but would caution him about who he could trust. She also zeroed in on the thing that had been puzzling to Jackson from the very beginning. If Rex Duncan was not a part of the conspiracy and did not believe in white supremacy, why was his ascendency to the White House so critically important to the group? Reba was going to work on this question with her husband.

But she also was steadfast and determined to do one more thing, which was to clear Jackson's name. She kept saying to him, "You don't deserve this. You are a decent man, who tried to do the right thing. It is time for you to stop having to run like a common criminal." Just in hearing her talk about his freedom made Jackson wince. Over the last few days, he had gotten so used to looking over his shoulder, it was now a way of life for him. It is so strange, he thought, how quickly one adapts to one's environment, no matter how radically different it is from the old one.

The evening ended with a detailed conversation about Sweeney. They all offered condolences for the loss of his friend. Jackson also indicated that he clearly remembered the smiling Uber driver watching and waving to he and Amy while they kissed.

But the more intriguing discussion about Sweeney centered on his computer skills and his relationship with the U.S. government. When he first related the essence of his story, Ronnie and Jenny exchanged glances. Both knew full well about the division Sweeney had been dealing with. But the glances between them also confirmed that Sweeney was an invaluable asset that they could deploy now to stop whatever these conspirators had in mind.

Ronnie whispered something to Jackson, who looked at Ronnie, then nodded yes.

Jackson then spoke, "Sweeney, we could use your expertise to stop these bastards, whoever they are. We feel like you are safe where you are for tonight. But tomorrow, if you are willing, we can pick you up in the morning so you can work with us to nail these guys."

"Fuck yeah," Sweeney blurted out. "I am all the way in." Then remembering that Reba was there, he blushed and quickly dropped his head. "I am sorry, Mrs. Duncan. I did not mean to curse like that."

She smiled and said, "The fuck you didn't, Joe. Now got get some rest, so you can help them get these assholes."

Ronnie leaned over to Jackson and whispered, "I think I am beginning to understand why you liked Amy so much, especially if she was half the woman her mother is." He patted Jackson on the arm and they all got up to leave.

There was still much work to be done.

———————

Just before Jackson Lowery met Reba Duncan, Roger Tyler reconvened his group with for an updated strategy call. Tyler had spoken with General Brock a couple of times during the day but now, with the Carrs on the call, the group had to make some final decisions.

"Jim, Susan, I want you to know that the General and I have spoken earlier and more and more we think that we should move forward with an abbreviated plan. Is that possible as soon as next week?"

As usual, Susan responded. "We just hung up with our scientists and we can be up and running by Tuesday or Wednesday. We looked at the numbers involved. Now, mind you, it is just a handful of cities, but we think the poison can reach over a million children in these targeted areas."

Ever the field marshal, General Brock had questions. "Thanks, Susan. But what will be the collateral damage? How many of our people will get taken out?"

Susan turned that question over to her husband. "Honey?" she asked.

"General, Susan is right. We estimate that we can access about 1.2 to 1.3 million children. We estimate, all told, that about thirteen to seventeen per cent will be pure white kids."

The general blew a loud whistle. "That could be up to 200,000 of our own people. Can't we get that number down some?"

Jim did not back down. "Not on such short notice, General. If we had another year or so, we could access ten times as many children and get the collateral number down to around five per cent. To move into action by next week increases the risk and grows the collateral damage at the same time. Sorry."

Thinking out loud, the General said, "Ten million killed. We would definitely reclaim our country after something like that."

Susan steered him back to the matter at hand. "For sure, General. But that is not where we are. Now, Jim and I know we will take a hit from this if we move forward, so we are ready to go underground for a few months or even a few years. We say this knowing that once you are positioned, General, that you will be ideally suited to recruit even more to the cause. Within a few short years, you will have a team in place to get your ten million. We are sure of it, sir."

Tyler spoke, "I am too, Susan. I never thought I would say it, but this could be a blessing in disguise. I like the idea of wreaking some immediate havoc and then following up from there."

Jim Carr finished for him. "And all the while, our guy is secretly preparing for a bigger bang."

"Exactly," Tyler said.

"Sounds like we are all getting on the same page," the General said. "One logistical question: is Monday possible? I know that it is just a couple days away, but I just don't like the idea that this Jackson fella is out there and that he may be able to connect with Reba Duncan."

Jim said, "Yes, Monday is possible. It will be somewhat difficult, but possible."

Tyler intervened. "But General, depending on how we play things with Merchant, we do not have as much to worry about regarding Lowery and Reba Duncan. Our tech folks are working on emails and other documentary evidence that will link Mills and Merchant to the poison we release next week. Though we cannot be sure that Jim and Susan will be inoculated as suspects, we can make it look like Mills and Merchant were the sole leaders and organizers. That would satisfy both Reba Duncan and the black college professor."

"But you mentioned the key to all of that, Roger, which is how we handle Merchant."

"Correct. How we handle him is key. Suicide is the only way. He is not viewed as a strong man, by any means. Let's go through it. The tech group will have the emails and evidence ready today. We have to have the suicide take place sometime over this weekend and keep his location under surveillance so it isn't disturbed. Near his body will be a suicide note confessing his role in the poisonings.

"Next, Jim and Susan will distribute the poison, hopefully by Monday, no later than Tuesday. The country will be devastated. Then, within twenty-four hours and maybe even because of something Reba Duncan puts out, people will start looking at Mills and Merchant. The emails and other evidence will be found. Then we will make sure that Merchant's body and note are found. Rex Duncan will lead the healing process, become president, and voila - we are set for bigger and better things in the future."

Tyler allowed the group time to let all of that soak in.

"Where will we have Merchant stored, provided we do it this weekend? I am sure he is probably looking to go to his own bunker. Should we stop him?" the General asked.

"I think we should have the contractor set up the suicide today while Merchant is in his home. His team can make sure that no one goes into the house until next week," Tyler said.

"And that, gentlemen, is a plan that will work," Susan Carr said.

"It most certainly is, Susan," the General said. "Let us know ASAP if things can be a go by Monday. It is time to go into crisis mode."

"Will do, General," Jim said.

———————

Bill Merchant was more than ready to be in Australia. His hideaway was in the Australian outback, far away from civilization, but had all the comforts one could ever imagine. Merchant's property could only be described as regal, and it was peppered with Aboriginal house servants and gardeners. One thing he really loved about Australia was that the dark skinned people knew and accepted their place. He also liked the fact that the dark, fine haired Aboriginal boys would share his bed without any worry of sneaking around or hiding from the police. Yes, Merchant could not wait to be back in Australia.

Of course, Livermore's techies knew about Merchant's Australian hideaway - and his penchant for Aboriginal boys. In fact, through their contacts, they had a story about one of those abused boys ready to go out over social media over the weekend. The story contained pictures of Merchant walking with the boy while in the outback. Significantly, the story also has quotes from Merchant emotionally denying the sexual abuse allegations, even though the so-called reporter never talked to Merchant. The seeds for Merchant's death were being put in place.

As all of these schemes were being finalized, across the street from Merchant's house, Livermore and R.J. got the call they had been waiting for. Strother told them about the change of plans, but he also emphasized to them how it all must be done. To that end, they were not to make a move until they received a handwritten suicide note prepared by the techies that looked almost identical to Merchant's penmanship. Strother told them that Mason should be there any minute with the note. He confirmed the instructions and then hung up.

Ten minutes later, Mason pulled up and gave them the note, which was inside a clear, plastic envelope. "Be sure to put it in the right spot," Mason said as he was leaving.

Livermore and R.J. then walked to Merchant's house. Livermore went to the front door, while R.J. went to the back door. When both were in place, Livermore tapped lightly on the front door. As Merchant walked to the door, he recognized the face on the other side of the glass diamond shaped window on the front door. In an immediate panic, Merchant turned around, planning on going out the back door. That door had already been picked open by R.J. who stood by the doorway, blocking Merchant's path with a smile on his face.

Merchant turned back to Livermore. "I can pay you both whatever you want," he said. "Anything!"

Livermore shook his head. "We all know that it is too late for that, Bill. It will be a lot easier if you relax and just let things happen. For once in your life, man up, Bill." He snickered as he pulled out the letter and the other materials he would need.

Merchant started to whimper, "This is not fair, this is not fair," he kept repeating.

R.J. agreed with him. "No, it is not fair, Bill. Especially for you."

FRIDAY

ONE

Rex Duncan was in a momentary state of shock when his wife told him the whole story. As he focused on how things had unfolded, like his wife, his shock turned to anger when he thought about eating dinner in his home with his daughter's murderers at the very time they were having her killed. He clenched his fists, saying, "I am going to kill Merchant with my own hands."

For a minute, Reba thought he meant it.

Just as quickly, however, the senator and likely next president of the United States became presidential. Looking at his wife and placing her hands in his, he said, "Honey, thank you for continuing to push this. Our family owes you a debt for honoring Amy's memory."

Reba lowered her head, accepting the praise.

Rex continued. "But even more than that, our country owes you a deep sense of gratitude. There is obviously a sick, vile cancer growing in the most influential sectors of our business and government leadership. I am going to dedicate the rest of my career, hell, the rest of my life to ridding this country of that cancer."

Rex then let go of his wife's hands and walked to their bedroom window. He always seemed to think better looking out windows. Down below on his street, he could see the two secret service agents. He knew that there were two more in back of the house. He took a deep breath and turned once again to face his wife.

"Reba, I am going to make a couple of calls. Once I get what I want from those calls, I want you to call professor Lowery. I will let you know what to tell him. My suspicion is that between he and his friends, they know a bit more than what they told you at dinner. That's okay. Under the circumstances, I would have held back too. When you deliver my message to him, he will hopefully be more forthcoming. After talking with professor Lowery, you and I are going to make a fresh cup of coffee, sit in our living room and figure out why these sick people would benefit by having me in the White House. If we have to brainstorm all night, we will do it. These bastards need to be stopped."

He then picked up the phone and began making his calls. Reba, feeling a rush and closeness to her husband that she had not felt in years, was about to go to the kitchen to brew a fresh pot of coffee.

She stood up, then hesitated, saying, "Rex, like you, I need to be kept in the loop on what information comes your way." She was looking squarely at her husband.

Rex understood. "I will make sure to do so, sweetie. You can count on it," he said.

Reba just nodded and headed toward the kitchen.

Jackson, Ronnie and Jenny were back at Bryce Mountain when Reba called that Friday morning. They had agreed to regroup at Jenny's hideaway for a few hours before paying Bill Merchant a surprise visit at his Great Falls home. Jackson answered the phone, placing the call on speaker.

"Hi, Reba. I have you on speaker with Ronnie and Jenny."

"Hello, everyone. My husband told me to be quick and to the point. I told him everything and, as he said to me, his new mission in life is to 'rid our nation of the sick cancer' that led to our daughter's death and your unjust persecution. He has made calls to the new F.B.I. director, the U.S. Attorney for D.C., and the D.C. Police chief. You are no longer public enemy number one. As Rex put it, the government dogs have been called off of you."

Jackson, Ronnie, and Jenny had to let all of that sink in. They each looked at the other. Jenny was the first to smile.

Jackson said, "Reba, that is great news. I, I don't know what to say. Thank you. Thank the senator as well."

Ronnie jumped in. "Reba, that is great news. But the killers out there are still looking to hurt us. We still have to get to the bottom of all of this."

Reba said, "We know that Ronnie, and we understand. This is why Rex wanted me to ask you if there is any information you didn't share with me yesterday - he needs as much information as possible to stop these people."

Ronnie pointed to the phone's mute button. Jackson nodded saying to Reba, "Reba, I am putting you on hold for two minutes. Don't hang up."

"Okay," she replied. Jackson muted the call.

Jackson said to Ronnie and Jenny, "What do you think?"

Ronnie said, "I think we need a little more time. We need to have our talk with Merchant and put Sweeney to work."

"I agree," Jenny said. "With Sweeney's skills, I can help guide him to get what we need from these food folks. I would feel more comfortable if we have a clearer picture to paint for the senator."

Jackson nodded. He took the phone off of mute, saying to Reba, "Here is what I think, Reba. First, we need thirty-six hours. We will give you all we have no later than Sunday morning, but we have to connect a few dots before we give you speculative thoughts. Second, sometime on Saturday afternoon, please ask the senator to release a statement indicating that I am no longer a suspect in your daughter's murder and that I am working with his office, national, and local law enforcement officials to bring her killers to justice. The words are important here, Reba. Make sure his statement says killers, not killer. Got it? The press will want more, but make sure that he and law enforcement stick with that statement alone, at least for twenty-four hours. Once the bad guys hear that I am working with law enforcement, they will try to scurry for cover and make a mistake. We can then get to the bottom of this thing."

"Got it, Jackson," Reba said. "I will deliver the message to Rex and don't see any of this as a problem. Oh, and Rex wanted to me to pass along that we'll make sure you're kept safe and protected when you come back to DC – just make sure you let us know where you end up. Keep us posted and Godspeed to you all."

"Thanks, Reba," Jackson said, about to sign off.

"Oh, Jackson, don't hang up. There is one other thing," Reba said.

"Sure, Reba. Go ahead."

"My husband said that Ed Harrington wants you to call him."

Jackson felt a shock to his system. It was not a bad shock, but hearing that name from his past was unexpected.

"Ed?" Jackson said. "Why does Ed want to talk with me?" he asked. The others in the car looked at each other, noticing that the name had struck a nerve in Jackson.

Reba said, "I don't know, but I was supposed to give you his direct line. Here it is." She then gave him Ed Harrington's number.

"Uh. Ok. Thanks, Reba," Jackson said signing off.

Jackson fell noticeably quiet, with a blank look on his face.

Ronnie was about to exit onto I-81 east toward Jenny's hideaway and commented, "Hey, man. You ok? It feels like we have gotten a get out of jail free card, but you don't look too happy. How do you know the new F.B.I. director?"

Jackson jerked his head toward Ronnie. "The new head of the F.B.I.? Ed Harrington? He is a D.C. judge," he said.

Jenny jumped in. "I know you have been on the run, Jackson, but two days ago, President Coleman appointed him Acting Director and transmitted his name to the senate for confirmation as the full time director.

"Whew. Oh, no," Jackson said, blowing a whistle. Having gathered himself, he remembered that the previous F.B.I. director had resigned due to health reasons a couple of weeks ago.

"Well, we all need to hear the back story, but thirty-six hours does not give us a lot of time," Jenny said. "We need to go to work and being here in Bryce is not really conducive. Now that you are a free man, Jackson, how about we go back to your place in Georgetown, which is closer to the action? Let's clear out of my hideaway, go get Sweeney, then camp out at your spot. While Sweeney and I do our research, you and Ronnie can finally visit Merchant in Great Falls." Jokingly, Jenny added, "and on the way back to D.C.

you can tell us about your good buddy and new F.B.I. director, Ed Harrington."

"Well, the truth is, Jenny, he is not my buddy. If Ed Harrington is the head of the F.B.I., I may need to go back into hiding," Jackson replied, only half-kidding.

Ed Harrington was the U.S. Attorney for the District of Columbia when he hired Jackson Lowery, fresh out of law school, to be one of his prosecutors. Things between the two started well enough. But before long, they turned sour. Jackson was extremely talented, efficient, and hard-working - all qualities that make a great prosecutor. But, he was also a loner. Ed Harrington, on the other hand, was the perfect social leader. Harrington bore a striking resemblance to Harrison Ford, but unlike the well-known actor, he always seemed to have his reading glasses perched midway on his nose. He kept them close by, attached to a spectacle cord or strap that hung around his neck. Among the staff at the U.S. Attorney's office, he was playfully referred to as "Glasses". However, there was no negativity associated with the moniker. Harrington was tall, affable, engaging with his staff, and admired by all.

Jackson knew that Harrington never understood why Jackson was not as social as his colleagues. Harrington used to talk with Jackson about his aloofness to no avail. Then, ironically, Jackson's success in court made things worse. Within three years, Jackson became the best trial lawyer in the office. Jackson shook his head thinking back on those times. Admittedly, his ego was out of control. He recalled Harrington railing at him about sharing his success with others on his trial team. Jackson once told Harrington, "Everyone has a role during trial. I am the closer. I bring it all home. The team knows that. So, do I. And so, do you."

That attitude drove Harrington crazy. He believed that Jackson was selfish, arrogant, and not a team player. Remembering the man he was during those days, Jackson agreed with that assessment.

Basketball made it worse. Harrington and Jackson played on the office's team in the city lawyers' league. Harrington was a world-class basketball player. But so was Jackson. Both had had successful college careers. Both wanted to shoot. Neither passed the ball to the other. During one game, when they passed the back and forth during a fast break, the rest of the team clapped and kidded them both. Harrington began to derisively call Jackson 'hotshot'.

The nail in the coffin of their doomed relationship occurred when Jackson's affair with his younger assistant was discovered. Harrington was livid, rightly thinking that it was another example of Jackson's selfishness. After months of the silent treatment, Jackson left the office. Soon thereafter, Harrington was appointed to be an associate judge on the Superior Court of the District of Columbia. Jackson had not had a meaningful conversation with Ed Harrington since he left the U.S. Attorney's office and further buried himself in his bunker at American University.

Ronnie and Jenny absorbed all that Jackson had told them. Jenny simply shrugged and said, "I wrote down the number," as she dialed it on her phone. "Here you go," she said, handing him the phone.

Jackson grabbed the phone just as Ed Harrington answered. "Ed," he said. "It's Jackson Lowery."

"Jackson Lowery. Well, it looks like you have been busy, as usual. Dating your students, now, huh?"

Jackson had the phone on speaker. Upon hearing Harrington's first words, Ronnie rolled his eyes and Jenny arched an eyebrow. Jackson decided to ignore the jab. "Ed. I hope that we can get beyond our past just to get through this crisis. The threat to these children is real and we need to stop it."

"I am well aware of the threat, Jackson," He said curtly. "And, I know it is real."

He paused. "Also, I am sorry you have had to go through all that you have experienced this week. But, Jackson, you are not a one-man band. You cannot stop these folks by yourself. You have always had a hard time working with others and if you are holding back now to be the hero, it could cost lives."

Jackson continued to take the high road. "Ed, I totally agree with you. Look, a lot has happened since our days at the U.S. Attorney's office. I am not trying to hog the show here, but I also don't want to give you theoretical or speculative information that would lead to you using resources to follow a wild goose chase. We just need a day to make sure our hunch has some basis in fact. That's it, Ed. Just one day." Jenny gave him a thumbs up.

Harrington said, "Alright, Jackson. You have your day. You also have my number. We are here for backup when you need it."

With that, he hung up.

Jackson said mockingly, "Thanks, Ed. See you soon, friend." He then said to Ronnie and Jenny, "Now what?"

"Time to go back to work," Jenny said, as Ronnie headed toward D.C.

It felt odd for Jackson to welcome Ronnie and Jenny into his Georgetown home. Over the past few days, he questioned whether he would ever see his apartment again. More than that, however, Ronnie and Jenny's presence reminded him how lonely a life he led. He had no real close friends. No girlfriend. He generally went to work, then home. The highlight of his life was hanging out with his son, Eddie. Eddie.

Thank God he would be able to see him soon. While they were cleaning out Jenny's hideaway, Jackson had called both Eddie and Pam. He told them that it would all be over soon and that the news will be exonerating him later in the day. Eddie was overjoyed. He asked if he could spend the next week or so with him. Jackson was looking forward to that. When all of this was over, he also wanted to take stock of his life. No man should be so alone.

Jenny did pay him a tiny compliment. "You have the making of good taste here, Jackson. You just stopped. For a small fee, I will help you finish decorating this place."

"You're on, Jenny!"

They had called Sweeney as they neared Georgetown and shared with him the working plan. Since Jackson lived in Georgetown, Sweeney said he would walk to the apartment. They gave him Jackson's address. On the way back, they had also stopped at a grocery store. They had just finished unloading the groceries when Sweeney rang the doorbell.

Jenny was obviously in a playful mood. As Sweeney walked in, she said, "Team Jackson is now complete. The ragtag bunch!"

"I like that, Jen. We are definitely a motley crew," Ronnie added.

Jackson showed Sweeney his desktop while also handing him a cup of coffee. "You do drink coffee, right?" he asked.

"Yes, I do. With cream and sugar, please."

"Of course, you do," Jackson said. "Like my son. All growing boys add cream and sugar. Here ya go," he said, handing him a mug and the cream and sugar.

Jenny had pulled out her laptop and positioned it on the table next to the desktop. She and Sweeney were side-by-side, ready to go to work. They all shared with Sweeney their theory centered around the poisoning of kids in school districts through the food. They then went through the major companies with existing school district food service contracts.

Sweeney could not believe what he was hearing. "These fuckers are bat shit crazy!" he exclaimed. "We have to stop them."

Jenny then laid out the game plan. Well, as best she could. Her shoulder had been hurting her quite a bit and she was in obvious pain. Jackson and Ronnie had made her promise to go to the hospital soon to get patched up.

She said, "We need to find out all we can about the leaders of Claremark, Jawer Foods, and Honeyberg. We also need to find out who is pulling all of these strings. Sweeney, with your skills, you should be able to identify and locate these guys. They have some solid tech folks. That was how they were able to find me. They also have access to satellite technology. They were using it to try to follow Jackson and Ronnie. Anything and everything you find is important."

Sweeney laced his fingers together and pushed them outward. He then started rotating his neck from side to side like an athlete preparing to do battle.

"I got this," he said.

Jackson and Ronnie looked at Jenny, Sweeney, then each other.

"Jack," Ronnie said, placing his arm around his neck, "we are out of our element, my brother. Let's go do our thing."

Jackson looked out one of the windows in his apartment and noticed that it was getting dark. "It is the perfect time. I'm ready."

By then, Jenny and Sweeney were fully absorbed in their computers. Jackson and Ronnie had some hunting of their own to do. They had a date with Bill Merchant.

TWO

Using binoculars, Jackson and Ronnie lay on the roof of the Great Falls Elementary School and peered down at Merchant's palatial Great Falls home. The house was dark on the inside, with the exception of a light coming from one of the upstairs windows, probably a bedroom. Ronnie pointed to the black SUV parked across the street and halfway down the block from Merchant's house. There was one occupant inside. "He is waiting on us, Jack," Ronnie said with a smile. "I am surprised he is alone. Maybe they traded off since it is so early. At any rate, the way he is positioned will not stop us at all." He was pointing to the back of Merchant's house. We can park on that back street by the playground, park area, cut through those two yards and walk in Merchant's back door. The genius in the car will not even know we were here."

Jackson looked at the park area and eyed his way from there to Merchant's back door as outlined by Ronnie. He then stood up. "Let's go, Ronnie."

R.J. was sitting in the SUV where he had been all last night and most of the day. Livermore had gone back to the command center in Fairfax. He had gotten word that things would be winding down. R.J. was fine with that so long as the cause continued. Livermore had confided to him that a bunch of darkies were going to be poisoned on Monday. *Good,* he thought. *There had been too much race-mixing as it was. It felt good to be on the right side of this fight.*

Looking up at Merchant's house, he was wondering if the body was beginning to smell. *I am glad that I don't have to go back inside that place,* he thought. There was nothing worse than the smell of rotting human flesh. R.J. settled back into his seat and closed his eyes. He figured that it was okay to get a little shut-eye. No one was coming to visit a dead man.

As R.J. closed his eyes for his nap, Ronnie was beginning to pick the lock on Merchant's back door, when he noticed that someone already had done so. "Jack," he said while turning to face his friend, "someone has already picked this lock. The door is open."

Both men went inside, immediately wishing they had come the day before when Ronnie had first suggested it.

The smell hit them as soon as they entered the kitchen from the back door. Jackson put his right arm across his nose and mouth. Ronnie said, "Damn. Let's find him."

They walked through the kitchen, then a large dining room to an insanely huge and opulent foyer, which was the entry point for anyone coming through the front door. A giant chandelier hung from a ceiling that stretched up to the second floor. A winding staircase seemed to wrap around the chandelier. Jackson and Ronnie walked up the staircase. A few paintings of Roman and Greek gods adorned the foyer and staircase walls.

At the top of the stairs, Jackson and Ronnie headed down a long hall. They passed a couple of closed doors along the way. They guessed that the master bedroom would be at the end of the hall. The smell got more intense as they headed in that direction.

The master bedroom was, indeed, at the end of the hall. The door was open. The room was also large, befitting the grandeur they had seen in the rest of the house. A California King bed draped with silk sheets and a floral bedspread was positioned along the back wall, to the left. To the right was a sitting area, complete with a mauve love seat, two antique French side chairs, and a white marble fireplace. An ornately designed gold-splattered coffee table sat in front of the love seat. The ceilings were inordinately high. Another chandelier was in the center of the room. Hanging from a rope tied to the chandelier was Bill Merchant. He was wearing dark blue pajamas, house slippers, and a red silk robe. His neck was obviously broken, with his tongue hanging out.

Jackson looked at Ronnie, whose eyes then scanned the room. He motioned to the bed. Lying in the middle of the bed was a note.

Frightening in content, the note was to the point.

'I have lived a lie most of my life. In many ways. I am sorry about one personal lie that has now been publicly revealed. But, my biggest lie has been my acting like all humans are equal. They are not. Just like any species, some are superior to others, in intellect and overall functionality. Genetics prove that the ethnic white species is superior to the dark skinned species. We now live in a world, however, that wants to treat all species the same. In order to stop the spread of this poisonous view, I am proud that my co-collaborator and I will be using real poison this week on the next generation of dark skinned people. Once we limit their proliferation, they can be better placed into service for the superior white population. I am honored to die while bringing the truth to light.'

Bill Merchant

As they were reading the note, Jackson was closer to the bed, squatting down, while Ronnie was leaning over his right shoulder and reading it as the same time. Out of nowhere, Jackson heard a noise, turned to his right and saw an object come down on Ronnie's head. Ronnie must have felt the blow coming, because he lifted his right arm just before impact, taking some of the sting from the blow. The blow still hit him hard, however, and Ronnie let out a moan and fell to the floor. Jackson looked up and saw the man who hit him still holding the poker from the fireplace in his hand.

Jackson did not hesitate. Before the man could wind up for another swing, Jackson lunged at him from his squatting position, tackling him like a blitzing lineman takes out a defenseless quarterback. The poker flew across the room. Jackson could tell that the man was a little surprised. Both struggled to gain leverage on the other. Jackson was not a fighter, but his father did teach him to box.

Always tall and skinny, his dad told him that boxing was the best way to ward off bullies. "Funny thing about being able to box, son. When you show you can, no one messes with you. It helps your reputation big time." Jackson's dad was right. After a few lessons when he was eleven, Jackson regularly sparred with his father. At thirteen, he had his first and last fight. A big kid who had been teasing Jackson for a couple of years purposely knocked Jackson's lunch tray out of his hands. The kid then squared up to Jackson in front of the entire lunchtime crowd. Jackson squared back in return. The big kid threw a wild right, which Jackson easily escaped by ducking to his left. He then swiftly unleashed a left hook to the kid's gut, quickly followed with a right to the head.

The kid went down. Jackson was suspended, but no one ever bothered him again in school.

That experience, however, meant nothing to Jackson at the moment. The man hopped to his feet and assumed a Kung Fu stance. Feeling that his aggressiveness had helped him get the poker out of the man's hands, Jackson jumped up as well, but did not strike a pose. He faked a left, then threw a massive straight jab to the man's face. He heard bones snap, both his and the man's. The man went down, grabbing his face. Jackson jumped on him, swinging away. A week's worth of frustration, emotion, and fury was wrapped into each swing.

While the man stopped trying to fight back, his next words served to freeze Jackson. "You can hit me all you want professor. On Monday, there will be a million less of your kind. Less of you to mix around our woman. Like your girlfriend, who I enjoyed getting rid of."

Jackson stood up, stunned. He noticed that his right hand was throbbing and hurting like hell. It was full of blood. The man was trying to get up, but was woozy and stumbling while trying. It looked like he was attempting to reach into his pocket. Jackson was going to stop him when he heard a spitting sound and saw the man fall backwards, with blood flowing from his left temple. With that, he was dead. Jackson looked to his right and saw Ronnie standing next to him. The smoke was still coming from the silencer on his gun.

———————

Jenny was amazed at Sweeney's abilities. She had heard of the savant computer types and even knew about kids like Sweeney who were so good the government paid them not to be on a computer. To

Jenny, that never quite made sense. It was like keeping a race horse in an eight by eight foot box. You can never really stop people from doing what they were born to do.

Jenny especially remembered a kid she saw on 60 minutes several years ago. It was right before Mike Wallace died. Computers were becoming more a part of American life and Wallace had found a young black kid from Harlem who was a computer genius. The kid, Anwar Jeffries, was about twenty-two years old at the time and he was wearing a baggy embroidered jacket like the nineties hip hop group Kriss Kross. The kid was so good that he transferred a million dollars from the federal reserve into Mike Wallace's bank account and then moved it right back. Wallace was blown away.

The government was paying the kid to stay away from computers. But they had to keep paying him more and more money. Corporate espionage was coming into vogue and major companies were offering the kid hundreds of thousands of dollars to test their internet security, design better computer protections, and even hack into competitors' databases. Jenny had actually met the kid years later in Quantico. He looked totally beaten down after being muzzled and marginalized by his own government. He was held hostage by his own skills. Watching Sweeney work for the last hour inspired Jenny to make sure that the story of Anwar Jeffries did not apply to Sweeney.

Between the two of them, they found out that the leadership of Claremark, Jawer, and Honeyberg seemed honest enough. Claremark has been, by far, the biggest player on the school lunch scene and they had sketchy contracting practices. It was clear that they bribed contracting officers, used some shady lobbyists, and did not mind crossing ethical lines. With just a little digging, Sweeney found evidence of payoffs and even a couple of offshore accounts. Jenny was not interested in any of that.

Sweeney then found something that was very interesting, possibly revealing. The CEO and founder of Claremark, Austin Nicholas, grew up in Alabama, where he attended the University of Alabama in the 70's. Apparently, while at Alabama, Nicholas was the campus head of the KKK. It was all kept under wraps and none of the information was easily accessible online, but Sweeney had the goods. Seemed as though Nicholas was following in the footsteps of his old man, who publicly supported the Klan.

This was all Jenny needed. She reached out to Jackson and Ronnie to update them on all that she and Sweeney had discovered. She tried them both a few times, but got no answer. She then told Sweeney to focus his attention on the local co-conspirators. She believed that they had enough to take to the senator, but she wanted to make sure.

Sweeney went to work.

SATURDAY

ONE

Saturdays are slow news days, even in Washington, D.C. But, not on this particular Saturday. The press was having a field day with the announcement coming from senator Rex Duncan's office. The senator's press release indicated that Jackson Lowery was innocent in the killing of the senator's daughter and that Lowery was working with law enforcement to bring the killers to justice. There was no mention of Lowery's whereabouts or what was meant by the reference to killers, not killer. Strangely, no leaks followed the release. None from the senator's staff. None from the US attorney. None from the police.

The collective 'no more information' approach made the story bigger and bigger by the hour. The cable news channels flooded the airwaves with their talking heads and political pundits wildly speculating on how to interpret the senator's press release. The feeding frenzy had grown out of control. At the same time, a social media story was circulating around the internet alleging that ITM CFO Bill Merchant had a history of abusing young boys in Australia. The story featured an exclusive interview with one of the boys who was interviewed along with his mother.

Amidst all of the media attention, Roger Tyler deemed it appropriate to have one final call with his group. This was a watershed moment for Tyler. All the years of silent frustration followed by hopeful organizing was coming to a head. He was doing all he could to keep things on track. For him, the plan was the only alternative. As soon as he got the General and the Carrs on the phone, he gave them an update.

"Well, as I am sure each of you know by now, Reba Duncan did connect with Jackson Lowery and they have all joined forces. But as we agreed during our last call, this ultimately can be a good thing. It certainly is playing out that way. Merchant is done and his letter is in place. We have people watching his place.

The General spoke, "I agree wholeheartedly, Roger. I can share another bit of good news that also suggests things are playing out well. I received a call from Senator Duncan asking me to come visit he and Reba at their home in the morning for breakfast. They said they need my help working through all that has happened in the last few days. I told them I was eager to help."

Tyler then directed the conversation to the Carrs. "That is good news, General. Jim and Susan, our main issue now concerns whether we can get this thing off the ground on Monday. I am increasingly worried about us being able to stretch it even one more day."

Susan said, "As you know, my husband is the expert, but I can happily report that our scientists are ready, as are our distribution centers. The packaging idea works perfectly. Trucks roll out Sunday night. We are proud to report that all is good to go."

"That is awesome news, Susan. Just terrific."

"We are excited," she said. "One question. What will we do with the ground team and the command center?"

"Great question," Tyler said. The General and I have been talking about that. There will be a lot of heat following Monday, so they will slip underground, many back into the bowels of some of the agencies where we have friends. Livermore will be able to access them on an as-needed basis in the future. As to the contractor, we don't need him anymore. Since he never disposed of Lowery, he will not get his bonus. Unfortunately, he lost a lot of his men, so he will have to regroup on his next project. I have told Livermore to shut down the command center by Monday morning. Until then, we need to be able to keep an eye on Merchant's house and have the techies clean up all we need to clean."

Jim stepped into the conversation. "Shouldn't we at least have them finish off Lowery? He has been a pain in the butt."

Tyler answered him. "Strother probably wants to, as do Livermore and his number two, R.J. But as far as I am concerned, that is not as big of a priority today as it was yesterday. Our folks know that if he gets in the way of our Monday plans, they are authorized to take him out, but now that Jackson has been exonerated by the feds, his death could look suspicious at this point. Our sole focus now is to make sure Monday is a success."

"We agree," Susan said. She then added, "Jim and I will be gone tomorrow morning, so this will be the last time we chat with you for a while. As we say goodbye, we want you to know how honored we have been to contribute to the cause of preserving the right humanity."

Jim simply added, "I agree. Stay true to the cause, gentlemen."

"Thank you both," Tyler responded. "For everything. Going forward, under the General's leadership, the best is yet to come. Godspeed."

"Hear, hear," chimed in the General.

With that, the most powerful white supremacy group assembled since the civil war officially disbanded, with the ardent belief that their efforts would bear fruit on Monday with the killing of over a million U.S. school children.

One of the most understated and overlooked D.C. landmarks is Lincoln's Cottage at the Old Soldier's Home in northwest Washington. Sprawled over two hundred acres, the site served as the summer house for presidents such as James Buchanan, Rutherford B. Hayes, and Chester A. Arthur. However, no president is identified with the site as much as the great president, Abraham Lincoln. Between June and November in 1862, 1863, and 1864, Lincoln and his family occupied the house to escape the swamp-like conditions at the White House and the wartime congestion of the capital.

It is said, however, that Lincoln did not escape the Civil War and his burden of leadership. Every morning he mounted his big gray horse and rode the four miles to the White House to carry out official business, returning to the Old Soldiers' Home every evening. As a historian, Jackson admired Lincoln greatly and loved being on the grounds of the Old Soldier's Home. Standing near the cottage, Jackson could visualize Lincoln mounting his horse, complete with his dress jacket and stovepipe hat, enduring D.C.'s summer heat on his way to work to save the nation.

Jackson had suggested Lincoln's Cottage to Reba Duncan as a place for them to all meet that evening. It was time to tell the senator all that they knew. Ronnie and Jenny agreed that it would be best done in person. But finding a place to meet was not easy. Since CNN broke the news regarding the senator's press release, the media had been stalking the senator and his wife. Forty news cameras were in front of their Kalorama home. Fortunately, secret service was keeping them at bay.

Ronnie and Jenny also suggested that Jackson call Harrington immediately after meeting with Rex. They had to be careful not to antagonize the new F.B.I. director, who was looking for a reason to clamp down on Jackson.

Lincoln's Cottage closed at 4:30 pm on Saturdays. Run by the Park Service, no one could get on the grounds after hours - unless, of course, you were a U.S. senator and possible future president. Rex liked Jackson's suggestion and, after a few calls, paved the way for everyone to meet at the one-time home of Lincoln. Jackson, Ronnie, and Jenny arrived in the Grand Cherokee half an hour before Rex and Reba Duncan. They settled into one of the cottage's rooms that had a conference table and waited.

Based on all that Jenny and Sweeney were able to find, Claremark was the likely co-conspirator. They also had hundreds of school district contracts. It was impossible to determine which cities were the probable Monday targets. Getting the senator and law enforcement involved was now essential. With the information they had found, including Bill Merchant's suicide note, prosecutors could obtain search warrants to gain access to all of Claremark's distribution centers. Subpoenas could also be used to gain access to company documents.

Thinking about this, however, bothered Jenny. She was hard pressed to see how search warrants would gather more information than Sweeney could get. She kept making that point to Jackson as they both were being checked out for their injuries. Ronnie had gotten an old marine buddy who was a doctor to come to Jackson's apartment to examine them. Even though Jackson was no longer a fugitive, he still felt uncomfortable going to a hospital. Jenny's gunshot wound was healing nicely. Jackson had a couple of bloody, broken knuckles. Ronnie's doc friend reminded them both how luck they were.

While his colleagues went to Lincoln's Cottage, Sweeney had decided to stay at Jackson's apartment to finalize his research on the local conspiracy team. Sweeney was enjoying watching the watchers. He did not find joy in a voyeuristic way. Rather, he appreciated knowing what he did not want to do with the rest of his life. He did not want to use his gifts to harm others.

Already, he had uncovered many pieces to the puzzle. Mills and Merchant had been in regular contact with an ex-Navy seal named Brent Livermore. Livermore worked closely with an R.J. Nevers, also an ex-Navy seal. According to his identification, the man that Jackson had fought and Ronnie had killed in Merchant's bedroom was R.J. Nevers. He also was the one who said he had killed Amy.

Through phone records and countless other name identification searches, Sweeney was able to put together a list of nearly twenty former special forces, navy seals, black ops types working with Livermore. He also pieced together about six or seven computer tech experts. Digging deeper into the recent phone records of Livermore and R.J. Nevers, Sweeney also unearthed the names Dick Strother and Russ McNair.

Quite simply, these men were hired mercenaries, something Ronnie had been calling them for the last several days. When Sweeney showed everyone their pictures, Ronnie quickly identified them as the two fishermen and the two men who looked into the window of the Newport, Tennessee diner. Jenny swore that Russ McNair was the same man she shot.

Through watching Livermore and his crew, Sweeney had learned a bit more about the operation. The tech guys had been instructed to fabricate information between Mills and Merchant to make it seem like they were operating alone.

Finally, they all had been operating in a nondescript building located in Fairfax. One of the reasons why Sweeney wanted to stay behind was because he had accessed the camera on one of the computers of a techie in the Fairfax building. He was able to hear and see almost everything being said on that side of the room. Sweeney noticed that there were four other computers with cameras in the rest of the building. He could only look at one at a time, so he recorded sound and video from the others. He would look at the tapes later - he wanted to make sure that he was thorough.

It was evident that the place was in wind down mode. Before they left, Jackson, Ronnie, and Jenny watched and heard Livermore bark orders and spew out racial epithets. Sweeney thought he was a real racist prick. They even heard him give out the future agency placement information for some of his team. He liked to throw his weight around and treated his team like shit. He had been up in arms because R.J. had not checked in. He talked about sending someone to Merchant's house, but got distracted trying to make sure they were shutting things down in the right way.

From all that Sweeney could determine, the plan was for the place to be vacant tomorrow, Sunday morning. Sweeney wanted to keep listening just in case he picked up on some information that could help them stop the dreaded Monday attack.

Back at Lincoln's Cottage, Senator Rex Duncan and his wife Reba entered the conference room and headed straight for Jackson. Reba hugged and kissed him. Introductions were made. Jackson, Ronnie, and Jenny told them all that they knew. Everything. Each of them realized that the only chance they had to stop this thing was to have the full support of the powerful Rex Duncan. Jackson and Ronnie capped off the update by telling them what they found at Bill Merchant's house and how they were attacked. They recited the letter word for word. They even told them what R.J. Nevers said about Amy. On hearing that part, Reba cried out softly. Rex's fists clenched.

Rex and Reba took it all in, holding back any strong emotions they were feeling. It was a lot for them to absorb. When they were finished, Rex said, "Well, folks we have a lot of work to do to stop these bastards. Let me get to it. Reba has given you all of our numbers. We should all stay closely connected between now and Monday. And please, let us know as soon as you get any new information from your computer guru. Also, I will take care of making sure Merchant's house is cleaned up, including this Nevers guy. I wish I had been with you at Merchant's. I would have loved to have pulled the trigger. Mr. Thomas, thank you for avenging our daughter's death." Looking at all three of them, he said, "You all are American heroes. I will do my level best to honor your work and finish these guys off."

He then paused. After a moment or two, he started shaking his head. "You know, when I was in college with Michael Brock, he started talking this white superiority garbage. He never stopped. And, it all came to this. We've lost our daughter and the lives of a million kids are at stake. I promise you, I will rid the country of this poison."

With that, Rex rose and walked out the room, with Reba following behind him waving her goodbyes.

As was previously planned, Jackson, Ronnie and Jenny sat back down. They were to wait another half hour before leaving, just in case some press had followed Rex and were lingering a bit.

"What do you think?" Jackson asked.

"He will be a good president," Ronnie said. "I like his go get 'em style."

"I agree, Ronnie," Jackson said. "But, what do you think about where things stand? Do you think we will get these guys?"

Jenny was deep in thought. In fact, even during the meeting with Rex and Reba Duncan, she seemed a little distracted.

"I cannot lie," she said. "I just know we are missing something. We are. Think about it. With Sweeney's skills, we should have been able to find some direct links from Austin Nicholas to Livermore, the folks in Fairfax, Merchant, Mills, something! And there is one other thing. When we heard that a bunch of hedge fund money was being funneled to Caremark to help he them more competitive for these bids, we all thought of Steve Mills. Well guess what, Sweeney checked. There was no link, not one dollar between Mills and ANY of the food service provider companies. We may be totally off on this thing. Even our premise may be wrong. What if it isn't the food? How about water? This thing is spinning me all around."

Jackson and Ronnie both understood Jenny's frustration. They were feeling the same way. She merely gave a voice to their collective hesitance. Still, Jackson picked up the phone to brief Harrington, hoping his uncertainty would go away.

On Saturday evening, the Duncans hosted dinner at their home for their long time friend, General Michael Brock. The General was his usual gregarious self, though he was appropriately observant of the recent tragedy of Amy Duncan's murder. In fact, it was the General who broached the subject of Amy's killer as they all began to eat roast beef, steamed green beans, and signature Idaho potatoes.

"Folks, I saw the statement that was released about that professor Jackson Lowery. I was glad to see that you were able to rule him out as a suspect. In your statement, Rex, you also used the word killers instead of killer. What in blazes is going on, my friend?" Once he asked the question, the General dug out of his plate a forkful of potatoes lathered in ketchup.

Rex coolly glanced at Reba before replying. "Well, you are not the first one to notice that distinction, Michael. My office has been inundated with calls and darn it, that one word has been their main focus. As I told you when I asked you to visit us, that is one of the reasons why I think you can help me, actually, us, Reba and me," he said, motioning to his wife.

"That is why I am here, Rex. You know I am always here for the both of you." He smiled appreciatively.

"We do know that, Michael. Tell you what, let's finish this meal my bride made for us and then retire to the living room to talk through everything. How's that?"

"You know I think better on a full stomach," the General said, eating more roast beef.

They all engaged in meaningless small talk while they finished their dinner. Boise State basketball, hunting in Montana, the changing work ethic among our young. As they moved to the living room, Reba carried in a tray with a fresh pot of coffee and three cups on it. The General sat in his favorite chair, while Reba sat on the sofa, with her left elbow resting on the sofa's arm.

Rex did not bother to sit. As was his habit when he was thinking, he had to move around. He walked to the living room window, looked outside for a minute and paced over to where his wife was sitting, elegant, legs crossed, back straight.

Then Rex cut to the chase.

"Michael, we have been best friends for a long time, so there is no need for there to be any bullshit between us. Reba and I have one question, why? How could you be a part of something so evil, so insidious that it could lead to our daughter's death. Why?"

The General had been smiling and relaxed when he entered the living room. In an instant, his whole demeanor changed. The smile on his face was replaced with a stoic recognition that his career was over. No Secretary of Defense. No possible presidential run. It was all over. But, the General did not blink.

"Rex, as much as I have been fond of you and our friendship, I have detested your tolerance for those who are inferior. In school, I could not believe how much you embraced this equal rights for all bullshit. For years, I have been telling myself that deep down, you really get it. I am hoping you understand that. We are losing our country to wetbacks, middle easterners, and darkies of African descent who are genetically

283

inferior to us. There are many of us - far more than you realize - that are ready to stand up and fight. To take our country back. That is the answer to your why, Rex. It is time for us to act like the ethnic purists that we are, and to hell with whoever gets in the way."

Reba spoke, almost for the first time all morning.

"Like Amy, Michael? Our baby? To hell with whoever gets in the way, like Amy. Is this what you and your military friends call collateral damage, Michael? It's okay to lose a few of our own, so long as we win the war. Is that what Amy was, Michael? Collateral damage?"

The General was unmoved. "Reba, I am truly sorry about Amy. She should have never been brought into this and certainly never should have died. I am so sorry and will forever feel partially responsible for her death. But those of us who are born to lead need to lead no matter where the chips fall."

Rex was back at the front window. Only this time he was signaling to the F.B.I. agents outside. Reba had her head down, slowly, deliberately, shaking her head.

Looking at Rex's back since Rex was still facing the window, the General asked, "How did you know?"

Rex turned around and looked the General in the eye. "Actually, it was easier than we thought it would be. Once Jackson Lowery told us what Amy heard, Reba and I poked each other's brains about the list of people who stood to gain personally should I become president. Then we considered who, among that list of names, would have the lack of moral fiber or the lack of an ethical compass to allow them to be a part of something so inhumane. There were about fifteen to twenty people on the first list. Once we applied the second criteria, you stood alone, my friend. You stood alone."

At that moment, three F.B.I. agents entered the room. General Michael Brock stood tall and erect as he was read his rights and the handcuffs were placed on his wrists. During that process, Reba got up from the sofa and walked to where her husband was standing. She leaned into his arms as he held her and rested her head on his chest.

No other words were exchanged between the two lifelong friends. They did, however, share an intriguing look between themselves. It was almost as if Rex was sending the General to war. Reba noticed the look and squeezed her husband's hand as the agents escorted the General out the door and into the waiting black sedan.

———————

The scientists in the windowless building situated in the southern Pennsylvania hills had finally given their bosses the news they wanted. The re-engineered poison would integrate perfectly with the food being processed in the ten Carr warehouses across the United States. The poison had been administered to the plastic packaging covering the food. According to the scientists' testing, the poison from the plastic would infect the food within minutes.

Before the Carrs went underground, they gave specific orders to each of their plant leaders to make sure that their trucks completed all of their deliveries by 7 am Monday morning. On occasion, in the past, some deliveries ended up being late. The Carrs made it clear to their managers that individual paychecks would be docked if any delivery was late. The managers were also told that no delivery should be stopped, no matter who pressured them to do so. In order to make sure that things were executed properly, the Carrs arranged for their chief operations officer to get a six-figure bonus provided that each delivery was clocked in by 7 am. There was no way that any of the deliveries would be stopped or be late.

SUNDAY

ONE

On Sunday morning, Dick Strother was visiting Russ McNair at the Fairfax County hospital when three F.B.I. agents walked into his friend's hospital room. McNair had extensive nerve and ligament damage from the bullet he got from Jenny Roberts. He had stumbled in the field near Delaplane, Virginia, and finally gotten picked up not far from I-66 near Haymarket. He was incoherent, disoriented, and confused.

One of his fellow team members took him to the Fairfax County Hospital where he underwent surgery. The bullet had nicked an artery and McNair had lost a lot of blood. He had just been placed back into his room after his second surgery when Strother dropped by to check on him. As soon as Strother saw the suits entering the room that Sunday morning, he knew that his ticket had been punched. There were three of them. G-men all the way. Arrogant pricks. Strother was thinking that it would be better to go out with a bullet.

The agents read him his rights and led him out of the hospital. As he was leaving McNair's room, he looked over his shoulder at his unconscious friend. One of the F.B.I. men was in the process of handcuffing McNair's good arm to the hospital bed. *Assholes*, Strother thought to himself.

Claremark Foods was based in Cleveland, Ohio, but they had ten food distribution centers across the country. Between late Saturday night and early Sunday morning, F.B.I. agents raided all of the Claremark properties. Agents also raided the home of Claremark CEO Austin Nicholas, which was located in the exclusive Cleveland suburb of Chagrin Falls. Nicholas was shocked by the raid, asking "What the hell is this all about?" He figured that one of his payoffs went bad.

There were still ten people, including Livermore, at the Fairfax command center when the agents converged there late on Sunday morning. Each of the ten were read their rights and escorted off of the property. The agents knew the exact whereabouts for everyone on Livermore's team. They would be in custody by noon. Ever full of himself, Livermore looked surprised by it all. His face said it all. He could not believe that they'd been found out and that he was being arrested.

Bravado aside, it is often the biggest mouths that hold the smallest amount of courage. The Feds took Livermore to their D.C. headquarters on Pennsylvania Avenue. He was there by mid afternoon. Since they had not gotten much from the other raids, particularly of the Claremark properties, they were going to squeeze Livermore as hard as possible. At first, Livermore played it tough. But he had actually been caught off guard by the raid. He truly believed that he and his co-conspirators were smarter than others in the government.

The F.B.I. smartly chose two black field agents to interrogate Livermore. Gary Smith was six feet, five inches and over three hundred pounds. He was a former defensive end at Penn State and as mean as they come. Tom Williamson was lean, balding and bespectacled. He was the agency's best interrogator. He was known for playing mind games with suspects and breaking them down. Blessed with unmatched patience, Williamson would legendarily question suspects for thirty to thirty-six hours straight without breaking a sweat. In this instance, however, both Smith and Williamson were told they needed answers yesterday. Ed Harrington, the new F.B.I. director implored them both to "do whatever you need to do to get information form this guy as quickly as possible. As far as I am concerned, he never existed."

In all his years working both in the field and at headquarters, Tom Williamson had never received that kind of directive. He nodded at the director, rubbed his hands together and pushed Smith to walk ahead of him as they both entered the room.

Sweeney had been monitoring all of the F.B.I. activities through his computer. He was already wired into the F.B.I. headquarters cameras in their interrogation rooms. Having heard the conversation between Williamson and the director, he knew that the interview was not to be missed. He yelled to Jackson, Ronnie, and Jenny to come watch the interrogation with him. They had all gotten back from their meeting with the Duncans and were grabbing something to eat.

"This is must-see TV, guys. Harrington just gave the green light to do whatever they need to do to get information out of Livermore. I wouldn't be surprised if they started waterboarding this fuck."

"Let me get this straight, Joe," Jackson said. "This is live?"

Sweeney was leaning back in his chair. "Yep," he said.

"Coming directly from an interrogation room at the F.B.I. headquarters downtown?"

Sweeney was loving it. "Yep, that's right."

Ronnie then followed up. "Is there anywhere you cannot break in - electronically?"

Sweeney leaned forward again in his chair, giving the question some thought. He then leaned back in his chair and said, "Hmmm, I don't think so, Ronnie."

Jackson and Ronnie looked at Jenny, who proudly folder her arms across her chest and arched her eyebrows.

"Here we go," Sweeney said as they watched Smith first, then Williamson enter the room. "Let me turn up the volume.

Smith started up first. Standing over the former navy seal turned-terrorist, he went right at Livermore.

"So, I hear that you think you are superior to me, you fuck. Is that so?" He pushed Livermore hard out of his chair. Livermore fell on his elbow, letting out a yelp. He was sitting on the floor holding his elbow when Smith continued.

"You crying, little white bitch. Did you hurt your elbow? Well, I am just getting started, you fuck. He then wound up and threw a devastating punch to Livermore's right jaw. The unusually loud 'pop' sound from the blow was jolting. Williamson did not flinch. For a moment, Livermore did not move. Watching it, the blow looked like it could have been fatal.

"Did he kill him?" Jackson asked.

"I doubt it," Jenny said. "Maybe broke his jaw. Let's see how he sounds when he talks."

Dazed, Livermore started to regain himself. He was holding his jaw, looking fearfully up at Smith. Any bravado he had entered the room with was already gone.

Smith used his two mitts masquerading as hands and picked Livermore up, slamming him against the wall. He then grabbed Livermore by his shirt collar with his left hand, holding him against the wall. Smith then reared his right arm back, as if ready to make another strong blow to the face. Before administering the swing, he whispered to Livermore, "They said I could kill you. I am going to make it hurt."

Through all of this, Williamson was sitting on one of the chairs at the table looking nonchalant and uninterested. With his thick, dark glasses, he looked like he was sitting in a public library observing a minor disagreement over computer access credentials.

Smith was about to administer his next blow to the flinching Livermore when Williamson calmly said, "Stop for a minute, Gary. Just give me one minute and I will leave you and Mr. Livermore alone."

Livermore cast his panicked eyes in the direction of Williamson, looking at him as if he were his personal savior. He then looked up at Smith, who was agitated, trying to make up his mind whether to accede to Williamson's request.

Smith put his hand down, then backed away from Livermore. Williamson then pointed to the overturned chair. Livermore picked it up and sat down, all while still keeping an eye on Smith's movements.

Smith positioned himself right behind Livermore, who could not see him but could more than feel his presence. Livermore was sitting at one end of the table, with Williamson at the other end.

Williamson did not waste any time. "Mr. Livermore, I will say what I am about to say one time and one time only. This is not an interrogation. We are not sure what it will end up being. That is up to you. But it is not an interrogation. There are no rules. Depending on how you respond, there are three possibilities regarding your future. You will either live the rest of your life in a country club prison or you will be in a general population prison with only blacks and Hispanics who know that you are the white supremacist who developed a plan to kill innocent black and brown babies while they were in school. Understood?"

Livermore nodded, clearly broken down. He looked quizzically at Williamson, who read his mind. "Do you have a question, Mr. Livermore?"

"Yes, sorry sir. But you said there were three possibilities about my future, but you only mentioned two of them. Sir."

Williamson did not smile. He showed no emotion whatsoever.

"You were listening and you are correct. The third possibility is that this room will be the site of your death. If I think you are lying to me or not telling me everything you know, Mr. Smith will kill you very slowly. We have been given twelve hours to ask you questions. My question will last thirty seconds. If I am not satisfied," he put his head down and looked at his watch, "Mr. Smith will use all of his allotted eleven hours and fifty minutes to kill you. Slowly. Very slowly. Do you understand?"

Livermore nodded. "Yes, I do, sir."

"Here is my question. Will you tell me everything you know?"

Without hesitation, Livermore proceeded to do just that.

TWO

The ultimate plan was to reverse the growth and influence of the minority population in the United States. The plan was created by a group of six well-connected individuals who came together around the principles of white supremacy several years ago. Since then, they had been quietly and selectively recruiting members from both inside and outside of the government. Steve Mills and Bill Merchant started the group. Livermore's main contact was Mills until he died. Since then, his contact had been a major corporate figure. Livermore never knew his name and the man always called Livermore. Livermore did not know the names of the other members.

The plan had three phases. Phase One was, in effect, the research and development phase. During this time, the six key group members would recruit surrogates, develop the right poison or toxin, and prepare for Phase Two, the implementation phase. As Team Jackson had figured out, the original plan was to poison the food of children in large, predominately minority school districts.

One of the group's leaders had a relationship with one of the companies providing food to a variety of school districts. This contractor was also providing food for small colleges and community colleges as well. Livermore did not know the name of the food service provider. The group had a number of scientists working on the right ingredients for a poison that would work the best. They had been waiting for some time for the scientists to refine the poison.

During Phase Two, the poison would be distributed to millions of people on the same day at about the same time. The expectation was that millions of young people of color would die as a result of the plan. Yes, there would be collateral damage, but that was to be expected. Indeed, the ultimate evidence of the insanity behind the plan is that thousands of white kids would die along with the million kids of color. Clearly, those behind the plan were so focused on the end goal that they were okay with murder on a large scale, regardless of the races of those killed.

Phase Three was the police state phase. The expected fallout from millions of deaths was that it would lead to anarchy. The group was expecting that the uncertainty would force the president to activate the military, and giving the Secretary of Defense heightened power. In that role, the Secretary would use clandestine surrogates to stoke, then stifle riots and create a national police state under which was expected the rampant jailing and killing of countless more minorities and dissidents.

As an added benefit, during this police state, the Secretary of Defense and his minions would be able to strategically identify, discredit and even kill leaders challenging their authority. The group believed that the impact of a fully executed plan with all of its phases would alter the course of history in America, permanently ensuring that whites maintained political, economic, and social superiority in the Western Hemisphere for years to come.

Of course, if the plan ended up not as successful as expected, the conspirators would still be well positioned for the resulting chaos and race war. The leaders of the plan were determined to follow the vision laid out in *The Turner Diaries*. Deconstruct. Destabilize. Destroy.

Later F.B.I. conversations with General Brock confirmed that he and his co-conspirators believed that he was positioned to be Secretary of Defense in a Duncan administration. The Secretary of Defense was the key player during Phase Three of the plan. The conspirators needed the right person in that job. They were banking on General Brock filling that role in a Duncan administration.

Jackson, Ronnie, Jenny, and Sweeney were all riveted while watching the F.B.I. agents completely break down Livermore. Ronnie, not always one to wax philosophical, made an astute observation when Livermore finished sharing all that he knew. "The power of the mind and the psychological control that can come with that power is amazing. Agent Smith only hit Livermore one time, but Williamson controlled him as if he had been their captive for years. They had taken control of his mind and his will. I actually think they could have gotten the same information from him without throwing one punch. Something else," he said, shaking his head.

As Livermore was spilling his guts, however, Jackson's inner voice was working overtime inside his head. He was thinking back to what Jenny had said to them earlier about missing something. Hearing Livermore triggered Jackson's thinking. In fact, while Livermore was still talking, Jackson stood up and walked away from the computer. Whatever was gnawing at him was trying to come out, but he just could not grab it. In his mind, he was breaking down Livermore's words. He also went back to his case solving approach of looking at the who, what, when, where, why, and how of the situation. The 'how' was his focus now. He was close. But it was now Sunday and close was not good enough. Jenny had been in touch with some of the F.B.I. contacts and the agency was beginning to believe that they had dodged the bullet by arresting all of the leaders—they could find no evidence of imminent threat for Monday.

As soon as they had stopped watching the showdown between the F.B.I. agents and Livermore, Jackson asked Sweeney to turn down the volume. Ronnie could sense Jackson's agitation.

"What's going on, Jack? You have been fidgeting since the middle of Livermore's confession."

"I know. I know. Earlier, Jenny was right about us missing something. This Claremark thing is not fitting. But, I have a thought on how these SOBs were going to do this and stay undetected. Joe, please go back to the part of the Livermore confession where he talks about the school districts. Hold it right there."

Sweeney punched some keys on the keyboard and said, "Done."

"Thanks. Now, Jenny: pull out your briefing notes on the various food service providers. Remember when you briefed Ronnie and me in Asheville? You gave us the background on all the major players."

"Sure, I remember. I was looking at the notes earlier, because this has been bugging me so much. They are right here," Jenny said, lifting up a stack of papers.

"Great. You told us about Joe Charles and his goals and vision after winning the Chicago contract. But part of his vision extended beyond K-12 school districts. Remember? What exactly did you tell us about his vision?'

Jenny looked at their notes. "Is this what you are talking about, Jackson?" She then started reading from her notes, "He gives cooking classes and has trained community members in the hood. He even has talked about bidding on food service contracts at small colleges and community colleges catering to minorities."

Jackson stopped her. "Yes, that's it, Jenny. That is exactly it! Now Joe, play back the Livermore interview about the plan."

Sweeney found the spot in which Livermore said, "This contractor was also providing food for small colleges and community colleges as well."

Sweeney stopped the tape.

If a pin had been dropped anywhere in the room at that moment, it would have been heard.

Jenny broke the ice. "Bartlett Foods. Joe Charles. He is such a good guy. He wouldn't be involved in this."

"No, he would not, Jenny," Jackson said. But neither would Rex Duncan. But like Rex, he could be an unwitting pawn."

"Wickedly sadistic and brilliant," Ronnie said.

Jenny looked like she might pass out. She then gathered herself, saying to Sweeney, "Joe, can you verify that the other food service contract providers have their own food distribution sites that they own and control? Also, does Bartlett Foods?"

Sweeney went to work on his computer. While everyone waited, the tension in the room was palpable.

Three minutes later, Sweeney spoke. "Caremark, Jawer, and Honeyberg all have their own food distribution centers. Joe Charles and Bartlett do not." Sweeney then pushed a few more buttons on the keyboard.

He continued, "Bartlett has an exclusive agreement with one food distributor. In their agreement, which I have pulled up, Bartlett has promised to use this food distributor for all of its contracts, even - and this is the exact language - 'food service provider agreements between Bartlett Foods and small colleges, community colleges, and historically black colleges or universities."

Jackson asked the obvious next question. "Who is the exclusive food distribution provider for Bartlett Foods?"

Sweeney looked up from the screen. "It is the Carr Company, wholesale food distributors owned by Jim and Susan Carr."

Jackson, Ronnie and Jenny contemplated what they should do next. Pacing around Jackson's apartment, each of them felt the physical effects of their week-long odyssey. Jackson and Jenny had been popping pain pills left and right since going to the hospital. Ronnie was now asking them to share some of those pills with him. The blow he had received to the head from R.J. at Merchant's house may not have given him a concussion, but it did give him a nagging headache that was still there.

Adding to the physical injuries was the stress related to the plan to poison kids. They had to stop this thing. If not, each would feel personally responsible. The pressure was mounting. Based on what they had told Rex Duncan, all law enforcement was fixated on Claremark Foods. It would look crazy for them to turn around and suggest that community icon Joseph Charles was about to poison a million black and brown kids.

Indeed, when Reba Duncan called Jackson to let him know that she and Rex had figured out that the esteemed General Michael Brock was a part of the group that hatched the plan, he tried to explain to her that in order to be thorough, Rex should have the authorities look at Bartlett Foods. Reba scoffed at the idea. "Oh, come now, Jackson, we can't waste the bureau's time on suggestions like that. Joseph Charles is on the right side. He fights this stuff everyday."

Jenny could not argue with Reba's logic. In fact, she reminded them, many people feel the same way about the Carrs. "Look, guys. I always thought that Jim and Susan Carr were hippie types. I have seen them on television talking about healthy eating and organic foods. Just like Reba said about Joe Charles, it is a tough sell to convince anyone, without any evidence, that the Carrs want to kill a million kids."

Jackson responded, "But, isn't that the beauty and the power of the group Mills and Merchant brought together. Most people would never suspect them. General Brock? And, who is the new guy? The one that took over for Mills? Weren't you tracking him down, Joe?"

Sweeney nodded. He had been busy. He had just tracked down the number of the caller who was communicating with Livermore when Mills was removed from the picture. During the interview they had all watched, Livermore said that the guy who took Mills' place always called him. Sweeney tracked down the calls made to Livermore's phone and noticed that the same number had made several calls with Dick Strother, their gun for hire.

As if everyone wasn't shocked enough, Sweeney told them that the number belonged to Hampton-Powell board chair Roger Tyler. When Sweeney dropped Tyler's name, Ronnie plopped down hard on Jackson's sofa. "Man," he said, "it never ends, does it.

I've always liked this Tyler guy. So, has my son, Ronnie, Jr. He is into computer hardware and he almost worked for Hampton-Powell. He decided on Dell instead."

Jenny was biting her nails, something Jackson had never seen her do.

Ronnie continued, "I liked Tyler, just like Jenny likes the Carrs. How could so many smart, successful people buy into this ethnic supremacy bullshit?"

"That is a million dollar question, Ronnie," Jackson said. "I am sure there are psychologists and psychiatrists who can give you nice wordy reasons why. From my vantage point, so much of this stuff comes down to basic human frailties surrounding money, power, greed, and control. For some sick, insane reason, many of us feel better about ourselves when we can look down on someone else."

Jenny then said, "True, and we still have to stop this poison tomorrow. By the way, have we now identified all of the group members?"

"I believe we have," Sweeney said. "We passed Roger Tyler's name on to Harrington's folks and Tyler will be arrested soon."

"Yes," Ronnie said, "but we have no proof regarding the Carrs. There is absolutely no link between them and the others. We will be hard-pressed to get the Feds or any local police force to stop their trucks."

Jackson asked Sweeney if he could locate the Carrs.

Sweeney said, "From what I can see, they disappeared two days ago. They literally dropped off the face of the earth. Trust me, that means something when I say it!"

"It truly does," Jackson said. "And you can see no link to the other conspiracy members?"

"None," Sweeney said.

"Damn it!" Jackson said. "I know it is them. We have to find a way to stop those trucks." He hesitated, giving the problem more thought. "And, you are right, Ronnie. When I go call Harrington with new and different information, he will bite my head off and may not do anything."

Jenny said. "Sweeney, how can we get to Joe Charles? Can you tell us where he is?"

Peering down at his computer screen, Sweeney said, "I have it all here. Joe Charles gave the keynote and was given an award at a big NAACP luncheon today in Baltimore. According to his iPhone calendar, he attended a follow up reception and met with some local Baltimore officials. He is about to have dinner with a couple of colleagues at his hotel and is scheduled to take one of the first flights back to his home in Chicago at 7 am. He is staying at the Royal Sonesta Harbor Court Hotel in the Inner Harbor."

Jackson said, "I have to say this. I am still in awe at how vulnerable we all are to the likes of people like you, Joe. Thank God you are a good guy, but in the wrong hands, access to that kind of information so quickly is downright scary."

Jenny said, "It is now 7:15. If we leave now, we can get to the Inner Harbor by 8:15. Toss me the keys, Ronnie. I'll drive. Sweeney, stay by the phone in case we need you."

Sweeney laughed. "Don't you realize that I will know when you need me before you will?"

No one else laughed.

THREE

Joseph Charles was feeling better about his business and his future. Last week, he had a great meeting with Senator Rex Duncan, who had promised to help him. Charles would definitely support the senator when he ran for president. *He will be good for the country*, Charles thought, *even though he is from Idaho*. Charles had to snicker to himself. How was he going to sell a white Idaho farm boy to brothers in the hood? By being real, that's how. One thing he did like about Rex Duncan, he was real and selling him would not be hard.

Charles also was having a productive time in Baltimore. The city schools were on his future bidding list, so any good publicity would help. This afternoon, Charles had been honored at an NAACP luncheon. The NAACP is headquartered in Baltimore so the ballroom was packed with well-known black politicos, celebrities, and other luminaries. In his speech, Charles hammered his usual themes of health, nutrition, and physical fitness. He also used his tried and true phrase that the only ones to 'save us, is us', his calling card for personal responsibility in the black community. He received a rousing ovation. More importantly, he had just been told that the Baltimore Sun would be writing a favorable piece on the dinner, with a focus on Charles' remarks. His source at the paper also told him that the Sun article would mention Bartlett Foods' highly successful school lunch program at Chicago Public Schools'. Yes indeed, this had been a good week.

Charles had just finished dinner at his hotel with two old college friends and was killing time, catching up on email and reading the news alerts on his smartphone. After his friends left Charles remained seated in the leather booth, looking out over the Baltimore Harbor. Glancing up from his smartphone, he smiled at the memory of bringing his twin daughters to the famed Baltimore aquarium when they were nine years old. The look on their faces during that visit was priceless.

Viewing article after article, Charles was especially intrigued by various machinations in the Amy Duncan murder. He felt horrible for his friend, the senator. Charles' feeling of anguish was followed by more guilt for being so laser focused on his selfish business needs at a time when the senator and his wife had to deal with such an agonizing situation. Apparently, however, according to the assorted articles, the case continued to take unpredictable twists and turns. The senator's press release from yesterday was fascinating in as much as it insinuated a conspiracy involving killers not just one killer.

Charles was looking at a picture of Jackson Lowery, the professor first suspected of killing Amy Duncan, when he felt someone's presence at his booth. He looked up from his smartphone and saw Jackson Lowery. Instinctively, he looked back at the picture on his phone, then up at Lowery.

"Uh, I was just reading about you," he said to Jackson.

Jackson looked down at Charles' phone, recognizing his own image and said, "Hello, Mr. Charles. You cannot believe everything you read. At least what you read last week. The articles today are getting better. We need to talk."

It was only then that Charles saw that Jackson had two people with him, an obvious military police type and a rather attractive, thin, but tough looking lady. He was more than taken aback and felt a little overwhelmed. He started to look around the restaurant.

"We are not here to hurt you, Mr. Charles. As a matter of fact, each of us admires you and your commitment to the community. But, sir, if you do not give your full time and attention to us for the next several minutes, millions of school children will die. Right now, you are the only one who can help us stop it," Jackson said.

He now had Charles' full attention. Charles put his phone away and opened his arms wide, indicating to the group that they could join him at the large booth. "Well, professor Lowery. That is one hell of an introduction. Now, who are your friends?"

Jackson introduced Ronnie and Jenny, who both shook hands with Charles. Charles reached out his hand to shake Jackson's right hand, saw that it was heavily bandaged. Jackson looked at his hand and shrugged, saying, "That, sir, is part of the story."

Jackson, Ronnie and Jenny then told Charles as much as he needed to know. They went into particular detail about what Amy Duncan heard which led to her death and the ensuing pursuit of Jackson. They summarily painted the conspiracy picture for him without sharing specific names. Through it all, Charles seemed interested, but could not see how any of this related to him. Jackson then tried to connect the dots for him.

"So, let me tell you why we are here and how you can help. We have confirmed that the group behind the mass extermination conspiracy has perfected a poison that they have placed in food that will be delivered to selected school districts tomorrow," Jackson said.

Charles looked stunned, but he still did not get it. "That is awful. Look, if all that you are saying is true, and I am not saying I don't believe you, it's just a lot to take in, but I will do whatever I can to help you. Candidly, I cannot do anything about my competitors food distribution system. Everyone keeps that pretty secretive. I compete with Caremark and the others, but am willing to call Austin or whomever. I am trying to see how I can help." Charles almost appeared to be pleading with them to show how he could help. Jackson made things clearer.

"Let me be blunt, Mr. Charles. The poison is not being distributed by Caremark or any of your competitors. It is being distributed by you. It is coming from the food distribution centers owned by Jim and Susan Carr. Mr. Charles, the Carrs are a part of this conspiracy that we have just described for you. Right now, the trucks leaving their warehouses are carrying food full of poison to kill over a million kids. You have to help us stop these trucks. Now!"

Charles face sank completely. "Jim and Susan? Is that what you said? They are a part of this? Impossible. There is no way... where is your proof?"

"Yes, there is a way Mr. Charles, and the Carrs found it," Jenny said. "They have been paying scientists for a couple of years to refine the poison. Now they have gone underground. We do not have the direct proof we need. But we know they are involved. We need you to stop those trucks."

Charles was beginning to gather himself. He still looked skeptical, but was not as unsteady as he had been. He spoke hesitantly, "I am sorry. This is incredible. Plus, it is late on a Sunday night. Is there anyone else I can talk to... you know?"

"To confirm what we just said? Is that what you mean?," Jackson asked.

Charles said nothing, but nodded weakly.

Ronnie, who had not been involved in the conversation up to this point, said, "Jack, we don't have time to waste. Get Rex and Reba on the phone."

Jackson did just that. On the drive to Baltimore, Jackson, Ronnie, and Jenny were trying to grapple with the lack of proof they had regarding the Carrs. They knew that Charles would not risk his whole operation and his future on a hunch. They agreed that the only person who could help them was Rex Duncan. Even though Jackson had tried to broach the subject with Reba earlier in the day, he had to talk with Rex directly and get him to agree to lean on Charles. It was the only chance they had. Jackson had called Rex and made his case. Like Reba, Rex was hesitant to embrace the concept that Charles could be involved in any way. Finally, Jackson made his final, emphatic point.

"Senator, please look at it this way. If we are wrong, over a million school kids will miss lunch for one day. Yes, there will be some finger pointing, but everyone will get over it. On the other hand, if we are right and do nothing, by this time tomorrow a million and a half kids will be dead, leading this nation to virtual chaos."

Sitting in the Sonesta restaurant, Jackson got the senator on the phone and handed it to Charles. Rex absorbed all that Jackson had said and then agreed to talk with Charles. After two minutes on the phone with the senator, Charles was a different man. He hung up the phone and handed it back to Jackson saying, "I am sorry. It just seemed so impossible. By the way, Reba Duncan says she is sorry she doubted you."

Jackson suppressed a smile.

Charles then said, "Let's go to work.

For the next three hours, that Sonesta Harbor Hotel restaurant booth served as a command center of sorts for the four of them. Jenny pulled out her laptop, while Charles was frequently using his iPad. Jenny had Sweeney on the phone.

Charles also got his administrative assistant on the phone as well. Jackson had gone to the restaurant manager offering a thousand dollars to shut down the section they were in for a couple of hours. He said fine as long as they were done by 10 pm, the restaurant's closing time.

As they got started, Jackson wanted clarity on the amount of kids involved. He asked Charles, "So how many kids do you service through your lunch contracts in the nine school districts?"

Approximately 1.6 million children. Keep in mind, it is not just lunch. We serve breakfast at about thirty per cent of the schools."

Hearing that, Jackson, Ronnie, and Jenny all felt a panicked jolt. None of them had even given consideration to breakfast.

"Wow," Jenny said. That gives us far less time. We were solely focused on lunch. Doesn't breakfast often get served before the first class starts?"

"That's right, Jenny," Charles said. In many cases, only a skeleton crew of staff is at the school when we start serving."

Jackson buried his head in his hands.

In the meantime, the first thing Charles did was to try and stop the trucks. He called each of the Carr distribution centers and spoke personally with the site leaders. He then tracked down the Carrs' COO, who confided that he was under strict orders not to stop the delivery, that there was no condition under which he would do so. Charles was flabbergasted.

Deep down, once he was convinced that all he had heard was true, he fully expected to be able to stop the shipments by making a few calls. To be stymied so quickly and so unequivocally was a surprise. The full weight of the conspiracy was settling in on him as it had on Jackson the previous week while he was on the run.

Of course, none of this surprised Jackson, Ronnie, or Jenny. They had been on a race against time for several days and understood how formidable the plan architects really were.

Charles and his assistant then sent emails to all nine of the school districts where he had contracts as well as the small and community colleges. His assistant reminded him that school administrators were often terrible with email responses and that they would be lucky if sixty per cent opened their emails by noon tomorrow. In addition, there were hundreds of individual schools in those nine school districts. With those kind of numbers, even in the best of circumstances, chances are that many of the schools would not get the word in time and thousands of children could die.

By now Charles had taken off his stylish dark olive sport coat that perfectly matched his sharply pressed, pleated blue dress slacks. He had also rolled up the monogrammed sleeves to his tailor-made blue pin striped shirt. Jackson could see that panic was creeping up on Joseph Charles.

"Jenny," he said, "can you and Sweeney give us some options from a technological point of view? Let's all think. What is the best way to communicate with school districts?"

Charles corrected him. "At this point, professor Lowery," he said, "we need to stop thinking about school districts and start thinking about individual schools. We have to figure out how to talk to all of them and keep talking to them.

Ronnie stated what would have been the obvious solution, if they had better proof against the Carrs. "Is there any way we could convince the police to go to every school and embargo the trucks?"

"A handful might do it, but so many would not. As you have been saying, we have to stop all of the trucks. Anything short of 100% still kills kids," Charles said.

"I wish there was a way for us to send someone to every school and make an announcement," Ronnie said. The word 'announcement' triggered something in Jackson.

"Announcement," he repeated. He looked at Jenny. She picked up on it.

"I think I get where you are going, Jackson," she said. "Most schools have morning announcements. Can't we do the same thing?"

Jackson continued, "Sweeney, can we tap into these schools public address systems?"

"Sure can," said the voice from the speakerphone.

By now, Charles was trying to figure out who the kid was on the phone. "Are you saying that this guy on the phone can hack into the systems of over a thousand schools by morning and make a group announcement at those schools?"

Jenny sounded like a proud mama when she responded. "That is exactly what we are saying and he can do it long before morning."

Charles looked confused. "If you have those kind of capabilities, my assistant and I can get you the list of every school," he said.

Jackson took a long breath. He finally could envision a remedy. He did not want to lose the momentum. By now, they had left the restaurant and had checked into a suite at the hotel. They all realized that they would be up all night. He checked the time and realized that it was after 3 am.

"Can we also leave group voicemail messages on each school's main number, as well as the numbers for the principal and person who runs each cafeteria?"

"I can do that, too," said the voice from the speaker.

Charles was shaking his head. "We can get you all of those numbers, as well."

Sweeney said, "That would be helpful, but as long as I have the school names, I can get to all the right staff."

By 6 am Sweeney had left voicemails for the key staff at each school serviced by Bartlett Foods. The message had been recorded by Charles and was short, but direct. 'I regret to inform you that the food delivered to your school this morning has been poisoned. It is toxic for human consumption. Under no circumstances should you serve the food or unload it from the truck. If it has been unloaded, store it in a place away from humans.'

Ronnie had been calling police precincts all night and almost half of those he reached said that they would send units to the schools to make sure that the food was not touched. Also, once it was clear that Charles could not get the trucks to stop, Jackson called F.B.I. Director Harrington. Harrington was skeptical at first, but he agreed to get the Feds involved and to

313

also lean on local officials. Both Jackson and Harrington worried that they may be too late. "That's a lot of trucks to be intercepted, Jackson," Harrington said. "There is still a chance that some may make it through. We all must continue to inform the local schools."

At 6:30 am, the public address system at all the schools began blaring a message from Charles. Sweeney ran the same message every fifteen minutes for an hour and a half. Soon, the word was getting out to the media and police departments that were at first unresponsive, started to respond. By 9 am, all of the thousand plus schools had received the message. Plus, many trucks were stopped by either the F.B.I. or local police. None of the food was opened. No child was injured or killed.

In Chicago, Charles had sent his staff to certain schools in order to seize the food from the trucks as soon as they arrived. Working with the Feds, his staff took the food to a lab on the south side of the city where a team of doctors and scientists examined the shipments. By noon, the experts confirmed the worse. All of the food was contaminated, having been wrapped in plastic packages saturated with poison. If any of it had been ingested by a child, that child would have died.

By the end of the school day, federal authorities had saturated each school. The authorities quarantined every school kitchen and took possession of every delivery truck they could find. The plan had been stopped.

AFTERMATH

ONE

It is often said that a civilized people are always on the brink of chaos. A faint spark of dissonance can lead to widespread revolution; a seemingly stable nation can become unglued in an instant. The organizers of the plan were banking on that incongruity, the fragility that makes our democracy precious and precarious at the same time.

Fortunately, it is also the resiliency and good heartedness of our people that allows us to bounce back, even during the worst of times. As word trickled out about the attempt to poison a million black and brown children, passions exploded. Yes, the crisis had been averted, but now the recriminations would begin. Some took to the streets, many talked of retribution, all were outraged.

It was at this moment when the calm, steady leadership of departing President Barry Coleman and Joseph Charles made a difference. Sensing the need to identify a hero, President Coleman publicly thanked Charles for his role in stopping the plan. Coleman reported that it was Charles who had suspected the diabolical plot hatched by the Carrs and their cronies. Coleman further said that Charles followed his own intuition by stopping the food distribution without having all the proof he needed.

The President called Charles an American hero who saved millions of lives because of his quick thinking and selfless actions. In turn, Charles credited Senator Rex Duncan, who refused to let friendship get in the way of doing the right thing when he exposed General Brock's conspiracy. Charles praised Rex and

Reba for 'not letting their grief stop them from finding out the truth' about their daughter's death. President Coleman effusively thanked Senator Duncan as well, fueling speculation that the president would be supporting the senior senator from Idaho to be his successor.

Three days after the plan had been stopped, Jackson woke up in a cold sweat. He was soaked. He sat on his bed and looked all around. It was still dark outside. He looked at the clock on his nightstand. It was 4 am. Jackson shook his head, got out of bed and started to take off his tee shirt. He was shivering. He grabbed a fresh shirt from his dresser and went to the bathroom. Still cold, Jackson decided to make some coffee. Once the coffee started to brew, Jackson sat at his kitchen table and tried to dissect his thoughts. He had dreamed of Amy Duncan for the last two nights. On this night, Rex Duncan was also in the dream. Amy was running from her father, while at the same time, calling out Jackson's name. "Help me, Jackson," she kept saying. "Help me!"

Jackson was wondering why he was feeling unsettled about Rex Duncan. What was bothering him? The coffee pot started to scream. Jackson poured himself a cup and walked to his living room, where he stretched out on his sofa. His thoughts returned to Rex and Reba. And Amy. *Was Amy trying to tell him something?*

Jackson closed his eyes, trying to make sense of what was lurking beneath the surface of his brain. He sat up, walked to his window and opened the curtains. There was no scenic view on Cecil Place, just the single lane street shaded by a few townhouses. If he strained a look to his left, Jackson could see the monstrous Whitehurst Freeway. Still, he often looked out his window as a means of channeling his thoughts. After a few minutes, he went back to sit on the sofa. Think in simple terms, he told himself. Soon, a thought came to him. More of a question. It was a simple question, which could lead to other questions.

Why does it seem that Rex is not devastated by Amy's death?

Is Jackson being unfair? People bear their grief differently. Reba was obviously destroyed, but Rex always seemed to be in control. Is that just the mark of a good leader? For some reason, that question kept coming to Jackson. But that in and of itself is a flimsy reason to think negatively about Rex. His show of grief - one way or another - doesn't prove that he was involved in the plan. Jackson got off of his sofa and walked back to the window.

There was something else driving his thinking. It was in the back of his mind, but was not coming through. Looking out the window, he noticed two of the famous Georgetown rats racing down Cecil Place, dutifully running the right way down the one-way street. The rodents passed by his house and turned right toward the newer townhouses across the street from him. 'Rex and the General,' Jackson thought to himself, naming the rats, while snickering. Then, it hit him. He knew why he felt that Rex Duncan knew more about the plan than he was letting on.

Jackson snapped his fingers, rushed back to his bedroom and got his phone. He called Joe Sweeney. It took a few rings, but Sweeney finally picked up the phone.

"Hello," he said softly, obviously having been awakened.

319

"Hey, Sweeney. Sorry to wake you up, but I need your help. It's important. How soon can you get here?"

Silence.

"Sweeney?" Jackson said.

"Jackson, is that you?" a sleepy voice said.

"Yes, yes, it's me, Sweeney. I need you. How soon can you get here?"

Sweeney was now awake.

"I'm on my way."

Just then, Ronnie walked into the living room. He was planning on getting Rose and Ronnie, Jr. from the bunker the next day. The fresh smell of coffee woke him up.

"Was that Sweeney on the phone, Jack?"

"Hey, Ronnie. Yeah, I asked him to come over."

"Right now?"

Jackson nodded.

Ronnie looked at his friend and turned toward the kitchen to pour himself some coffee. Jackson just watched him, saying nothing.

Ronnie came back into the living room, took a sip of his coffee and said, "So this thing is not over, is it?"

"Afraid not."

"Okay. Let me call Jenny. She better get on over here." Jenny was staying at the Crystal City Marriott, contemplating when she would be going back to Atlanta.

———————

Late that afternoon, Jackson, Ronnie, Jenny, and Ed Harrington were all standing on the Duncan's front porch of their Kalorama home. Sweeney was in class. Jackson knocked on the door.

Reba opened the door, smiling when she saw Jackson. As she looked at the others and noticed their expressions, she became concerned and said, "Did something happen?"

Jackson spoke, "No, Reba. We just need to talk with you and Rex."

Reba called out for Rex and let them in.

———————

Earlier that day, when Jenny and Sweeney got to Jackson's apartment that morning, he told them about his concerns and his hunch. He asked Sweeney to dig as deeply as possible into the work of both Rex Duncan and Michael Brock while they were at Harvard. Sweeney could not find any of their class work documents online, they both went to school there too long ago. But after much digging, Sweeney found the notes of some of Rex and Brock's professors, which had been converted to online documents stored in the University's secure file for professors. The files were not accessible to the public.

One economics professor, Jonas Schreiber, expressed concerns in his notes about the overzealousness of Brock and Rex in presenting, *Why Society's Pecking Order Works*, a paper they co-wrote. The paper argued that, "capitalism could only survive with a definable upper, middle, and lower class and that some people born in the lower class were best suited to stay there, particularly minorities." Curiously, Schreiber's later notes about the paper identify Michael Brock as the sole author.

When Sweeney read Schreiber's notes to Jackson, Ronnie and Jenny, they all became numb.

"Does this mean that Rex Duncan was a part of the plan?" Jenny asked.

321

"I don't think so," Jackson said. "At least, not an active participant. But I think it's possible that he knew about it through Michael Brock and supported its thrust."

"That's a pretty big leap, based on one college paper," Jenny said. "In effect, you are saying that our next president may have been okay with the killing of a million kids."

"I am not really saying that," Jackson responded. "I am just saying that we need to be sure. Look, it just has been bothering me that he doesn't seem as sad or devastated as he should be about Amy. I know he loved her and I don't think he had anything to do with her death, but it is almost as if he accepted it all too quickly. It made me want to find out more about him and Brock. But trust me, I know that has nothing to do with whether he was involved in the plan. It just prodded me to focus on him."

No one said anything. Jackson continued.

"Then it hit me. The main thing is this: Remember when we met the senator and Reba at Lincoln's Cottage? He brought up General Brock and I will never forget his words. He said, 'You know, when I was in college with Michael Brock, he started talking this white superiority garbage. He never stopped. And it all came to this. We lose our daughter and the lives of a million kids are at stake. I promise you, I will rid the country of this poison.'"

"Okay," Jenny said. "And?"

Jackson responded, "Duncan tells us that Brock never stopped talking about this garbage, yet we know that Brock never talked like that with anyone publicly or privately, except those with whom he was in cahoots. There is no way he would have gotten all of those stars and military advancements if his true sentiments were known. But, he continued to talk to Duncan about it. Duncan had to know."

Ronnie then spoke, "You may be on to something, Jack. If the General felt comfortable enough to talk candidly about his racism with Duncan and *still* believed he would be appointed the Secretary of Defense, you have to also point a finger at Rex Duncan. All of which makes Amy's death crazily ironic."

"And, truly sad," Jackson said.

Jenny chimed in. "But wasn't it the Duncans who fingered the General? If Rex knew about it, why would he turn him in?"

"Reba," Jackson said. "She was the one who pushed Rex to help her find the truth. When it became clear to Rex that we were getting close and that Reba would not stop, he had to make his friend a sacrificial lamb."

"I am still not sure. It all seems a little thin. The main question now is what do we do?" Jenny asked.

Jackson scratched his head and said, "I suggest we take it to Harrington and get his opinion. If he thinks it makes sense to go further with it, so be it. If he doesn't, I will be fine with that too."

"Will you, Jack?" Ronnie said. "Even if the man becomes president of the United States?"

They all fell quiet.

Jenny said, "Jackson, you have to call Harrington. It is unavoidable. We have to get his opinion."

Neither Jackson nor Ronnie said anything.

Sweeney then spoke. At times, the nerdy college kid felt in over his head around the other older, more knowledgeable adults. But he also felt safe, protected and nurtured around them. Increasingly, he was getting comfortable speaking up.

"You guys are scaring me. Look, I am still in college. We have to call in the F.B.I. It looks like Rex Duncan will be the next president. I was okay with that until I did this research. We have to stop him. If he gets in, he will find a way to hurt people. Is this the world I am facing in the future?"

"Not if we can help it, Sweeney," Jackson said. He playfully grabbed his neck. "And 'we' includes you. Your work is helping us make things right. Both you and Jenny are right. I will call Harrington."

After being brought up to speed, Harrington said, "Jackson, you may be onto something here. If so, we cannot let him get in the White House. But we need to flush him out. I think the best way to do so is through his wife. If I go talk to him alone, she won't be in the room. I think that you and your team should go with me for a surprise visit. You can then ask him about the college paper in front of her."

Jackson thought that Harrington's suggestion was brilliant. But he was wondering why Harrington seemed more accommodating. He said, "Actually, that suggestion makes a lot of sense to me, Ed. I have to ask, though, are you and me okay, now?"

"Jackson, it is no secret that I had major issues with your loner, egotistic tendencies. But, that was a long time ago. More than anything, over the last few days, I have seen you use the instincts and skills you've always had to help stop a catastrophe. And you have done so while working with your team. You have served your country well. Now, let's go see the senator."

TWO

When Senator Duncan saw all of them and the look on their faces, he winced, but recovered quickly.

"Hi, folks," he said, smiling. "How is everyone?" He looked at each of them and said, "Is everything alright?"

Reba walked to her husband and grabbed his hand.

By now, Jackson, Jenny and Harrington were seated on the sofa. Rex and Reba sat in the two side chairs directly across from the sofa. Ronnie remained standing, assuming a protector's stance.

Harrington looked at Jackson, silently giving him permission to lead the questioning. Under proper protocol, Harrington would do the talking, but his look handed the reins to Jackson. Jackson acknowledged Harrington's gaze and was momentarily distracted. He had not seen Harrington in over ten years. The man still looked fit. Jackson also noticed that Harrington still had those reading glasses hanging around his neck. Some things never changed. Jackson got refocused.

"Senator," Jackson began. "While you and General Brock were at Harvard, do you remember writing a paper together entitled, *"Why Society's Pecking Order Works*?"

Rex Duncan started turning beet red in the face as he stared at Jackson. He said nothing. Reba, confused, but sensing something bad, tried to step in.

"Jackson, what on earth are you talking about? And why are all of you storming our home in this way?

It is not about some college paper. You all need to say what you want to say."

Jackson took a deep breath, about to speak. Rex looked like he had been knocked off stride. At that moment, he knew that they knew. Like his friend, General Brock, the reality of not gaining the power and status that he had craved his entire life, was hitting him in the same way it had hit had Brock, and in very same room.

He stood up, held up his palms and said, "Jackson, I need to talk with my wife and then Director Harrington. This will not be played out in this way."

Now totally flummoxed, Reba stood and put her arm around her husband's waist.

For everyone else in the room, those words were the confirmation that they needed. Rex Duncan knew about the plan. Jackson was angry. All that he had gone through was coming to a head. Amy. The plan. Even the frailties of his past, highlighted by Harrington's reemergence in his life. All were weighing on him at that moment. Jackson's head was spinning. Not quite sure what to do, he also stood up.

He walked within six inches of the senator and said, "She deserved better."

Rex matched Jackson's stare and said, "Yes, she did."

Jackson turned to walk away, then, in a totally unexpected move, turned back around and threw a powerful left hook straight into the senator's stomach. The punch lifted Rex a little off of his feet. Rex grunted audibly, then dropped to his knees. It was a beautiful punch. Mike Tyson would have been proud.

For the next few moments, chaos ensued. As the senator fell to his knees, Reba screamed and rushed to his aid. Rex was having a hard time catching his breath. Harrington tackled Jackson and was assisted by several agents who were in the nearby kitchen and heard Reba's screams. The glasses hanging around Harrington's neck were shattered. Ronnie and Jenny initially moved to pull Harrington off of Jackson, but then backed away, correctly deciding that it made no sense to fight the F.B.I. agents.

Jackson was cuffed and roughly thrown on the living room sofa. Rex Duncan was still recovering from the blow, trying to catch his breath. He slowly began standing up.

Reba glared at Jackson, saying to Harrington, "I want that man arrested and out of our house!" Any fondness she had for Jackson previously was now all gone. Her eyes contained nothing but venom in them. Of course, at this point, she knew nothing about her husband's real relationship to the plan. Harrington took charge.

Talking to his agents, he said, "We have this under control. Toss me the keys to his cuffs and head back to the kitchen. Please close the door behind you." The agents complied.

To Rex and Reba, he said, "You two sit in your chairs."

Rex, who had his breath back, said, "Ed, you cannot order me around in my own home, especially after having been assaulted by the likes of him!" He aggressively pointed at Jackson. "My wife is right. If you don't arrest him immediately, you will never be confirmed."

Harrington stayed cool. "Senator, this is not about my confirmation. Nor is it about Jackson Lowery. It really is about you." He tossed the key to the handcuffs to Ronnie. Ronnie took them off Jackson, who had not said anything since he had punched Rex.

Harrington turned to Jackson, Ronnie, and Jenny. "You all can leave. I will be in touch soon."

As the three of them stood up to leave, Rex Duncan pointed a finger at Jackson, but he said nothing. Reba was crying with her head down. They walked out of the room, left the house and got into the Jeep. Ronnie was driving. Jenny was riding shotgun, with Jackson, as usual, in the back seat. They all sat stone-faced and quiet in the car as Ronnie navigated the streets in and around Rock Creek Park.

As soon as they got on Massachusetts Avenue heading toward Wisconsin Avenue, Jenny exclaimed, "Jackson Lowery! What the fuck? Where did that come from? Did I say that you were my new hero? What a freakin' badass!" She was beaming.

She then looked at Ronnie, who held up his hand for a high five and said, "Jack, I never, in a million years, thought you would go gangster like that. It needed to be done and I am glad you did it."

Jackson was somewhat surprised by his friends' reaction. He sure wasn't looking for accolades when he punched Rex. He was just at the end of his rope. Plus, Rex's arrogance lit a torch in him.

"Well, the best thing about it was that Harrington did not arrest me. When he tackled me and all of those agents piled on, I thought for sure that I was going downtown. Thanks, guys, for having my back."

"We did kind of back away. I had a sense that Harrington was going to let you go. Truth be told, I think Harrington liked the fact that you slugged that asshole," Ronnie said.

"Yeah, he did," Jenny said.

Just then, Jackson's phone rang. He answered, had a brief conversation and hung up.

"That was Harrington's office. He wants to meet us in two hours."

Jenny chuckled. "Your new best friend."

Two hours later, Harrington joined Jackson, Ronnie, and Jenny in front of the Mary McLeod Bethune statue in Lincoln Park on Capitol Hill. Team Jackson was there early, blending in with the other park users. Jenny had ventured over to the playground, where several mothers with strollers had gathered. Jenny was sitting on a swing. Three teenaged boys were passing a basketball between them as they cut through the park. A couple of them snuck second looks at Jenny, who smiled back at them. Ronnie was leaning on a tree, eating an apple.

While he looked unfocused, he was taking in everything and everyone in the area. Jackson was in a much better mood. The punch lifted a load off of him. He was kicking a few stones on the ground. The team all came together to face Harrington as he walked toward them. Four F.B.I. agents, with earpieces, fanned out around him. Harrington shook hands with each of team Jackson. The park goers watched them all assemble.

Harrington looked at Jackson. "You have changed. The Jackson Lowery I knew before would not have had the balls to take that punch."

"I did not think about it. It just happened," Jackson said with a very tight smile.

"Well, it was a helluva punch," Harrington said.

Jackson shrugged. "Thanks for not arresting me," he said. "And, sorry about your glasses."

Harrington waved his hands. "Forget it. That bastard deserves a lot more than an uppercut to the gut. In fact, let me bring you up to date."

Jackson, Ronnie, and Jenny all gathered in closer to Harrington.

"Officially, the senator admits nothing, other than he feels that it is best that he not run for president or re-election when his term ends. My impressions off the record is that Duncan had been tacitly supporting his friend, General Brock, behind the scenes. None of the other conspirators knew this."

Jackson cut in. "Why, Ed? Why would he do it? The man was running for president. Does he really believe this crap like the rest of them?"

Ed looked at his shoes, shook his head and said, "Jackson, more than anything, I think he was consumed with being president. The old humble, I am not sure stuff, was a joke. I don't know if he believed in white supremacy to the extent that the others did. He just saw it as one of many possible means to an end: getting to the White House."

Jackson shook his head. "Power. It was all about power. He did not care about the loss of lives. He knew he would be more revered if he provided order to a destabilized country," he said.

"Exactly," Harrington said.

"Even if it cost him his own daughter's life," added Jenny.

Ronnie then spoke for the first time. All this talk reminded him of his Black Op days in the government. While Harrington had been speaking, flashes of violence in war torn countries peppered his brain. He knew the extent to which men would kill for power.

"Rex Duncan is not alone. Power hungry men like that come in all colors, shapes and sizes. Duncan's mindset is similar to African rulers in places like Rwanda, Uganda and Sudan, where ethnic cleansing and starvation were used as political tools to keep leaders in power. Duncan is like all of them."

"Bosnia, Serbia, Stalin's Russia, the list goes on," said Jenny.

Shaking his head, Jackson asked, "How did Reba react to it all?"

Harrington bit his lip. "She was blown away. She immediately asked if the confrontation they had with General Brock was all an act, a big show. It obviously was because Rex kind of hung his head and did not answer. She sat down and kept saying, 'our daughter...how could you do this to our daughter?' He was begging for forgiveness. They are going to have a tough time."

Now Ronnie was shaking his head.

"They even had Brock's exit orchestrated," he said. "A true military man to the end, falling on his sword for his future commander in chief. I bet that Brock really believed that once Duncan got in the White House, he would still find a way to push the white supremacy agenda - even from jail."

"And, Amy is dead," Jackson said. "I feel bad for Reba, but Rex Duncan is getting off easy." Looking at Harrington, he said, "Ed, whatever you do, make sure that man is finished in politics."

"He is done, Jackson. But I am not finished with him yet. You can count on it."

"Thanks. Over the last few days, there have been a lot of arrests, but that poisonous mindset is out there. It has to be ferreted out."

Jenny asked, "Are we free to go, Mr. Director?"

Harrington gave her a slight smile. "For now. I will be in touch." He nodded at them and turned to leave.

Team Jackson then walked side by side, past the Bethune Memorial, got in the Jeep Cherokee and left.

THREE

Four days after the plan was thwarted and one day after the meeting between Harrington and Team Jackson, the senator announced that he would not be a candidate for president and that he would be resigning from the U.S. Senate at the end of the year. He and Reba moved back to Idaho. The conventional public belief was that he could not get over his daughter's murder, and that the grief was too much. Rex Duncan was never charged with any crime.

Consistent with Team Jackson's wishes, the contributions made by the four of them were never mentioned by anyone.

While all of the details were never made public, the names of all six of the conspirators were displayed all over the news. The media did their best to demonize each of them. Having been charged with conspiracy and treason, Roger Tyler and General Michael Brock accepted reduced sentences in exchange for naming names.

In addition to the regular occupants of the Fairfax command center, over two hundred people both from inside and outside of the government were indicted. Most were convicted and jailed, including the scientists and researchers working out of the Pennsylvania building. True to their word, Jim and Susan Carr disappeared completely. No traces, no leads. Rampant speculation and media coverage about their whereabouts never led to any information whatsoever about where they could be hiding. They were nowhere to be found.

Jackson Lowery spent the next several weeks trying to figure his life out. He kept his promise to his son, Eddie, by having him stay with him for a couple of weeks. It was the perfect antidote for a troubled period. Jackson took a leave of absence from American University. He had been completely exonerated publicly, but was unsure about standing in front of a classroom on a regular basis.

Rather, he used his time to play tourist in his city - have seafood dinners at Sequoia's, vegan soul food dishes at Kephra's on H Street, tour for the first time the new African American museum on the Mall, people watch at Eastern Market, and listen to jazz at Blues Alley. When he took his son to the famed jazz club to see saxophonist Gerard Albright, Eddie said afterwards, "I guess having all those instruments playing was cool, but there wasn't any real beat."

Jackson elbowed his son on his shoulder saying, "Uh, there is a beat and the instruments playing is kinda the point." Jackson was genuinely enjoying his time off.

But, the scars remained from Jackson's journey. He often thought about Amy Duncan, wondering if his attraction was part of a brief infatuation born out of a middle age crisis or the real thing. He was not completely sure. He did know, however, that he missed her without really knowing her and that speculating about what might have been could be worse than knowing exactly what he was missing.

Full of gratitude for those who helped him, Jackson sent cruise tickets to Rahim by courier, for Rahim's mom and her sister. Rahim had answered the door and after seeing what was in the envelope, he made the courier wait while he wrote a note to be given back to Jackson. The note said, "Thanks, Mr. D.A.

Made my momma's day. But this is exactly why you are no longer locking peeps up. Too big a heart, man. Glad you got your payback! Sorry about your girl. Oh, and this don't mean I owe you. We still even." He added a crooked smiley face.

A special bond now linked Jackson, Ronnie, Jenny, and Joe Sweeney together. Each of them was trying to move on with their lives after the adventure that had united them so closely together. Ronnie fetched Rose and Ronnie, Jr. from their bunker so that they could settle back into their Marietta, Ohio home. Jenny went back to work, at least temporarily, but she was having trouble transitioning to her old nine to five job. Sweeney wanted to drop out of school, but finally acceded to his parents' wishes, promising to get his degree from Georgetown in December, the next year. He was taking twice the load for the next two semesters to make it work.

A few days after Eddie went back to Pam's, Jackson had dinner with Ronnie, Jenny, and Sweeney at the 1789 Restaurant. As good as it was to see each other, a heavy cloud hung over them. Their traumatic and exhilarating experience together turned on a switch that could not be turned off by reintegrating into their old lives. Sweeney, who was still full of the exuberance of youth, boldly said during dinner that they "should all start a business, work together and stop bad things from happening to people."

They laughed, but the seed was planted. Jackson knew at that moment the four of them would intimately be intertwined into each other's lives. He just did not know when or how it would happen, and what exactly it would entail. Later, when Jackson and Ronnie were alone, the two friends reflected on all that had happened.

"Ronnie, I never properly thanked you for being there when I needed you. I honestly had nowhere else to turn. Thanks."

"Hey, man. That's what I am here for. It is what I have been trained to do. But, you know Jack, I am the one who should be thanking you."

"Why," Jackson asked, seriously confused.

"Let me tell you why. The most challenging part of my military career was when I went undercover, trying to stamp out the white supremacy cancer. I got so caught up in the us versus them mentality that when I got discharged, I immediately started working on my own hideaways, my bunkers. Just like the rich folks. Just like the supremacists. We all want to be able to separate ourselves from others and from the world around us if the water gets too hot. Going through all of this with you has shown me that you can't really hide, Jack. You really cannot disappear. Once you get to the point where you feel you have to be so separated from society, you take away from yourself the very reason you have to live. You cannot live while always looking over your shoulder."

Jackson mulled over his friend's words. Ronnie had grown quite a bit after their ordeal. So, had Jackson. The bond between them was now unbreakable.

Smiling, jackson said, "Well said, Ronnie. Spoken like a true historian. In the meantime, let's not get rid of your hideaway anytime soon. At any given moment, I may need your help getting off the grid. It may be a while before everyone starts thinking like you and me."

EPILOGUE

Heidelberg, Germany is a beautiful city. It is also historic. Situated in southwestern Germany on the River Neckar, a major tributary of the Rhine River, Heidelberg is known for its rich culture, beautiful vistas, and resilient people. Heidelberg's origins extend back several hundred thousands of years. Modern Heidelberg can trace its beginnings to the fifth century, when the town became an important political site for the Catholic Church.

Since then, Heidelberg has always been influenced and sometimes overwhelmed by religious and political conflicts. In the 15th and 16th centuries, Heidelberg was a hub of activity in the era of humanism and the Reformation and the conflict between Lutheranism and Calvinism. Heidelberg University, founded in 1386 is one of Europe's oldest institutions. For centuries, thought leaders from around the world have come to the University to shop their ideas and test their intellectual prowess.

Unlike many German cities, Heidelberg was not destroyed by air raids in World War II and therefore still has original buildings from the late Middle Ages and early Renaissance. In fact, one of those structures, the strikingly elegant and Gothic Church of the Holy Spirit located downtown in Heidelberg's marketplace area has been shared by both Catholics and Protestant for hundreds of years. After centuries of being at the center of political and military conflict, the people of Heidelberg are among the most welcoming people on the world.

Three months after they thwarted the plan, Jackson Lowery, Ronnie Thomas, and Jenny Roberts were sitting in an outdoor cafe in the Heidelberg marketplace drinking lattes and munching on German pastries. While admiring the Church of the Holy Spirit across the square, each found themselves impressed by the friendliness of the ancient, hardy town of just over 150,000 people.

"Have you noticed that everyone is smiling here?" Ronnie said.

"They are awfully nice, aren't they?" Jenny said, as crumbs from her pastry dropped from her mouth.

Ever the historian, Jackson had to put it all into perspective. "This town has been through a lot. In an odd, interesting way, all of the wars, all of the religious debates, and all of the intellectual discussions have helped the people here feel very comfortable with who they are. There is no pretense here. The people like each other. It's funny how you can feel that spirit, that energy."

"Thanks, professor," Ronnie said while grinning. "But, on that one, my friend, I would have to agree with you. I remember when Rose and I were here when I was stationed in Frankfurt. It always felt different, more peaceful whenever we visited. Nice place."

Wiping her mouth, Jenny said, "Is it time to go, boys?"

Jackson looked at Ronnie, tilted his head in Jenny's direction and said, "Always a woman of action."

The three American tourists paid their bill, noticing that the grinning young waitress waved goodbye to them as they were walking out the door. Looking at her two companions, Jenny said, "Maybe it's a Stepford Wives thing."

They hopped into their rented white Peugeot, with Jenny sitting behind the wheel. Ronnie sat in the passenger seat, while Jackson sat alone in the back seat.

"Why is it," he asked, "that I am always the one in the back seat?"

Ronnie responded. "Duh, you are always the one we have to hide."

They were headed southwest toward Offenburg and the famed Black Forest region of southern Germany. Instead of taking route 5 on the Autobahn, Jenny steered in the direction of road 36 south, the local highway the follows the Rhine River.

The Rhine River remains one of the most vibrant and active rivers in the world. All day long, barge after barge travels up and down the river along with other cargo and tourist boats.

"This is definitely the more scenic route," Ronnie said, but his tone had changed. The playfulness between the three of them from earlier in the day was now gone.

"We have about a one hour drive," Jenny said. "Should we go over things?"

"Yes, let me pull up my notes," Jackson said, punching the notes app on his phone.

Two weeks earlier, Jackson had been sitting on a bench facing the King Memorial in D.C. when Ed Harrington sat down next to him. Jackson looked around and saw four F.B.I. agents positioned, as usual, strategically near them.

"I was surprised to get your call, Ed," Jackson said. "This must be important."

"Harrington was still all business. "It is, Jackson. When do you plan to go back to teaching at AU?"

"I don't know about that anymore. I do need to make some decisions about what the heck I am going to do with my life. Lord knows I love teaching, but I am a different man now."

"Look, I wanted to talk with you confidentially and it does relate to your future, so hear me out."

Jackson was thinking that Harrington wanted to offer him a job.

"Oh, no! I know that the two of us are making progress, but you are now ready to offer me a job?"

Harrington grunted. "This ain't no buddy-buddy movie yet, Jackson. And, it really isn't a job, per se. Just hear me out. That thing you went through. The evilness behind it. You and I know that there is more of it out there. Not just the white supremacy crap. There is evil in every form. Now that I am settling into this job and gotten all of the briefings, I know that there are time bombs all over. Like it or not, as some of my predecessors have told me, sometimes the best way to fight this kind of evil is outside of the government."

Jackson laughed. "C'mon, Ed. I am no James Bond or Jason Bourne."

Harrington did not laugh. "No, you are not. But you have something valuable, Jackson. You have good instincts. That is one of the reasons why I hired you all those years ago. That is what made you such a good prosecutor. You also work well outside of normal channels."

"What are you asking, Ed?"

"Give me a minute. You also are a good leader. I know we have had our differences, but you have grown as a person. I saw how you handled your team, how much they respect you. You really did put them first and valued their roles. You may not know it or not, but as motley as your crew is, they are very effective. Here's the deal, Jackson. I just got this job. I do not want to be taken by surprise on my watch by the likes of what you just had to deal with. I cannot allow these hidden forces to plot major destruction while our government sleeps. I want you to work off the books with me and the rest of the intelligence community to ferret out these bad guys and stop them. I want you and your team to do what the government cannot do. And at the right time, you can decide when to call in the Calvary. I want you to work for our country."

Jackson leaned forward and slapped his knees with his hands. "That's a helluva thing to ask, Ed. I still don't know what it means." He then paused, giving himself time to think. Harrington said nothing.

"Are you talking about a salary, budget, all that?"

"You put all of that together. Like half the people in D.C., you would set up a consulting firm with you and your crew as employees. Your main client will be a shell company funded by the government. I have talked to the heads of the CIA and secret service. The appropriate folks at the White House have also signed off on this. The intelligence folks have prepared a list of suspicious activities that they cannot break through. Once you are ready, we will go over the list and you can pick the ones you want to take a crack at. The only people who will know about this are you and me."

"How black ops do you expect us to be?"

Harrington caught his drift. "I do not expect you to be assassins. Defend yourselves as needed. Uh, that also means you can use that vicious left hook of yours." Even Harrington had to smile at the thought.

"But seriously, you decide when the time is right to call us in."

"This is a different kind of ask, Ed. I will give it some thought and talk with the team. Give me a couple of days."

"Okay," Harrington said. "That's fair. I will wait for your call. In the meantime, I have something you and your team can work on to see if this kind of thing appeals to you."

He looked like the cat that had just eaten the canary.

"As part of the plea deal with General Brock, he told us that each of the conspirators had built their own bunker getaways. He doesn't know where they all are, but he suspects that the Carrs are in theirs."

Jackson's thoughts went straight to his conversation with Ronnie about bunkers and the article Ronnie made him read.

Harrington then handed Jackson a sheet of paper. "The one thing that the General did tell us was that his co-conspirators shared some info with each other about the kind of layout they should each have in the event of a longtime stay. One common feature they talked about was an elevator. Here is the list of the major elevator manufacturing and installation companies in the world. Our folks have looked at the list and done what they can with it. It still is a dead end. Something tells me, however, that you and your team can get further that we did."

Jackson shook his head. "You remembered how much I like to tie up loose ends, didn't you?" he said.

Harrington had a twinkle in his eye. "Yes, I did." Harrington had a thought then said, "Usually by yourself." The twinkle in his eye was gone. "At any rate, I know that the whereabouts of the Carrs has been bugging you. By the way, the C.I.A. also signed off on this since we presume you will be going overseas."

Harrington stood up and began to walk to his car. All four agents gathered around him in unison, whispering into their earpieces. Jackson called after him, "Ed?"

Harrington stopped and turned around. "Yes?"

"When we find the Carrs, do we bring them back?"

This time, Harrington did smile. "Preferably. But you make the call." He then got into his car and drove away.

———————

While Jenny was driving them toward the Black Forest, Jackson reflected a bit on his conversation with Ed Harrington that day at the King Memorial. He particularly thought about how Harrington had given him the power to decide the Carrs' fate. They were almost at that point.

Following up from his meeting with the Harrington, Jackson called his team to his Georgetown apartment for dinner and a discussion. Ronnie and Jenny both pressed him about the subject matter, but Jackson merely told them that they all needed to meet as soon as possible. Sweeney walked to Jackson's from his dormitory.

Needless to say, they were all excited about the F.B.I. director's proposal. There were a lot of details to work out, but the direction was clear. Jackson then gave them copies of the list that he received from Harrington, explaining to them what he had been told.

Jenny had said, "If we are now officially employed, I need to quit my job and find a place here.

I need three days." Looking at Sweeney, she said, "You are in midterms, right?"

Sweeney nodded, saying, "They will be done this week."

Jenny turned back to Jackson. "Sweeney and I will get on this three days from now. Go back and get some money so we can go to work."

Grinning wide, Ronnie said, "I will help you prepare two budgets, partner. One to get us going on this and then a larger budget for the start of our venture."

As Jackson expected, Jenny and Sweeney worked their magic. Jenny was able to lay out the criteria needed to whittle down the elevator company search. Jackson was pretty amazed at how she came up with the variables. She assumed, for instance, that if the core white supremacists, like the Carrs were going to hide out, they would want to be in a location where whites were a majority. So, she told Sweeney to look for underground projects in Europe or Australia. She had Sweeney list the work orders in which no names were attached to the project. She told him to pay attention to projects done on behalf of a corporate entity not based where the construction was taking place. She also made sure he paid attention to the projects paid with offshore money from the Caribbean or Switzerland.

Sweeney went to work. After a day or so of Jenny and Sweeney increasingly narrowing the variables, they had a link they liked. Stevenson Elevators' mainline business consisted of installing elevators in the homes or small offices of the super rich. Rarely did they install an elevator traveling more than three floors. Over a year ago, Stevenson contracted to install an elevator completely underground for a shell corporation based in the Bahamas. Sweeney had viewed all of the documents associated with the contract. There was no contact person listed, nor was any phone number listed for the buyer. The main red flag that struck Jenny and Sweeney was that there was no contract price on the contract itself. However, when Sweeney tracked down Stevenson's wire deposit receipts, he found a two million dollar deposit from a Bahamas bank. Going through bank records, he was able to link the Bahamian company listed on the contract to the bank account.

For some time thereafter, Jenny and Sweeney pored over the Stevenson files trying to ascertain a location for the construction. Jackson and Ronnie joined in the search. They could not find the location. They did see a strange notation under the note section. It said, "Digging site: gray tree, 50 north." Ronnie was able to break the logjam. The contract was several pages long, most of it legal boilerplate. Ronnie kept asking why would they include all of the boilerplate pages when it was obviously a loosely structured deal. In looking at each of the pages, he saw a random number (only one) on every page, often in the middle of a sentence. He wrote down each of the numbers and began playing with them.

The next day, he had it. When read together, the numbers represented coordinates. He was able to discern the longitude and latitude coordinates for the location of the elevator project. It was near Germany's Black Forest. Jackson then offered a suggestion regarding the digging site entry. He said, "I think I understand this. Let's be sure to bring a compass with us."

With Jenny still behind the wheel, they were making good time. The Peugeot had some pick up. They did not have an exact idea of what they were looking for, but from Google maps they knew the coordinates were on part of the seventy-five acres owned by a German doctor and his wife. They had three kids and lived on a mansion on the Rhine. Many of the homes near the Black Forest had a look and feel similar to Transylvania in Romania from the Dracula legend. Throughout the Rhine region the trees are a dark, rich hunter green color.

Access to most of the mansions was often a long, scary, tree laden road, sometimes so far from the main road that the house could not be seen until you were right upon it. Jenny and Sweeney could find no link between the doctor and the Carrs. In fact, they found no link between the doctor and anyone in America. They seemed to be a hard working upper middle class family.

Jenny initially missed the driveway to the doctor's mansion and had to turn around.

She then turned up the driveway, which seemed more like a road. The doctor's mansion was about three-fourths of a mile away. Jackson was looking left as Ronnie looked right. They were looking for a gray tree. Jackson got excited when they first turned onto the driveway, but every tree he saw was dark brown or black. The shade from the trees made it dark even though it was two in the afternoon. Jackson could see how the creepy Frankenstein and Dracula horror genre grew from this environment.

They reached the end of the driveway without seeing a gray tree. Both he and Ronnie were disappointed, not understanding how they missed the gray tree. Outside of the formidable mansion were three kids playing. The kids were between the ages of nine to fourteen. They ran to the car. Then the mother came outside. This did not feel like the hideaway for attempted mass murderers.

The Black Forest family was nice. They had never been to America and wanted to talk about New York City, LeBron James, and Kim Kardashian. Jackson, Ronnie, and Jenny were antsy to leave but knew it was important to be genial with their hosts. Ronnie, who spoke the best German, slyly asked about major construction on the property. The doctor's wife told them that the government did major excavation work on their property a couple of years ago. The family had been told that it had to do with a drainage issue from the Rhine. The workers were finished after about three months. After finally extricating themselves from the family, Jenny coasted down the road back to the main street.

Halfway down, Ronnie called out, "I see a gray tree!"

Jenny pulled into the woods as far as she could and positioned the car behind another group of trees. She wanted to make sure that the doctor would not see the car, if it was still there when he came home.

They got out of the car and walked to the only gray tree within eyesight. Jackson stood next to the tree, pulled out his compass and rotated around the tree until the compass was pointed due north. He then walked fifty paces, with Ronnie and Jenny following him. When he reached fifty paces, he walked around a bit and finally stepped on a metal plate, similar to the plates you see on the street during street repair construction. He looked at Jenny and Ronnie. Both pulled out their weapons. With Ronnie having been stationed in Germany for several years, he still had significant military contacts in the country. He was easily able to get them all guns.

Jackson poked around until he found a handle connected to the medal plate. He pulled it hard. The plate came off easier than expected. You could see ladder steps going down to a concrete floor about eight feet down. He looked at Ronnie and Jenny again, took a large breath and climbed down the hole. Ronnie and Jenny followed.

Once at the bottom, Ronnie and Jackson turned on their flashlights. To the left of the ladder was an elevator. Ronnie said, "Just like that."

Jackson pushed the down button. You could hear the elevator pulling up to their floor. When the door opened, they all walked in and pushed the down button. There were only two buttons inside the elevator: one with an arrow pointing up and one with an arrow pointing down.

The elevator started to go downward, traveling the equivalent of two floors.

When it touched the bottom, the door opened and two people stood there to greet them. The man was tall and lean with an obvious toupee. He had a weather-beaten face that had gotten much sun over the years. Although, he was wearing khakis and a yellow golf shirt, he had a rugged, cowboy look about him.

The woman was very dressy and made up. She had blonde hair full of hairspray and was wearing a long flowered sundress. Thin and attractive, she reminded Jackson of a country western singer. Both were in their sixties.

Both held guns pointed at them.

"Hello, Mr. Lowery," the woman said. "I see you refuse to give up, don't you? How much white blood do you have in you?" Her smile and all that it represented made Jackson want to strangle her.

"Susan Carr, I presume?" Jackson said. "Shall we sit down and talk?"

She looked at her husband, while Jackson snuck a peek at Ronnie and Jenny. He was surprised that Ronnie had not already started shooting. Both had their guns cocked and ready to fire.

The Carrs apparently also recognized that Ronnie and Jenny were ready to shoot. Unlike their visitors, the Carrs were not prepared for a gunfight.

"By all means," Susan Carr said. It was quite evident that she spoke for both of them.

"Let's."

She and her husband eased backwards away from the elevator and kept backing down a long hall. They clearly were not used to walking backwards. Susan Carr stumbled a couple of times in her heels. Ronnie and Jenny were all business. Ronnie held himself firmly in the ready position, while Jenny matched his focus.

After thirty feet or more, the hall opened up to a large great room full of impressionist paintings and tall plants. Jackson recognized the famous painting of the woman knitting. Jackson liked the room, and thought the paintings worked well. He then thought how odd it was to be thinking about something like that while everyone in the room had guns trained on each other. A giant picture window was off to the right, displaying a high-rise view looking down on Central Park in New York. Jackson could see the birds flying in the park and people jogging below. He started to comment on the view, when it struck him that he was watching a tape or some kind of live feed. Another reminder of Ronnie's article.

Susan Carr motioned to a sofa off to the left. The sofa was facing two high back chairs. A coffee table with two glasses of water was positioned between the sofa and the two chairs. Jackson sat on the sofa, as the Carrs each sat in one of the chairs. Jenny stood behind Jackson to the left of the sofa, while Ronnie stood behind him to the right. His posse was in place.

"So, Mr. Lowery, can I get you something..."

Jackson cut her off. "Ma'am, we do not want any food or drink you may be serving."

Jim Carr chuckled at this. Jackson shot a glance at Ronnie, recognizing that his friend might shoot the man right then and there. Jackson looked at Ronnie as if to say, "cool it".

Susan Carr said, "Of course. I understand. So now what?"

Jackson tersely said, "You have only two options. You can leave with us now. Or we can call our U.S. intelligence friends who will shortly storm this place. It is up to you."

Both Carrs still held their guns, but not with the same conviction. They looked at each other. "We are not going with you," she said.

"Then, I am going to have to ask you to put down your weapons," Ronnie said, speaking for the first time. He pointed his gun at Susan Carr's forehead.

She looked at the husband, then gently laid her gun on the coffee table. Jim Carr did the same. Jenny hurriedly picked up both of their guns.

Susan Carr looked again at their husband and leaned toward him to kiss his cheek. She then reached down and grabbed the two glasses of water, handing one to him. They gave a toast by touching their glasses and while looking into each other's eyes, gulped the water down.

At that point, Jenny lowered her gun and softly said, "Cowards."

Ronnie lowered his gun as well and sat on the sofa next to Jackson.

Jackson leaned back on the sofa, staring intently at the Carrs.

The end came quickly. The two of them held hands just before they both began to look sleepy. Susan lowered her head first. Jim Carr made a coughing sound and then dropped his head. They were dead in less than two minutes.

Jenny was now sitting on the sofa as well, having laid the Carrs' guns back on the coffee table. The three of them looked at the Carrs for a long time. Jenny took a few photos and emailed them to both Sweeney and Harrington. They then walked back down the hall, got on the elevator and left.

Ronnie eased behind the wheel for the drive to the Frankfurt airport. When Jackson reached for the passenger side door, lifting up the seat for Jenny to sit in the back, she paused, then climbed on in. For the first time since the three of them had been in cars together, Jackson sat up front. Ronnie started the car, noticed Jackson sitting in the front seat and looked back at Jenny, who smiled and said teasingly, "About time you took a turn up front, Jack."

Jackson alternated looks between his two friends and said, "It is a brand new day. I'm not hiding anymore." Jenny nodded a smile as Ronnie gunned the Peugeot for the airport.

Author's Note

For the past 15 years, I have been deeply immersed in the national education reform movement. As a result, I have written three non-fiction books and opinion editorials that have appeared in nearly every major newspaper in the country. Indeed, most of my writing has been directly related to that work. All of which begs the question: Why would someone like me write a book like this?

Quite frankly, I have always loved reading political thrillers, mysteries, and action-filled suspense novels. In recent years, even while engaged in writing exclusively about education, I have frequently mused about writing a novel. Those thoughts became more crystallized during the 2016 presidential campaign. The growing prominence of the white nationalist movement during that campaign, along with the increasingly divisive nature of U.S. politics, prompted me to write this book.

Politics aside, I thoroughly enjoyed accompanying Jackson Lowery on his journey.

As my first foray into fiction writing, I had no idea how much fun it was going to be to put together all of the necessary pieces of the story. As much as I love writing about education, none of it compares to the liberating freedom associated with writing a novel. Writing *The Plan* was an incredibly satisfying and rewarding experience. I look forward to book two of the Jackson Lowery trilogy.

Of course, writing is an easier process when you have people around who you can count on. The person I have relied on the most for copy-editing and organizational advice for my last two books has been

Alyssa Devlin. Alyssa is, quite simply, terrific. I am looking forward to working with her on many future projects. Sincere thanks as well to Terrie Scott for jumping in at the end of this project and providing a superb job of editing and formatting.

I also thank my book agent extraordinaire Anne Bohner, for her wise counsel and friendship. Thanks to Mike Presky, Jaime deBlanc-Knowles, and Sloane Miller for their encouraging writing tips.

Special thanks to the popular and talented Indie thriller writer, Rafael Amadeus Hines, for his willingness to offer guidance and help wherever needed. He is such a good guy. Thank you, my brother!

I have been blessed to be surrounded by an incredible family and an amazing network of friends. Thanks to all of them for their steadfast love and support. In particular, my sons Kevin and Eric patiently guided me through the ups and downs of the story-telling process as I wrote (and re-wrote) *The Plan*. They did not hesitate to share their views. Thank you, sons! I also need to give a shout out to my step-son, Kalijah, who always seemed to know the right time to interrupt my writing by asking if I wanted to go to a movie. Those breaks kept my mind fresh. Thanks, K.

Finally, this book is dedicated to my wife, Amber. She is the sweetest, most love-filled soul I know. Her love, motivation and encouragement has made me a better man. For that, I am eternally grateful. ~ Kevin P. Chavous

About the Author

Kevin P. Chavous is a noted attorney, author, and national education reform leader. Born and raised in Indianapolis, Indiana, Mr. Chavous spent most of his professional career practicing law and engaged in public service in Washington, D.C. As a former member of the Council of the District of Columbia and its education committee chair, Mr. Chavous was at the forefront of promoting change within the District public school system and helped to shepherd the charter school movement and school choice into the nation's capital and around the country.

A prolific writer and much sought after speaker, Mr. Chavous' opinion editorials have appeared in most major newspapers and he has given speeches on the topic of education in nearly every state. Former Indiana Governor Mitch Daniels calls Mr. Chavous "the most effective advocate for children in America". Mr. Chavous is also an accomplished author, having published three books of nonfiction: *Serving Our Children: Charter Schools and the Reform of American Public Education, Voices of Determination: Children that Defy the Odds,* and *Building A Learning Culture in America.*

Mr. Chavous loves reading political thrillers and was inspired to write *The Plan* in response to the increased prominence of the white nationalist movement during the last presidential election. Just before he began writing this book, he discovered that his great-great-grandfather's name was Jackson Lowery. He decided to give *The Plan's* main character his ancestor's name. Mr. Chavous is currently working on book two of the Jackson Lowery trilogy.

Visit his website:
www.kevinpchavous.com

Follow him on Twitter:
@kevinpchavous

Like him on Facebook:
www.facebook.com/KPChavousBooks

42037364R00213

Made in the USA
Middletown, DE
10 April 2019